SOLEDAD
or Solitudes

Number Six in the Texas Tradition Series
Tom Pilkington, Series Editor

SOLEDAD

OR SOLITUDES

A NOVEL BY

R·G·VLIET

With a new Introduction by ANN VLIET
and an Afterword by TOM PILKINGTON

Texas Christian University Press
Fort Worth

Copyright © R.G. Vliet *1977*
Vida Ann Vliet *1986*

Library of Congress Cataloging-in-Publication Data

Vliet, R.G., 1929–
  Soledad, or, Solitudes.

  (Number six in the Texas tradition series)
  Rev. ed. of: Solitudes. 1st ed. c1977.
  I. Vliet, R.G., 1929– . Solitudes.
II. Title.   III. Title: Soledad.   IV. Title: Solitudes.
V. Series: Texas tradition series; no. 6.
PS3543.L5S56 1986   813'.54   85-40826
ISBN 0-87565-063-5

Design by WHITEHEAD & WHITEHEAD

For ANN *and* BROOKE,
and to the memory of MARSHALL BEST
and TONY GODWIN.

We live in an old chaos of the sun

—WALLACE STEVENS,
Sunday Morning

These people, living as real people might have lived, these towns, placed where real towns are or may have been placed, are fictitious.

INTRODUCTION

I imagine the curious reader's first thought on picking up this reprint of *Solitudes* will be "Why change the title?" If he compares the texts he'll find a lot more change: not only an epilog and several new scenes added, but cuts and insertions in almost every line.

Solitudes / Soledad is proof that even after publication no text is really inviolate. And in this case we can be glad, because *Soledad* is now the book that the author had wanted *Solitudes* to be. Why it took so long to finally "get it right" is a study in the relationship between a developing novelist and the shifting exigencies of commercial publishing. So I thought that in order to satisfy the curiosity of those who read introductions, to perhaps give some insight into the ongoing development of a novelist's work, I might try to recall here the making of *Soledad* while it is still somewhat recallable.

Except for the stylistic reworking (mostly tightening up, toning down, pointing the narrative line), all the new material in this definitive edition, including the title *Soledad*, was restored from what was intended for publication in the first edition, brought out by Harcourt, Brace, Jovanovich in 1977. The scenario is, I'm sure, a familiar one: idealistic young novelist brings in a book that isn't quite there yet, realistic editors determine to shape it up. Suffice it to say that after the smoke blew away the author was not really happy with the result.

To begin at the beginning: I don't know if many writers can top Russ's record for having editors retire or die on him at crucial moments. Pascal Covici, Sr. was the first. He was instrumental in getting Viking to accept Russ's first book of poetry and first novel, but died before negotiations were completed and as a consequence (at least so Russ felt) *Rockspring*, written in 1963–1964, wasn't published until 1974. It's hard to recall exactly what happened at that time, but I believe it was this: Viking offered a contract accepting both books and an option on a second novel, but would print the poetry only if it won the Lamont award, which subsidized publication. Russ called this shady dealing and besides, he claimed, he didn't have a second novel, he was a poet and a playwright. Russ's hindsight later convinced him that if Covici had lived he'd either have "Dutch Uncled" him through the contract or have talked Viking into waiting for Russ to discover his own bent. As early as 1954, his playwriting professor had told him he was really a novelist, but Russ had spent the next ten years trying to write plays and was still insisting that his *Rockspring* was simply an oddity, the exercising of a whim he would not repeat. One week after refusing Viking's offer, the idea for a longer novel jumped into his head and he began the ten years of research and writing that went into *Solitudes*.

I can't recall the exact sequence of the off-again, on-again relationship with Viking, but even before Marshall Best revived Viking's interest in *Rockspring* (which had to be 1973, just after its publication in *The Hudson Review*) they were planning to publish *Solitudes*. In 1969, when Russ asked them for an advance on the second novel, they came through with a contract and enough to enable us to stay a second year in Mexico. All this time (except for a year lost to radiation treatments) Russ was working on the book six days a week (five to six hours a day), in Pennsylvania, Texas, Massachusetts, Mexico, and Vermont, finally "finishing" it in the fall (I believe) of 1974 and thrusting it into my hands for immediate reading. At four o'clock in the morning, Russ waiting expectantly for my unadulterated praise, I turned the last page, wondering how I could manage to be both honest and tactful.

Because the feeling that had been rushing me all night—once past the first, delicious chapters—was anger. I was angry at the shapelessness, the turgid detail, at the fact that after waiting for it for over ten years it wasn't the little gem of form (or was it just that I had grown more critically astute?) that the simpler *Rockspring* had been. The author seemed to be more interested in a blow-by-blow account of Texas life in the 1880s than he was in telling a story. Every bush, every brand name, every artifact of daily existence was examined in detail. You had to take time to count the legs of every centipede, and then you would come suddenly upon a passion being torn to tatters side by side with the most mundane observations about dipping sheep.

Nevertheless, Marshall Best, who had put off full retirement until he had seen *Rockspring* through the press, wanted Viking to publish the second book, and would have been willing to nurture it through revision, but he was now retiring completely and, since Russ felt that the only younger editor willing to take on *Solitudes* would have treated it as a genre Western, there came another parting of the ways.

Fortunately Harcourt, Brace, Jovanovich immediately took up the book, apparently not worrying about the problems in the second and third sections—they simply assigned him Tony Godwin, an editor whose ability to get the best out of an author was well established. This was the first time that Russ (who wrote everything like a poet, taking time to chisel out every exact word) had ever revised anything once it was completed, or had ever let anyone get another finger in the pie. My horror at the second, third, and maybe even fourth versions, as he tried to take Godwin's specific advice for getting "the breath of narrative running through it," is all too easy to recall. For years after it was published I could never remember how the book ended, I'd read so many different versions, the worst one completely losing the point of the book in a good old-fashioned posse chase. Then one day Russ called Godwin's office to tell him that at long last the book was done. He was put on hold, transferred from one voice to another, and finally was told, "I'm sorry Mr. Vliet, but Mr. Godwin has just died."

I don't recall how many editors got their hands on the book after that or where they all went, but Russ himself got rid of the posse chase and one of them insisted that the title had to go—the Soledad prison episode was current and the editor was afraid the title would be misleading. Another—or was it Tony Godwin?—got rid of the epilog on the basis that it was out of place in an essentially tragic book. Most of them—as did Russ—worked unsuccessfully to turn Soledad herself into "a less literary character." I even got my two cents in, chagrined that most of my sage advice was not taken. No one, thank God, touched the character (the wildness, the realness) of Clabe, who comes through even in the first edition despite all attempts to pull the book toward some kind of stereotypical norm.

(Russ's problems with the market-place didn't end with the publication of *Solitudes*. When Harcourt, Brace, Jovanovich asked for an outline of the next novel, Russ wrote back saying that if Faulkner had submitted an outline of *The Sound and the Fury* it would never have found a publisher, but, since they insisted, outlining pretty accurately what came to be *Scorpio Rising*. Harcourt, Brace, Jovanovich dropped the book sight unseen. Fortunately, Random House picked it up, left Russ alone with the book, extended deadline after deadline, and this time his editor, Rob Cowley, stayed with the house until the book was safely in the bookstores. And this time Russ was so determined to get the book right before he himself had to abandon it that he staved off death for weeks to revise the last five chapters. As soon as Cowley read the manuscript he vowed to get Random House to handle the paperbacks of not only *Scorpio* but *Soledad*. However, Random House's paperback division was cutting back, and that brings this publishing history full circle: once again Viking, the house Russ always thought of as his publishing home, welcomed him back to its list.)

In the meantime, even after *Solitudes* was published Russ would worry about it, talking about revising it, and I would worry about his putting that ahead of his new novel, wanting him to get on to something better, afraid he would dissipate what energy he had left before his illness returned, which it did in the fall of 1981. But the pressure of limited time, or the new chemotherapy, or whatever caused the sudden clarity he claimed descended on him one day early in 1982, determined him to revise *Solitudes* when work on his new book was too taxing. We replaced the dining room table with a bed so he could be close to the woodstove, and he spent his days there in that blizzardy Vermont spring, scribbling away on yellow pads and then carefully copying his revisions into the already published book, cutting pages from magazines (where parts had been published separately) to restore hunks of lost material. The following spring, in the sun at J. Frank Dobie's Paisano ranch near Austin, while he was undergoing more treatment and racing time to finish *Scorpio Rising*, I typed out the new manuscript from his revised text and was amazed at what a good book it now was: the narrative line was perfectly clear, the detail that was left seemed to fall into its natural place, the disparity between styles disappeared into a rich organic form. Left alone to percolate in the back of Russ's mind, it had finally become what it could be.

So when Texas Christian University Press asked in the spring of 1984 to reprint *Solitudes*, the revised manuscript was ready and waiting. And Russ was not the only one to benefit from his hard-earned lessons. For all my anxiety over his earlier "wasteful" groping with genre, his self-destructive stubbornness in the face of editorial necessity, his agonizing insistence on the slower, organic path in coping with narrative shape, I perceive it now as a triumph for the human spirit that when everything said "Give up and rest, don't bother with it, it's not worth the agony," Russ managed to conquer Fate by leaving both *Scorpio Rising* and *Soledad* in their right, intrinsic forms.

I speak for him here in thanking Texas Christian University Press and Viking Press for helping him rescue *Soledad* from oblivion.

ANN VLIET

Kyle, *1985*

ONE

ONE of those Texas blizzards that come
down from the high north or northwest, the back of the hand
of God Almighty, and smack the land low. That thin blue
streak on the horizon northwest rises up fast, like lifting a window shade onto night. Then the wind slices out from under
the hefted dark and stings the trees, fetches a screech across
the sleet-scratched stones. The air is one long slant of buckshot cold and powdery snow. Thirty minutes ago it might have
been a spring country. Now a man sucks ice in his tin cup.

February 16, 1881

THAT wind can blow. That wind can blow from here to the Gulf of Mexico, and he wished it'd take him with it. For two days the weather had gone wholesale. It was a blue norther that could have shifted Hell eastward and frosted the corners. It had whipped the cows down from the Concho River section. They had come down in big drifts, their heads low, their tails tucked, knots of ice on their humped-up backs, their hocks scraped hairless from puncturing the crust. They had left a blood track. Now they milled around on the pond, a little ways up the brushy draw, lowing, trying to find water, a cloud of steam that you could smell the brute odor of lifting off their backs.

Shit, he'd had that wind up his back most of his life, yes, twenty-four years of it. *What the hell was he doing out here, playing this four-handed game of freeze-out?*

Look at that sonofabitch Emmitt over there, putting an edge to his knife. Back and forth, back and forth with the blade across his boot top like he was playing some damned fiddle.

"Emmitt, why don't you quit? Open the goddamn peaches."

Emmitt's head jerked up. He stared out from under his hat brim at Claiborne through two little pig's eyes. He had a flat, slanted sort of face that when it looked at you always seemed like it was aimed at you crooked. His ma must have put a sadiron to his face when she'd seen what she'd bornt, hoping to press out a blotch on her life.

"What the hell's the matter with you, Clabe?" Emmitt said.

"Red's got a spider in his dumpling," Lige said. "Don't you know that?"

"Shit," Claiborne said.

"Never knowed you when you didn't," Lige said with a grin.

"Shit," Claiborne said.

Lige laughed.

Yes, you can laugh, you sonofabitch. You've got seventeen of my good dollars in your feedbag. Lige and Neal, those two bastards. Last night. At Y.O.'s place. Passing the time until we come out here. "How's about a little game of pitch?" Oh, that wind can blow, blow, high across the night. Them two bastards've been playing together so long, they know what the other one's got by the way he leads. The cards never broke my way. Every deal, almost, Lige says, "Mmmmmm, Red, I brung your saddle home." "Uh huh, Red, I kinda brung your saddle home." Shit. Neal leads with a trey. I put down a jack. Lige gets it with a queen. I ain't got no trumps. Christa'mighty. "Yes, and you can keep my damn saddle home, you sonofa*bitch!*"

For a minute the sun came out, as if the wind were blowing it across the sky.

Look at Y.O. over there, putting his quid one side of his mouth to the other. Back and forth, back and forth. Why don't he quit?

Y.O. spat. He ran his sleeve across his beard and looked into the coffeepot, which was trying to boil on the scarce, wind-whipped fire. "Near to coffee as she's gonna get," he said. He dumped in a handful of snow to settle the grounds.

Lige reached into the grub wallet. "These biscuits is all crumbs," he said.

"The old lady bakes 'em too short," Y.O. said. "They don't take travel."

"They'll do," Claiborne said. "Let's eat and git."

Emmitt whacked an exact cross with his knife in the top of a can of peaches. "Froze," he said. He set the opened can on some coals and poked ashes around it with the blade of his knife.

That cedar elm burning smells like piss.

Sure, Emmitt was all right. Lige was all right. Y.O. was all right. To hell with them.

Claiborne stuck his hand into the snow. There was a rope burn on his left hand, a sugary sore that wouldn't close. The cold felt good.

"Hey!" Emmitt said. "She's quit!"

"What, for Christsake?" Claiborne said.

"The weather. She ain't blowin' no more."

The men looked up. High in the sky the sun stood still. A far-off wind, so high up you couldn't hear it, dragged the last webs of cloud from off the sun and hauled them southeastward. The new sun hurt Clabe's eyes. The brush in the draw was still. Even the stock on the pond was still.

The fire leaped up around the coffeepot. Emmitt fished the can of peaches off the coals.

"Just like always," Lige said. "Them bastards let up quick as they come."

"Let's eat," Claiborne said. "I need somethin' to put a bottom on my stomach."

"I figure Neal's about set up down below," Y.O. said. "We'll drive the stock right down the draw. They'll go. They're crazy for water. Keep 'em back from eatin' the willer branches, though, or they'll cake up and die on us."

"Some of them damn cows has got rail hides," Emmitt said. He crooked his head toward a small, mealy-nosed steer at the edge of the herd. The letters AMON were burnt the length of its side.

"I want to cut out the unmarked stuff, sell the marked stuff over to Fort Croghan," Y.O. said. "Hagerman'll butcher 'em at the fort tonight. All we got to do is bury the hides. The other stuff, we swallow-fork the right ear, crop the left, slap an iron on. That goes to San Antonio. You goin' to Santone with us, Clabe?"

"Nope," Clabe said.

"I'll need a good man."

"I go as far as Fort Croghan. Then I take my cut and git," Claiborne said.

Y.O. said, "Suit yourself."

"Yep," Claiborne said.

"Red's got to get back to Cherokee in time for prayer meetin' Sunday night, ain't that so, Red?" Lige said.

"You takin' Johnnie Lee Chant to prayer meetin' again tomorrer night, Clabe?" Emmitt said.

"Ever' Sunday," Lige said. "Ever' Wednesday, too. Her grandma's real religious." Lige laughed. Y.O. laughed. He spat.

"Goda'mighty, I'd like to light into some of that," Emmitt said. "That gal's so purty it hurts your eyeballs to look."

"How the hell do you do it, Red?" Lige said. "You take 'em to prayer meetin', next thing you know you got 'em down on their backs yellin' hallelujah."

Emmitt grunted. His eyes were shut tight like he had Johnnie Lee Chant locked in big as life behind them. And that's as close as he's ever going to get, the ugly wood tick. So goddamned ugly he has to sneak up on a dipper to get a drink out of it.

To hell with them. That Emmitt, that Lige, that Y.O. don't know shit from wild honey. They ain't never been stung. Something was stinging him. But Clabe went right on trying. He couldn't keep himself from it.

Last Wednesday evening. Fetching Johnnie Lee home from meeting. Off the road, sparking in a hired rig under a live oak. The air so still, the leaves in the tree so still. Johnnie Lee kept holding that prayer book on her lap. Clabe couldn't get up past the prayer book. Johnnie Lee was laughing like crazy, Clabe's hand buzzing around like a bee betwixt her knees. She must've had on sixteen dozen petticoats. "Grandma's waitin'," she says, over and over. "Grandma's waitin'." And the telltale kind of a laugh that it don't take but one mite bit more of a shove to get them over the far edge of it, make their breaths come fast. And once he was there, in there amongst the brush, there wasn't any holding him back—all the wildness in him came out, like he was trying to get back at something, like he was going to knock a few stars out of God's black sky. They liked that. And then lie there with some woman or other under him, what he'd sweated and worked over, him foundering in a spread of empty dark, the world still out of plumb.

He might have made it last Wednesday night, excepting that wind came up. It hit them slam-bang like somebody'd kicked open an icehouse door. They like to froze. He didn't know how he got Johnnie Lee home. Well, he was going to get up her back stairs yet.

Up on the pond a cow lowed. Four long-haired horses were hitched to a nearby live oak. They were spooky and ornery. One of them kicked, causing a commotion in the bunch. Sonofabitch, Clabe's hand hurt. And this new quiet round about made him nervous. The air was still. Already the sun was hot and bright. The glaze on the brush in the draw had begun to thin and drip. He had to get back to Cherokee Sunday night.

"Dish up the goddamn peaches, Emmitt," Claiborne said. "We ain't got but till Christmas."

Y.O. said, "Somebody better go tail up them cows. There's a couple down on the ice."

"Some of them cows is so bad froze their hoofs is gonna drop off," Emmitt said.

"Damn it to hell," Claiborne said. "Let's eat and git."

"Shut up! Look up there," Lige said. He stood.

Above, on the ridge on the north slope, about sixty yards up the draw, a man sat a horse.

Emmitt and Clabe grabbed up their rifles. They stood.

Y.O. stood. He whipped his hat from his head and waved it. "*Halloo!*" he hollered. "*Come down here.*"

"Put down them guns," he said to Emmitt and Clabe. "Start pourin' the goddamn coffee."

Lige and Emmitt and Claiborne hunkered back down around the fire. They kept their rifles close beside. The sun bore down. The grass was beginning to poke through the melting snow.

Up on the ridge the man touched a heel to his horse's belly. Clabe watched from under his hat brim. The horse fetched forward, but its head stayed low. Clabe could tell it was bad gaunted by the way it picked its way extra careful down the slope, sitting its haunches. Sometimes it didn't even bother to go around a bush, it just rode the brush.

Emmitt's claybank nickered under the liveoak. The other horses shifted, pulled at their halters.

"Give me the peach tin," Claiborne said. "He can use my cup."

The horse skirted the pond. The rider never paid the cattle any mind, but came straight on. Horse and rider came on terrible slow, it seemed to Clabe—a hunk of stone pushing through the air. The horse put one foot down in front of the other so awful slow. Its nose swung close above the ground. But it was a blooded animal, you could tell that, for all it was so rid down—not gelded. A big, blood black with a white blaze and three quarter-stockinged feet, hefting around twelve hundred pounds, plenty of chest and bottom, good and solid, and likely, when it was fresh, no daylight under it. But it looked now like it'd been rid through the weather until the bottom had plumb dropped out. It came on powerful slow.

The man wore a black sombrero and a yellow slicker. He rode straight-backed and stiff. Atop him the tall, pointed crown of the sombrero looked like it could punch a hole in the sky.

"Divvy up the peaches," Claiborne said. Emmitt knifed out the peaches into the four cups and left some in the can. The coffee was still hot. Lige lifted the pot from the fire and set it at the edge, on some stones.

"Well," Emmitt said under his breath, "it don't look like he's from one of the Concho River outfits."

The black horse had come to a stop a few yards off and the rider sat looking down at them. He was an old man gone past his prime, a Mexican, and it looked like this trip had frazzled the ends some. His face was weather-beaten and wrinkled, his hair was white, his great handlebar mustache white—Mexican silver against the dark brown of his skin. He wore plain mule-ear stovepipe boots. The spurs had long gooseneck shanks and Mexican rowels with lots of points— what they call a sunburst rowel.

Y.O. stepped up to the black and caught hold of one of the cheek pieces—it wasn't a bridle, but a Mexican hacka- more with a fancy, plaited bosal across the nose. The horse just stood there, its eyes wide, its legs shaking, it was that rid down. Y.O. looked up. He spat.

"*Buenas días*," Y.O. said. "Come rest your hat and coat." He kept hold of the cheek piece.

The man looked down at Y.O. He looked across to the three men beside the fire. If there was anything working be- hind that dark face, it didn't show.

His hand moved down the front of the slicker, unbuck- ling it. He flipped the slicker back, across the horse's rump. The man hadn't any side gun. There was a rifle under his knee, but not a business rifle. It was a Sharps Creedmore, a hunting rifle worth a pretty sum. And that hull wasn't just some old piece of Mexican trash, either. It was deep-dished, double-rigged, with pointed *tapaderos* and conchoed skirts. The trappings were all silver-garnished. It was no working rig.

It would have suited *el presidente*. It held down a first-rate heavy wool blanket.

The stranger gripped the large, flat saddle horn with both hands and swung down. The horse foundered to one side under the shift in the weight. The man swung down stiff and slow, like he'd just stepped out of another country that was slower than this, where a man's heart beats maybe once a minute and a mocker hangs half a morning to a note. He was old, and the blue norther had locked his joints.

Y.O. let loose of the cheek piece. The Mexican leaned for a minute against the black. Then he straightened up and unloosened the girts to give the horse's back some air. He peeled off the yellow slicker and flung it over the saddle. The horse didn't shy at the spooky slicker. It stood stock still, nose down, shanks quivering. It didn't even give the hull a shake the way a horse does that's just come out from under a heavy weight.

He was a big man, tall and lean and straight in his back as a fence post, for all he was past his prime. He was dressed fit to kill: good-grade black wool britches, stovepipe boots, a clay-worsted riding jacket, wool vest, Mexican sash. His shirt was bleached muslin, with a fancy tucked-out front of white linen. A three-day norther hadn't knocked the stiffness out of that starch-proud shirt front. You'd have thought he was on his way to a Mexican *baile* when the weather had caught him. He'd had to use his slicker for a coat.

"Have a bite," Y.O. said. "We was just fixin' to eat." The Mexican stood there and looked at Y.O. "*¿No habla inglés? Venga a comer,*" Y.O. said.

"*Muy bien, gracias,*" the Mexican said. It was a croaking noise in his throat, like he hadn't used his talk box in years. "*¿Tiene algo que comer para mi caballo?*"

"Lige, fetch some feed for this horse," Y.O. said.

Lige grabbed up a half-full tow sack of corn from beside the fire, stood up and fetched it to Y.O. The thawing, still-icy

grass crunched beneath his feet. The Mexican pulled a feedbag from under the slicker. Y.O. shook some hulled corn into
it and the old man put the bag onto the horse's nose and
slipped the headstall up over its ears.

Y.O. said, "*Vamos a comer.*" He turned and walked
to the fire. "No speeka da Engleesh," he said to Clabe and
Emmitt and shrugged his shoulders.

In a minute *el hombre* followed him. Lige came along behind. The old man walked stiff and slow. Even the workings
of his hands and arms were slow. The crisp ice crunched.
Raw, wet grass squeaked beneath his feet. Something about
him made Clabe want to back off. The sun was high. Up on
the pond the cows bawled.

The whole business stuck in Clabe's craw. Where had
the old greaser blown in from, like some stick tossed down
by the wind? The Mexican was almost to him. The closer he
came, the taller he looked. The tall, black, varnished sombrero. His eyes kept looking from one man to the other, but
not from fear. It struck Clabe that the man was looking for
someone. Something grabbed in Clabe's chest. It grabbed so
tight he gave a sharp little laugh. It surprised his own ears.
The old Mexican was looking at him. He looked again from
Lige to Emmitt to Y.O. and smiled, a tight little smile at the
corners of his mouth. Then his eyes lit back onto Clabe, like
a hawk that's skimmed the ground pounces down to its own
shadow. The hair lifted on Claiborne's neck. He hated the
dark sonofabitch. Them fancy duds. That blooded horse. The
Sharps Creedmore. He'd likely shot them off a white man.
Claiborne shivered with rage.

The ground was still icy, and Clabe pressed his hand
against a patch of slush. Lige squatted back down by the fire.
Y.O. pointed to a place beside the fire, across from Clabe.
"Pull up a cheer," he said. The stranger eased himself down.
He had to reach behind to keep from falling back. He let out
a sigh when he sat, straightened up, blinked back the sweat
from his eyes. He looked at Clabe.

He likely had Indian in him. But his cheeks weren't high. It was the long thin face of a Spaniard, one of those white Mexicans, but the dark had crossed him. He looked at Clabe. Claiborne looked down at the ground. The man wore fancy spur leathers: an ℞ was tooled on top of both leathers, across the front of each boot. Clabe looked back up. The sonofabitch was still staring at him. Clabe jabbed his boot heel into the ground. "Come on, Emmitt, dish out the goddamn peaches," he said. Emmitt passed the cups around. Lige dumped a handful of biscuit crumbs into each. The Mexican got Claiborne's cup. Clabe got the goddamned can. California canned goods, and an Indian maid kneeling like a statue on a rock. Her eye filled half her face. She was blue-eyed, same blue as the badge of sky around her.

The Mexican looked at Clabe. He held up Claiborne's cup and nodded his head. "*Gracias,*" he said.

To hell with him.

The tin can smelled harsh and metallic. The insides had turned black. They always do that. Claiborne pulled a pewter spoon from his vest pocket and stirred the crumbs in with the peaches. He stirred with his right hand. His left hand hurt. In two months he hadn't got used to all the time having to use his right hand. The sonofabitch was still looking at him. Claiborne didn't pay him any mind. He spooned out the mush from the can and supped at it. It tasted like hell. It tasted like the turned-black can.

Across the way, the Mexican was putting his down fast. You'd have thought he hadn't eaten in a month. His head was back. His Adam's apple worked in quick jumps. The silver mustache scratched the rim of the cup. Clabe dumped his peaches on the ground.

"Reach me that coffee," Claiborne said. Lige put a cedar stick through the wire handle and lifted the pot across. Clabe poured a little coffee into the can, sloshed it around and tossed it on the ground. The hot liquid steamed in the thawing grass and the grass snapped. Then Clabe filled the can

with coffee, black and hot. It rammed like a red-hot poker
down his gullet, knocked the back of his brains awake, hurt
all through his chest. That felt good. His hand didn't hurt
so much now. Clabe closed his eyes and supped the coffee.
Johnnie Lee Chant laughing in the hired rig. Clabe could
smell the might'near readiness in her hair. He supped the hot
coffee. Come Sunday night . . .

The old Mexican was looking at him. His cup was
empty. He likely wanted a cup of coffee. Let the greaser wait.
Claiborne supped his own coffee, took it in like good whiskey
across his hot teeth. He looked up, above the rim of the tin
can. The Mexican was staring direct across. The sonofabitch!
Claiborne took a loud, slow sup, but it might have been ice
going down his gullet now. His eyelids narrowed. He stared
the bastard right back, looked him square in the eye. But the
man wouldn't faze. There wasn't any scare in his eyes at all,
only a kind of sadness there and back of that a dark fierceness
looking out at Clabe, knowing what it was looking at, the
flesh all loose as feathers around the eyes—like a hawk Clabe
had come on once, hurt, dragging its wing, hissing at him
from the shade of a scrub cedar. Mostly the hawk's fierceness
had been in its eyes. Claiborne had seen that. He had hated
that look. The hawk wouldn't back off. It was like it was
somehow better than Clabe, stronger, held some of the whole
sky in its feathers. Then Claiborne had killed it. He'd been
glad to do it. He had laughed like crazy, chunking stones at it,
watching it flap, last of all smashing flat its head and eyes.
The same fierceness was in the old man's eyes. It made Clabe
want to back off, to be shut of them, of the dark in them.
And at the same time something inside Claiborne craved to
reach across, touch the man, touch whatever it was in his
eyes. He wellnigh did.

The old man nodded his head. Clabe's heart took a hitch.
Coffee spilt from the peach tin, dripped. Clabe busted out
laughing again. Lige and Emmitt and Y.O. looked across.

"What the hell's got into you, Red?" Emmitt said.

"Shut up," Claiborne said. He closed his eyes, swigged off a hot slug of coffee. He'd like to spit it in that bastard Emmitt's face.

"Johnnie Lee Chant's got him high as a cat's back," Lige said. "She's got him climbin' fence rails."

Clabe looked at Lige. "Go butt your brains out on a stoopin' post oak." Lige and Emmitt and Y.O. laughed.

The Mexican looked at the four men. He smiled. "*Sí, sí,*" he said.

"Looky that," Emmitt said, jerking a thumb at the old man. "He looks as happy as if he had good sense."

"Pour the bastard some coffee," Lige said.

"Pour it your ownself," Clabe said. He pushed the pot back toward the fire with his boot.

"Hey. You want coffee?" Emmitt said to the Mexican. Emmitt pulled off his hat and reached over and grabbed the pot handle with the hat brim. He poured himself a cupful and passed the pot to Lige. "Sonofabitch, that's hot," he said. He fanned his coffee with his hat.

"*¿Qué?*" the Mexican said. He looked at Y.O. "*¿Qué dice?*" he said.

"*¿Quiere café?*" Y.O. said.

"*Bueno. Muy bien, gracias.*" The Mexican nodded his head politely, like he figured it was some damned social. The rim of his sombrero joggled a mite. Claiborne thought of the smashed hawk flapping under the scrub cedar.

Lige started to pour himself a cup of coffee. A pebble plinked against the pot. He looked up, annoyed.

Y.O. clucked his tongue and shook his head, his eyebrows knotted and lips puckered like some old granny that's got a whippersnapper's hand reaching across her plate. "Now that ain't *manners,* Lige," he said. "We got company. Reach him your cup, Pancho," he said to the Mexican. "You're the guest of honor. Ain't that so, boys? Lige, pour the man a cup of coffee."

"*¿Perdón?*" The Mexican said.

"*¿Comprende?*" Y.O. said.

"*Yo no comprendo,*" the Mexican said.

Y.O. grinned. The Mexican smiled. He nodded his head vigorously. The rim of the black sombrero flapped. Y.O. laughed.

Emmitt said, "The old codger makes about as much sense as last year's bird nest with the bottom punched out."

"Let's pick up and go," Claiborne said.

"Don't get all in a hassle," Y.O. said.

Lige poured black coffee into the stranger's cup. "*Gracias,*" the old man said. He picked up the hot cup and looked across again at Clabe. Then he drank from the cup, slow, sad almost, his eyes all the time moving, watching the four men.

Lige filled his own cup, handed the pot across to Y.O. Y.O. poured himself a cup of coffee.

Clabe drank his coffee. Up on the pond the cows bawled. All around, now, the ground was beginning to show—patches of wet grass streaked with new green. Clabe stared at the coffee grounds in the bottom of the peach tin.

Y.O. said, "Looks like we kinda lost our weather."

Emmitt said, "I allow as how the sun's gonna hold."

A blue-speckled lizard with two black collars came out of some rocks close by. It flattened itself on a warm rock.

The Mexican set his cup on the ground. "*Ah! Caballeros,*" he said, "*miren ustedes. Aquí tengo unos retratos.*" He reached inside his jacket and felt around through the pockets. Clabe's hand was on his rifle. The Mexican smiled. He fetched out two pasteboard-backed cabinet pictures, frazzle-cornered and splotched by thumbs—took by a camera in its black tent. "*Son de mi familia,*" he said and held one up in the air. He smiled and nodded his head. Over on the rock the lizard had turned its colors. Now it was green and yellow in the sun. Its eye was half closed. Its spotted throat lifted and fell.

The old Mexican showed one photograph around the circle. He reached the other across to Clabe.

"I ain't intristed," Claiborne said.

The Mexican leaned toward Clabe. He held out the photo. It hung like a dark window in the air.

"Shit," Claiborne said. "*Shit!*" He fetched back, flung the peach tin hard as he could. It hit Emmitt's claybank on the rump. The horse let out a squeal that would have done a hog proud. There was a general laying back of ears and widening of eyes and smacking of horseflesh and snorting and kicking and farting in the bunch. Mr. Lizard was back under his rock.

"Damn it, Clabe, quit," Emmitt said. "That horse has already got a hump in his back."

"Leave me be," Claiborne said.

"Drink your coffee and shut up," Y.O. said. The Mexican slipped the pictures back inside his jacket.

The horses quieted. The men drank their coffee. The sun held high.

The dark hawk flapped in Claiborne's head. It made a swishing sound. It spun around and around on its back under the scrub cedar. Its wing-tip feathers spread apart like fingers, scratched the lowest branches, whipped down a shower of rusty needles. Claiborne shut his eyes tight. A shower of rusty cedar needles, dust-filled feathers, the thin hawk screech. Or was it a wind screeching through the cedar branches, across the points of needles? A high wind, black. It hurt the back of his head. His breath tasted metallic. Clabe bit down hard. He grabbed hold of a swatch of wet grass. Something pulled at the back of his head, made his eyeballs start to turn up and strain back. That happened sometimes. To walk into a room and of a sudden nothing hold, the room moving apart at the corners, his boot not quite on to the floor, a lamp tilting at the edge of the table. His hand would grab out quick and touch nothing, his eyes wide, like stumbling through a plunder-room without a light, trying to find the piece of harness he knew was hung somewhere. Then rage would bubble up in him. There was a grief in it, he didn't know why. It put a worse rage in him. Sometimes all he wanted to do was to tear the world apart when that rage came on. A queer whiteness would crowd up around him, the strain inside was so fierce. He hated that white. He wanted to bust through that white, mash in the face of the first sonofabitch that opened his mouth, smash the first live thing he came across, stomp it, yes, break a few bones, get back, get back at something . . . *Oh, God damn! God damn it!* Clabe opened his eyes. For a minute the whole air was dark. Something moved in the dark, hovering, beating its wings over him. He couldn't get back his breath. Then the dark broke up into splotches and then into the full light. Clabe stared at the black sombrero flapping. The Mexican smiled, nodding his head.

"Boys, let's get this stuff down the draw," Y.O. said. "They got to make beef tonight." He cut off a fresh chew from his plug of Star Navy and tucked it into his mouth.

Lige reached into his vest pocket and pulled out the makings of a smoke. He jerked a leaf out of the book of cigarette papers, commenced bundling up a new life of Bull Durham. Fished a burning stick from the fire and lit the shuck. "I'm set," he said.

The Mexican's eyes jumped quick as a jackrabbit from one man to the other. A net of wrinkles spread across his face. Claiborne stared at him.

The old man set the tin cup on the ground. He stood up. He didn't have an easy time doing it. It looked like he'd got ten years older since he'd come here, like even the sunlight was too much weight. "*Gracias, gracias para la comida,*" he said. He bowed stiffly, twice. The tucked-out shirt front crinkled at his breast. The rim of the black sombrero flapped— a horsehair hatband shone slick as a coiled blue whip snake around the crown. He pulled himself up straight. "*Bueno. Ya me voy,*" he said.

He turned and walked stiffly to his horse. He walked like he thought somebody was going to hit him between the shoulder blades. He spoke to his horse. He slapped its withers and the animal jerked its head up. He slipped off the feedbag and hung it from the saddle horn, flung the heavy toe fender up over the saddle, pulled the girts and cinched them tight and let the *tapadero* fall back down again. The silver conchos shone like a spread of Mexican dollars.

The old man took hold of the saddle horn with both hands and put a foot into the stirrup. Y.O. said, "Oh no. You can't leave."

Lige and Emmitt grabbed hold of their rifles and got up onto their feet.

The Mexican stood stock still, one foot in the stirrup and one on the ground. Y.O. shifted his leaf plug to the other cheek and spat. He said, "I'm sure sorry, Mister. It's just we can't have you spreadin' it around about what-all you seen here."

The Mexican stood there for a moment. Then he said, "All right." Leastways that's what Clabe thought he heard him say. He put his foot down from the stirrup. He turned and started walking toward Clabe. Clabe stared at him. The old man kept right on coming.

Sweat burned in Clabe's eyes. The Mexican swam through the blur, a fierce ripple brightness washing around him. That must be the sun. His shirt front was afire. Claiborne blinked. Then there were two of them, two dark strangers ringed with fire. Clabe scraped a sleeve across his face, trying to rub the sweat from his eyes. The man was still coming toward him. He walked solid and heavy, as if his jacket and boots and sash and britches were trappings of lead and the sombrero weighty as blackened silver. He stuck out his hand, walked toward Clabe like he aimed to touch him, like he had some sort of claim on him.

Somebody laughed somewhere.

Claiborne scrambled backward on the grass. He skidded himself back, fell back onto his elbow, his rifle in his hand. Now the man was almost to him. Up there above him. Dark shadow lifting. Wings. The explosion cracked the inside of Clabe's skull. The man smiled. He pulled his jacket open for

Clabe to shoot again, the bright shirt front, like it was a fact he couldn't be killed, couldn't be made to die. Claiborne fired again, a sharp, snapping noise. The black hat flew up, the man's hair was scattered light. The Mexican hunkered down to rest a mite.

Claiborne jumped to his feet. "What's he doin' over there?" he said.

Y.O. said, "You kind of cleaned his plow for him, Clabe."

Lige said, "It's dirtied his shirt some."

The Mexican lay stretched out on the ground over near his horse. The horse had shied back, and Emmitt held it by the cheek piece. Lige and Y.O. stood above the Mexican.

"Goddammit," Claiborne said. "What's he doin' over there?" He started walking toward them, wet grass screeching beneath his feet.

"You sure blowed the liver and lights out of him, Clabe," Emmitt said.

The sombrero lay on the ground in front of Clabe. Claiborne stomped in the crown, smashed it flat, gave the hat a kick. It skidded across the ground, stopped against the man's hand.

Y.O. said, "He must of jumped three foot in the air when it hit him."

The man lay flat on his back on the ground, breathing in little quick half-breaths, his eyes wide, staring up. His shirt front had sogged up the blood like a blotter. All the tucks were soaked red. The blood welled through in an even bigger splotch and puddled at his side.

"Lost enough blood to paint a house," Lige said.

"Who was laughin'?" Claiborne said.

"Ain't nobody doin' no laughin', Clabe," Emmitt said.

Y.O. shook his head. "Well, boys, we got us a Meskin for breakfast."

"Somebody was laughin'," Claiborne said. He looked down at the Mexican.

The man looked at Clabe. He opened his mouth, slow and careful-like, like a sand turtle trying to get a bite around a dewberry. His white mustache was a pair of pointed leaves shaking above the fruit. "Ah . . . *Alto*," he said.

"It's too late to stop now, *amigo*," Y.O. said.

The man shut his eyes and swallowed hard, his Adam's apple sliding under the skin. His neck and face were shiny with sweat. The left eye opened, looking up at Clabe like it was one big joke and he was winking, like he was any minute going to bust out laughing. He made a sniggering noise and opened his mouth wide and let out a laugh that if it'd come out any kind of sound would have scared the deer from the brush. The stock stirred and bawled at the edge of the pond. The old man gave a heave, his hand grabbed the grass, a twig of red sprouted from his mouth. His face went flat. His fingers let go, his flesh loosened its whole length. Only the laugh stayed.

"Close that damn mouth," Clabe said. "Close that eye."

Lige touched the head with his boot. It rolled over to the side and the eye stared out of sight against the grass.

"He wants puttin' to bed with a pick and shovel," Y.O. said.

Claiborne looked down at him. The body lay there, bigger than it ought to be because it was so solid and still, so dressed in its bloodied clothes and still. *No.* Clabe hadn't gone to do it. The bastard had kept coming at him, his black hat flapping, flapping. What was he doing over here? *Hell, shuck it off. It don't matter. He weren't nothin' but a Meskin.* Clabe couldn't tell one Mexican from another. *They're all alike. A Meskin don't count for much.* Then Clabe felt some better. Things shifted a little more into place, and yesterday was Friday and tomorrow Sunday and it was this sun and these cows and his goddamn hand hurt. *He ought not to of come up on us like he done. Put him under a counterpane of rocks.*

"He got a belt on him?" Y.O. said.

Lige bent down and pulled the man's shirt out of his britches. A leather strap was around his waist, across the sunken belly. The man's skin looked younger there.

"I must of missed him the first shot," Claiborne said.

"You never shot but once, Red," Lige said.

"That done it," Emmit said.

"Goddammit, I shot twice."

Y.O. said, "Shut up. What's in the belt?"

Lige unbuckled it and dragged it from under the man's back. An ℞ was tooled on one side of the belt, in the center of the back. Lige lifted the long flap and spread the belt open. "There ain't even no greenbacks in it," he said.

Y.O. said, "Chunk it." The belt looped and twisted through the air and landed in the bushes.

"What about them boots, Clabe?" Emmitt said. "They're about your size." For all how tall the man was, he'd had mighty small feet.

"To hell with it," Claiborne said.

"What about the hull and rifle?"

"I don't want none of it," Claiborne said.

Y.O. said, "He was sure all tricked out."

"Likely shot them off a white man," Claiborne said, "the sonofabitch."

Lige poked around in the vest and jacket pockets. "Poorer than skimmed milk," he said. "Here's them two pitchers. That's all there is." He flipped the two pasteboard-backed photographs onto the ground.

Y.O. sliced another chunk off his leaf plug. He spat the old chew out and tucked the new one in his mouth. "Emmitt, go tail up them two cows," he said. "Clabe and Lige and me'll take care of this." The pond was still hard-frozen, but there was water here and there on it. Cows walked around on the pond, mouthing whatever water they could find. Two steers were down. They lay on the ice looking like they were satisfied to stay there until they were dead and the rest was just foolishness.

Y.O. said, "Let's get him under. We ain't got all day. Toss me that fish." Emmitt pulled the yellow slicker from the saddle and tossed it to Y.O. Y.O. flung it across his shoulder. "Fetch up the hat," he said.

Y.O. took a wrist and Clabe a wrist and Lige got hold of the two legs. They heisted him up. He was heavy as a sack of feed. Claiborne didn't look at him. He kept his eyes on the ground. They started up the side of the draw. It wasn't easy. Brush snagged their boots and rocks rolled out from under their feet. "Jesus Christ, this is poor work," Lige said. When they got to the top they were breathing hard.

They lugged the body over to a rise about forty yards off from the edge of the draw—a round hump of a place covered with brush—and climbed on up. They put the body on the ground. Their shirts were soaked. Steam lifted from the brush. The sun bore down. Clabe hunted around until he came on a hollow place among the rocks, over where the brush was thickest. He kicked out the cedar needles and sticks, and Lige and Y.O. fetched the body over and dropped it in the hollow. The nose and chin and boot toes stuck up above ground level. The bloody tucks were like dark red crusts.

Y.O. said, "You missed them cuff links. That gold ring, *también*."

Lige pulled off the gold ring. He pulled the cuff links from the cuffs.

"That wind must of blowed him clear from Mexico," he said.

Y.O. said, "I think he kind of cottoned to you, Clabe."

"Shit," Claiborne said.

"I kind of took a shine to the old codger my ownself," Lige said.

"It don't sweat me none," Claiborne said.

Y.O. said, "Anyways, dead cocks don't crow."

That damned smile. Claiborne stared down at him, the dark length of him. *Dirt to dirt.* Clabe didn't want anything more to do with it. But of a sudden, out of the flesh, out of the bloody shirt and tucks and jacket a shimmering darkness lifted up, like heat from the ground. It hit Clabe's face. It stopped his breath, almost made him choke. It was a terrible energy lifting up. It wellnigh pushed Claiborne back. It seemed like that body might any minute shift, rub an elbow against rock, brush off the cedar needles, open an eye and wink at him again, *holy Jesus*! like he might sit up in that hole, shake the short death out of his old-man's hair, grin at Clabe. "C-cover the bastard up," Clabe said.

Lige tucked the slicker around the body. Clabe jerked the sombrero out of Lige's fist and chunked it down onto the face. Atop the yellow slicker it was a round, black sun.

Y.O. said, "All right, boys, start pilin' 'em on. There won't nobody smoke him out here." They piled rocks over the carcass. It was a quick business. "Leastways it'll keep out the skunks."

Some crows flew across overhead. Lige said, "Look at them tracks in the sky." He wiped his face with a dirty ker-chief. A red pissant ran out of the pile of rocks and onto Clabe's boot.

Clabe said, "Let's get the bejesus out of here."

When they got back down into the draw the two steers were off the ice. Emmitt was standing over by the black. He'd looped the reins to a cedar bush. He said, "He's a prime piece of horseflesh."

The horse stood spraddle-legged and trembling while Y.O. and Lige studied him. They ran their hands down its legs, lifted its hoofs, checked its mouth. It was a clean-limbed animal, straight-backed and slope-shouldered, big-veined, lots of belly, good black hoofs, shoes all around. It had a six-year-old mouth. Y.O. said, "He's a blooded animal for sure. What's his brand?"

Emmitt said, "It looks to be an upside-down stool. I don't know it."

Y.O. said, "Has he got a county brand?"

Lige said, "There's a **B** on his neck here."

"That might be Brown County," Y.O. said.

"There ain't no brand like that in Brown," Emmitt said.

Y.O. said, "Well, I don't want him around. We'll sell him up to Kansas."

Lige said, "His sweat's cold. His pulse is sort of thready."

Y.O. said, "Hand-rub his legs and give him a little water. I'll lead him. Clabe, unlace this piece of Meskin flash and hide it in the brush." He pulled the Sharps Creedmore out of its leather and broke open the chamber. Vernier scale. Pistol grip. It was a dandy.

Emmitt said, "I sure would like that saddle blanket."

Lige said, "We'll throw it in on a game of pitch. How 'bout it, Red?"

Claiborne said, "I don't want nothin' to do with it." Pitch neither, you sonofabitch.

Clabe uncinched the fancy Mexican saddle and dropped it onto the ground. He looked at his hand. The sore was raw and sticky. He untied the wipe at his neck and wrapped it around the hand.

Emmitt and Lige commenced rubbing the black's legs. Clabe walked over to his horse, the blue roan in the bunch. Old Beel didn't like to see him coming. He jerked his head and snorted. Clabe backed him off from the tree and tightened the girt and hit the leather. Beel humped his back and crab-stepped a little, but that was all. He was pretty well broke by now, except for mornings. Clabe rode over to the Mexican saddle, threw a loop onto it, dallied twice and dragged it up the side of the draw. He stashed the saddle under a cedar bush and covered it with trash—branches and such. It looked like something a cat had scraped together. Then he rode back down into the draw.

The blanket was behind Emmitt's cantle. The rifle was across Y.O.'s slickfork. Y.O. was mounted and led the black on a hair rope. He said, "Let's get these cows out of here."

Lige stood by the fire. "Emmitt, what about this here coffeepot?" he said. He dumped out the grounds.

Emmitt said, "Just let it set right there." He was about to mount. He caught the cheek piece in his left hand, pulled the claybank's head to him and lit on up. The horse spun around. It showed the whites of its eyes. It made a rattling noise in its nose, took three stiff-legged steps and quit the ground. Emmitt was wellnigh chasing clouds.

Lige and Clabe and Y.O. watched. The horse swapped ends with itself. It doubled up like it was trying to tie some kind of knot in its back. It put its nose down between its forelegs until it looked like it was going to hit the ground on its head. It lit on all four feet. Then it hunched down and jumped back up—way up. Emmitt came near having a bird's-eye view of the surrounding country. That claybank bucked sky eastward and sky westward, but Emmitt stuck it out.

Of a sudden the horse quit its pitching and took off on a run down the draw. Lige said, "If the devil would take that damn horse to Hell, he'd sure be adding to his collection."

Pretty soon Emmitt came riding back up. The horse was about played out, but it could still wring its tail. It was blowing hard. Emmitt reined it in. He said, "Now hand me the coffeepot."

Lige fetched it over to him and Emmitt tied it to his saddle.

Clabe's horse shifted. Clabe looked down. The two photographs were on the ground and in one of them a small, pretty woman was looking up. There in the photo, in her summer white. Her face white. The white face and the white dress shone like cold light in front of the dark, painted studio leaves. Her hand was on a gatepost. Clabe got down from Beel and picked up the two pictures. The other was of a Mexican squaw, old and fat. Claiborne looked at the first picture. There was some blood on it, already dry. She stood bright as new-bought china behind the blood sprinkle and the smudge Clabe's thumb made on it. All in her summer white. Round-faced. Hair pulled back. Black centers to her eyes.

Lige said, "Purty as a speckled pup under a new-painted buggy." He'd come up behind Clabe. Clabe turned the picture over.

Emmitt said, "Is that them pitchers, Clabe?"

Claiborne said, "I reckon."

There were some print words on the back side of the photo, stamped in gold, all squared-up fine. Claiborne shifted the card around to read it. He said, "I can't read Meskin. What's it say?"

Y.O. rode on over. He said, "That ain't Meskin, Clabe. It says *San Antonio*. That's where that pitcher was took."

Claiborne said, "Maybe that horse is from Bexar County."

"What kind of a lookin' woman is she?" Emmitt said.

Lige said, "She looks to be a white woman. Purty, too."

"Aw, hell," Emmitt said, "I didn't see that. Let me have a gander." He started his horse toward Clabe.

"Go ahead," Claiborne said. He sailed the picture of the old squaw through the air at Emmitt. The claybank shied back like somebody'd offered it a rattler.

"Oh, you sonofabitch," Emmitt said. The horse jumped around crazy as a hoptoad in a tack factory. It fencewormed and sunfished, the coffeepot clanging against its side like a fire bell in Hell. It was a real spasm. Lige and Y.O. laughed. Then the claybank took off again down the draw.

Clabe walked over to the picture of the old Mexican woman and picked it up. *What's a Meskin squaw havin' her pitcher took for?* He carried it to the campfire and dropped it on the coals. It humped up and browned a moment, then let up a thin blue smoke and popped into flame. Clabe tucked the other photograph inside his jacket. The shriveling picture burned down to a black chip. Clabe kicked the coals apart.

He picked up his cup and spoon and wiped them with a handful of wet grass. He looked at the cup. *Shit.* He flung it as far as he could up the side of the draw.

Emmitt rode back up. Lige said, "What you been doin', Emmitt? Takin' a bird census?"

"Go to hell," Emmitt said. Lige and Y.O. laughed.

Clabe mounted. Lige mounted. "Let's get a move on," Y.O. said.

They rode up to the pond. The cows didn't want to move. They stretched their necks and balled their eyes and lowed, a kind of deep-gutted misery cry. Some were standing on the sides of the draw and had to be rounded back down. Clabe and Lige and Emmitt worked the stock. Pretty soon they had them ginning around below the pond. Y.O. looked them over. "It's a good drift," he said.

Emmitt said, "It'll be killpecker guard tonight."

They started them down the draw. The cows moved slow, they were sore-footed. They drove them across the scattered campfire and the bloody grass.

Claiborne touched the stiff pasteboard in his jacket pocket. It was still there.

Somebody laughed . . .

Emmitt said, "Lookit that moon up there." The sun was at its height, the sky was a washed-out blue. And there was the three-quarters moon, in broad daylight. It looked like a scrap of cloud or a spook fingernail.

Lige said, "It's been gettin' bigger ever' night."

Emmitt rode beside Clabe. He said, "Clabe, you got that pitcher?"

Claiborne said, "I chunked 'em in the fire."

"Hell," Emmitt said, "what'd you go and do that for? You sure are ornery today."

Claiborne said, "Ain't that a fact." They rode on a way.

"You takin' Johnnie Lee Chant to prayer meetin' tomorrer night, Clabe?" Emmitt said.

Claiborne said, "I reckon."

"Look out there, Red," Lige said. "You're gonna get religion some one of these days, messin' around with women."

Claiborne said, "I ain't leadin' the life of a buck nun."

"Goda'mighty, Clabe," Emmitt said. "I wish I was in your boots."

Shit. You don't know nothin' about it.

Lige said, "It is hot as blazes."

Clabe looked up. The air was bright. The grass, thawed now, was a fresh, yellowish brown streaked with new green. Even the rocks, scrubbed by the blizzard and now sun-bleached, looked brand-spanking new.

The stock was hot and moving. The horses followed along behind, their saddles creaking. Emmitt opened his mouth and made like he could sing:

> O the night I struck New York,
> I went out for a quiet walk . . .

Damn them to hell. Clabe didn't like any man.

3

DARK. That's a rooster crowing in the dark, wrangling it up through the crick in its neck, ripping the satin dark. Not the real morning yet. The rooster crowed again, scraping it from its craw. And another and another rooster, farther and farther, all over town like spurts of light, struck lucifers. Somebody was turning a rackety coffee mill downstairs.

This damn bed sags. The cords need tightening.

Clabe was sunk in a feather tick like a thumb in puffed-up biscuit dough, between two sheets, a goosehair bolster under his head. He listened. A three-dollar clock ticking in the dark. Smell of glaze on new calico, rosewater, tar soap, lamp oil, lavender. Vanilla and warm skin. There she is on the far side of the bed, breathing. Even. Easy. Through an open mouth. So she finally let up. After all that fuss. Clabe slid his hand across the feather tick, between the sheets of domestic. Johnnie Lee, warm as biscuits, fat as mud. She turned from his touch, moaning in her sleep. Still in her medicated scarlets. Jesus H. Christ.

Old, deaf Granny Chant is grinding coffee downstairs. Maybe she's fixin' me breakfast. Sit up and take some fry, son. Yes'm. Take some butter. Did you en-joy my Johnnie Lee?

The rooster struck it up again, rough as a rasp, from the splotched top branch of its fig tree down in the dooryard. And another off yonder atop an old sawbuck, and another stretching its flesh upward from a grip on a hoe handle, and on a snapped-over cornstalk in last year's garden patch and on a wagon tongue and a picket fence and the town watering trough, *chark-o-cherokee*, the whole kit and caboodle working like hell to crack the nightshell apart, let loose that yellow yolk right here over Cherokee. Already the window was a different, gun-blue dark.

. . . Back from Fort Croghan about an hour to dark. That bastard Harney always hulls a short ration—two bits to Sam to bed Beel down proper and see he gets a good feed.

Washed in the basin in the bunkroom over the wagon yard. Plenty of Hoyt's Cologne. A clean shirt and his go-to-meetin' suit. Brass-toed boots. Wet his hair with water to flatten out the curls, parted it dead center from the front straight back down to the nape of his neck. Pretty fancy. Oysters and whiskey at the Buckhorn Saloon. Cove oysters, up from the Gulf, and a handful of crackers, a bottle of pepper sauce, nickel's worth of cheese. It makes a Christmas dinner in July.

And there was Johnnie Lee across the aisle amongst the women, the world is a trouble and a sorrow the only bright light is Jesus, singing hard, sometimes looking at him. Consider, the preacher said, the path of righteousness. Johnnie Lee had darkened her eyebrows with a burnt match, dabbed vanilla behind her ears. Clabe could smell it clear across the aisle—vanilla and warm skin. In her lace-trimmed Sunday dress, narrow shoulders, girl waist, lots of hip in a basket of bustle: bread of Heaven. The preacher flung his arms around like he was fighting bees instead of sin. Come up and be saved, come up and be saved. Next thing Clabe knew he was down on his prayerbones at the front bench, all choked on his sins like on a gulletful of sweet potatoes, the womenfolk crying and singing along behind, shouting across to the men to change their ways, get up there with him.

Amen. Amen. Rolled his sins like a dung beetle up to God. His pride, his laziness, his taking the Lord God's name in vain, his drinking, his gambling (he could smell the vanilla clear up here), his general disrespect of things religious. I thank

you, you good people, and Preacher Threadgill, that brung
me to see my sinful ways. These last three days he'd been
sweating it out, thinking on last Wednesday's sermon—The
Devil's Tally—and now he seen his way clear, clear to be
saved. Scratch his name, O Lord, tear out that page, inscribe
it anew in the *Lord's* tallybook.

*To hell with the Lord God Almighty, fetch Him down here,
let Him walk the brush, let Him see what it's like. All this God
stuff, all this Sweet Jesus stuff, all them words, for Christsake. You
can sing your psalms across a dead horse, you can heap up your
prayers until you get a mountain pile and never get out of this hell.
It don't fit the pieces back together, this whole damn world knocked
apart like a busted bale . . .*

I can't *breathe* in this place. It's too weathertight.

Now the window was taking shape, oyster gray, square as
a cracker. One star out there.

That fishlike hush just before dawn. The clock ticked
away in broken chunks.

. . . *Last night.* The hired mare cropping wet winter grass
next the fence. Clabe watched the lamplight drain out of the
kitchen and cross the parlor and settle in the downstairs sleeping room. It was awful quiet, except for the mare's chomping.
The light went out in the sleeping room. A lamp was still
burning in the room upstairs. Claiborne stepped down from
the buggy, caught the mare by the curbstrap under her chin
and led her into the lot across the road. He tied her to a tree.
Then he walked back across the road and opened the gate and
closed it careful behind him and pulled off his boots and stuck
them in a gooseberry bush. The swept yard felt good to his
bare feet, wet and cool. He picked his way across a garden
patch, past a peach tree loaded down with old horseshoes,
and started climbing up the outside staircase. There was moonlight enough to see by. The three-quarters moon.

Johnnie Lee opened the door a crack on its wooden

hinges. All Clabe could see was a strip of her face. She'd blown out the lamp inside.

"Claiborne?" she said. "What on earth!"

"You said you was going to lend me your prayer book, Johnnie Lee."

"Well I didn't mean *tonight*, for goodness sakes," she said. She giggled. Claiborne put his hand on the door frame, leaned down to her. "I figured to start right in studyin'," he said, "while the iron's hot."

"*Shhh*. Don't talk so loud. Is Grandma sleepin'?"

"There ain't no light downstairs."

"Well," Johnnie Lee whispered. She had her nose and mouth pressed to the crack between the door frame and the door. "Don't talk so loud." It was a pretty nose and mouth. Claiborne stuck his forehead into the angle of the frame and the door, close to her nose and mouth.

Claiborne whispered. "I sure have missed you," he said.

"I can't say as you've showed it, the last few days. You ain't been keepin' *me* much company."

"I been awful busy."

"So busy you can't keep a little company with me?"

"I'm keepin' company right now, Johnnie Lee. You're awful purty."

"Ummm," she said. He tried to kiss her. She slid down to the floor, on the other side of the crack. He slid down too, right along with her.

She said, "You didn't hardly say a word to me on the way back from church tonight. What'd you hire a rig for, I want to know, if we wasn't going to talk and visit and such?"

"I reckon I was all het up from bein' saved," he said.

"Awful religious," she said.

Clabe's feet were getting cold. He and Johnnie Lee pressed their faces to the crack, closer and closer, drinking in the breathy heat from each other.

"Did you really miss me?" Johnnie Lee said.

"Ever' minute."

Their mouths touched. She pulled back.

Claiborne reached his hand in through the door crack. He touched her face, her nose and cheek and ear and the streaked hair still piled up. Johnnie Lee kind of leaned her face into his hand, turned her head among the movings of his hand. The motions fitted.

He said, "You sure are sweet, Johnnie Lee."

She said, "You are, too, Claiborne."

He pushed at the door a mite. "You better go now," she said.

"Aw, Johnnie Lee, show a little Christian charity. Least-ways come set on the steps a spell with me. That's the softest hair."

He ran his fingers across her forehead, under the frill of hair and into the slight smooth dip at her temple and along her ear and through the warm nesty hair behind her ear, yes she liked that, and along her neck and chin (he could feel the lace of the high, tight collar scraping his wrist) and gentle across her soft-as-ripe-plums lips. She kissed his fingers, made upward pushes with her nose and mouth into his palm, like a wet calf feeding.

"All right," she said.

There was some fuss and fixing up inside. Then she came out onto the landing. She was still in her Sunday finery. Her shiny brilliantine dress threw back the moonlight like the dark silvering at the back of a mirror. Even her chestnut hair had some of that mirror silverishness. She had the prettiest face, chalk white in the moonlight. Black eyebrows and wet bright lips. Claiborne started toward her. Johnnie Lee laughed, stepped back against the door. "No," she said, "let's look at the moon." She sat down at the top of the steps. The stiff brilliantine rustled when she sat and piled up into a con-glomeration of yard goods around her. Claiborne sat down next her, close as he could get. She said, "It looks cold up there." The moon was a cold stone flung into the black. Clabe got an arm around her. They sat there admiring God's handiwork, the firmament and such. Pretty soon Claiborne was admiring more of God's handiwork—up and down her back, around her waist, on the nubbin of her hip. She was backbone all the way around, but he found the soft places. Thing is, she let him do it. A little at first and then a whole lot more. It was a muss of yard goods and kisses and catch. They tossed it back and forth like a Christmas orange.

Johnnie Lee pulled her mouth loose. "Oh, Claiborne, stop it, I got to quit," she said.

"All right, Johnnie Lee," he said. "I sure don't want to bother you."

She stood up, pushing back her loose hair and straightening her dress. She had a wild stare. Of a sudden she laughed. "You got the boniest feet," she said. Next thing he knew she was in the house.

He was right in after her. It was so dark inside he couldn't've found his nose with both hands. He wasn't looking for his nose, though.

"Claiborne Sanderlin, you get out of here."

"That night air's bad for my health, Johnnie Lee."

"Please, darlin', please."

"My *feet* are cold," he said.

She giggled. He caught her, over by the bedpost. "Oh, Claiborne," she said. Their teeth clicked when they hit. There was some fierce bussing and hugging and grapevine twisting. They sank down to the floor.

She got back her breath. "Quit," she said. "*Quit*. Grandma's right underneath."

"It'll do her good," he said.

"I've changed my notion," Johnnie Lee said.

His hands were everywhere, looking to pick grapes in the Lord's vineyard.

"My notion," she said.

Buttons and hooks.

Jacket and shirtwaist and shift and camisole. Lace and pleats, ruffles and overdrape. Worse than a goddamned shucking contest. Try to unhitch all that in the dark. Bone corset. Wire bustle. Bolts of brilliantine tacked around her waist. Poplin undershirts, layers of petticoats. Hooks and scalloped leather up her calves. Snaps and straps and stocking harness. Enough gear to outfit a team of horses. But he knew she was under there somewhere. Finally he got her worked back to her sateen bloomers. He hulled these down onto the floor. But she wouldn't take off her long johns—her medicated scarlets.

"No no no no," she said. "I ain't never had ever'thing all off at once before. Not even to take a bath," she said.

Like a steer, I can try.

He got her catty-corner onto the bed, lay this burden down. Slots and trapdoors in her medicated scarlets. He put a hand in through. There she was in all her sweet particulars, her flanks ribbed like a washboard from the corset. Pretty soon she was psalming right along, rolling around on the feather tick like a turned-loose horse trying to rub out the saddle marks. But she wouldn't take off her medicated scarlets. She must have figured with her flannels on it was almost like it wasn't happening.

Step smart. Drop your britches. Hell's bells, her in her long johns, him in his shirt and collar, it's right formal. It's Sunday for sure. Cold feet on the tongued-and-grooved floor. She was still psalming. He hopped back in bed, it being the Christian thing to do. Path of righteousness—up the draw, into the cave, loaded for bear. What a friend we have in Jesus.

These goddamned flannels. Might as well play up to an old horse blanket.

Got the back slot undone, spread it open around her hips. O pearly gates. O doodads and curlicues. Her legs were hiked up, her long johns stretched like a fence rail between her stifles—a fine howdy do. As soon worry sardines out of a half-open can, drink coffee with the spoon stuck in your eye. I've changed my notion, she said. No you ain't, he said. Yes I have, yes I have, she said.

Ike! she said.

He had the windmill going, valves and leathers and sucker rods. In the oyster of the world. But she wouldn't kick off the trace chains. She was as helpful as a notch on a stick. Until the long johns split. The red flannel parted company right up the crotch, her legs fell apart like a deck of cards. Clabe like to lost his ace in the shuffle. Then they were both bellying up to the bar. *Save me!* Clabe's back and his bones and his balls and his blood cried. But she was somewhere else, singing in the choir loft. He'd put her up there. Clabe's heart shook. This is the best of Hell. *Where is Your Almighty face and I'll blacken it with blood, hang it to a star.*

Here. *Here!* Here's Your damn tithe, right smack in the collection basket.

Light broke. It was a black sun.

Cold and slick as an empty oyster shell. Another starve-out proposition.

"Get off me. You're too heavy. It's too much."

He rolled over onto the bed. The bed turned slowly around in the dark, tipped up on one leg. Clabe grabbed hold of the tick.

"Oh, my God, what *was* that? What did. Me. It was awful, awful. I was . . . squealing, weren't I? My God, how could I? How *could* I? Oh. Give me a cloth or something. Oh, this is terrible. Oh, dear God, dear Jesus, forgive me, forgive me, forgive me, forgive me, that ain't never what I went . . .

"Just like some same as. Like a wild. Things. Oh, why'd you do it? Why'd you go to do that?"

The bed leveled off. The land leveled out. Here and there a stand of live oaks.

The cows milled around on the pond.

"Oh. Oh. It's gonna be the trouble times for me. It will. I know it will. Oh, it hurts. I bet that's what you was after from the start, weren't it? You bastard. Oh darling, is that what you was after? I should of knowed. Oh, you're disgusting. Ever'body told me to watch out. But you was so good to me. You was so sweet and purty, all that red curly hair. *Why'd you have to go and do it?* I'll never be able to look a body in the face again. They'll see. They'll all know. Oh, I'm so ashamed. Claiborne, you do love me, don't you? You do, you do. Darling. That's the first time ever I. Only with you. Only just with you. We shouldn't of never. I just went . . . went all to pieces. It was awful. You brung me to it. We got to make it right."

The cows were bunched up in the dark. They didn't want to go through the chute. *Fort Croghan.* Christ, he was burnt to the socket. He was really dragging his hub.

". . . like an old shoe. Is that what you mean to do? Is it? Well, I won't let you. I just won't let you. I love you, Claiborne, or I wouldn't of never. Never. Never. Never. Never. Dear. Sweet. Dearest darling dear. Are you asleep? *Are you going to sleep?* Oh you bastard, get out of here, get out of my bed, get out, get out. Claiborne? Claiborne, *please.* Please, darling, please. You can't *stay* here. Grandma's right downstairs."

She pinched him.

"Huh?" he said.

"Get up, wake up," she said.

"Could stand a dose of Kookman's Bitters," he said.

"Get up. Go away. Move over. Get out. Shhh! *Don't wake Grandma!* Oh, I hate you. Get up. I know you now, I know all what you are. You ain't no gentleman. Get out of my bed. Get up. You fart, you'll be sorry for this. You'll rue the day you ever done me like this. Get up. I love you, Claiborne. We'll settle this tomorrow. Get up. I wish I'd never set eyes on you. All that sweet talk, all them fancy promises. I should of been listenin' to what your hands said. Oh, Claiborne, don't you be so mean. I love you. We got to straighten this out. Get up. Oh, you'll pay for this. I hope God comes down and hits you with a thunderbolt. I hope you catch your awful dingus in a throw rope. *Get up.* . . ."

□

Something clicked against the window, beak and claws, then flew off. The rooster crowed again, down in the yard. The sky showed pale as bleached domestic stretched out tight. There was a star up there, like a bright hole in the cloth.

The sky began to lighten, first pink and then yellowish, spreading through the cloth like the watery stuff that comes after the first, hard bleeding of a bad wound. The bandages of light unraveled across the ceiling. They spread in streamers on the whitewashed walls. Streak of light around a washbasin rim, shiny belly of a crock.

A mourning dove sounded from a branch somewhere.

Johnnie Lee was hard asleep. Her head was back, her eyes shut, her mouth open a ways. Her hair looked wellnigh red on the bolster. Claiborne could smell the vanilla, but it was a dry smell now. Poor gal. She had the coverlid pulled up tight under her chin. And likely she'd be keeping her particulars tucked up under her chin hereafter. The next man along would have to climb a brier to get to it.

Claiborne put back the comfort careful. He eased out of the bed and stepped onto the floor. It was a cold floor. Clabe felt around on the floor, found his coat under a chair. The photograph was in one of the pockets, and he took it out. The white dress flashed.

Claiborne held the picture up to the light. He started to sit—jumped right back up. The chair was as cold as an anvil. Clabe sat on the edge of the bed.

The morning light seemed to move into the picture. It was like it was the same air and the same light in the room and in it. The light reached into the photograph, it ruffled across the painted leaves and in and out of the wrinkles at the bottom of the drop. Clabe could see the line between the floor and the drop. There was a carpet on the floor. It didn't look anymore like grass than a scatter rug does. The gatepost stood up into the air. Her hand was on it, and she was about to step out of the photo excepting that there was a wire grip up under her ears, in back of her head; that made her stay there.

The dress was as white as stripped milk. The high white collar lifted her head. Her body was prideful, upright in the bright dress. The long sleeves followed her arms. A crisp puff of white at each shoulder. Such white summer stuff! She stood upright and pert, but there wasn't any stiffness to her, not what was inside the dress. Her hands showed that. One hung loose from a sleeve and rested against the skirt. The other, the right one, with its wrist on the gatepost, drooped in the air, the fingers loose and relaxed. They were long, thin, particular fingers, without rings. A small black brooch like a beetle at her throat. Clabe craved to reach his hand into the picture, through the gloss surface, touch her face. He stared at her face. Well, she wasn't all that pretty. But her face was so *cool-looking*, and there was such a quiet to it. Her hair, black as a wet slate, was pulled back tight. It set off the round, white face. A touch of a smile to her lips. Almost not a smile. More a knowing than a smile. And if she was of a mind right now to turn her head or reach down with her hand and brush a wrinkle from her skirt . . . but she didn't move, kept looking straight ahead. Not at the camera or the black tent or who- ever was standing there behind, but right on through all that. She was looking at Clabe! Two bright spots in the black cen- ters of her eyes from the powder flash. *Oh, but she's so careful, that's what it is!* There she stood in the put-together world, gatepost and carpet and painted leaves, and her terrible quiet was she kept a *hold* on her self tight as the wire grip. She wore her body like her dress, moved it through the world, made it touch. She put her wrist to the gatepost.

Blood pounded in Claiborne's head. He stood up, stumbled over to the window, across a pile of clothes. The star was doused. The sun was about to come up. The ground out- side was wet with dew. There were some broken branches on the ground under the peach tree and under a fig tree over by the fence. A line of smashed-down bean-row brush in the gar- den patch. The blizzard. He'd clean forgot there'd been a norther two days back. But now it was spring, a wet morning.

Two brown hens were scratching and pecking down in the dooryard. Across the road Clabe's hired mare was cropping grass under the tree. They were going to cuss a blue streak at the livery stable when he fetched her back. Their best trotter. To hell with them. He'd pay. He had thirty dollars in his morral from the Croghan job.

The mare and the trappings and buggy were wet. The sky was brightening fast.

Her face shone in the picture. *Do you think you can find me?* A blood stain was near her chin and on the hem of her dress. A big splotch in one of the corners. *That old Meskin likely shot it off a white man, the sonofabitch. The blooded horse, too.* Bexar County! San Antone. They make a saddle like that there. *Yes, I'll find you, come hell or high water.*

What'm I doin', sittin' bare-assed here? Let's get goin'.

The window was shut tight. The air was close and still, stale. It pinched the back of Clabe's nose. He could make out things in the room now. The bedstead yonder, Johnnie Lee sound asleep, the counterpane half onto the floor and half of it pulled up under her chin. Even her pores looked closed. Her weekday dress hung on the wall. A chest of drawers with a heap of woman's truck on top: tucking combs, thread, a cracked saucer with hairpins in it. The pile of clothes was on the floor, bustle and petticoats and his string drawers—ragtag and bobtail from last night's tussle. It looked like the leavings of a spring twister.

Two scissortails flew by outside the window, a sign the frost season's over. Their pink sides flashed as they streaked past. A hawk swung slow in its circle way up high. Clabe heard old Granny Chant moving around downstairs. Smelled her coffee. It made him restless.

San Antone! It was a new day. It was all a big orange show.

Clabe dug around in the clothes pile, fished out his string drawers and britches and heisted them on. He grabbed up his coat. Johnnie Lee smiled. She was likely wrapping ribbon wire around a husband. She made a waking noise . . .

Clabe saw the sun for a minute from the top of the stairs. The hot bloody cap of it was bulging up. Then he was down the staircase four steps at a time. He reined in quick. Old Granny Chant straightened up from her work in the yard. She had on a big slat bonnet, an old black Ulster coat with a piece of blue apron hanging out below, and a pipe in her mouth. She looked at him bug-eyed. The pipe dropped out of her mouth. Her pruning shears clattered to the ground. "Oh, you tomcat!" she said. Clabe didn't stop for his boots. He didn't bother to open the gate—just sailed right on over. The pipe hit his shoulder and bounced into the road. Every sand-bur in the county was in that lot, and he was hopping all over the place. Old Granny Chant was giving him unshirted hell behind. Clabe didn't wait to study it. He jerked the reins loose, lit into the buggy, slapped the straps at the mare's rump. The mare took off with a snort, aimed straight for the trees. He gave her her head. Birds flew out of bushes and rabbits scattered. They hit the trees like spit through a screen door. He didn't know how they got through whole. Finally they came out on the other side. The mare pulled up a slope and back onto the road, about a quarter-mile from the house. The sun burned bright. Clabe felt damned good.

4

ALMOST nobody was in the street. Just the usual morning watch, Troy Huett, Frank Dillard, Asa MacGonagill and Scuff Price flat out on their backs in front of the Beehive and the Double O Saloons. Four hymnlike snores. Anson Hubble was opening his store. Smells of burlap, green coffee, harness leather, cheese, glazed calico and asafetida rolled out of the open doorway. The storefront was covered with nails and tack heads, sheriff's notices, snuff signs, funeral handbills.

The mail hack was in front of the store, Alf's new bay between the shafts. Fresh horse droppings glistened in the street. Clabe drove on past. There was plenty of space between business buildings. Here's the two chinaberry trees, boards slapped up around them—old Mrs. Shackleford trying to pretty up the town. The long morning shadows of the general store and the boot shop and the Family Hotel lay across the road. On the other side of the street the windows of The Ladies' Shop and the City Barber Shop blazed like mirrors. Clabe drove past the blacksmith's and the Missionary Baptist Church of Christ. The white sow that slept in the dumped bathwater under the barbershop quit rubbing her back against the foundation of the Missionary Baptist Church of Christ and looked at Clabe through blonde eyelashes as he passed. Clabe stopped at the town watering trough. The mare didn't want to drink, she kept looking in the direction of the stable. Clabe backed her, turned the corner and headed east. It was against the mare's nature. She wanted the stable. She kept pulling to one side of the road or the other. Clabe whipped her with the reins. They drove past some empty lots and pulled up in front of Hallie Splawn's place. Nobody was about yet but smoke was coming from the chimney at the back of the unpainted gray frame house. Clabe climbed from the buggy, hitched the mare to a gallery post. He walked on around to the back. A flock of chickens was pecking cornbread scatterings at the back steps. He waded through them and mounted the steps and crossed over to the door.

Hallie Splawn was in her kitchen, bent over, shoving a bake pan into the oven. She looked to be mostly rump. Her upper arms, in short sleeves, were as big around as hams.

"How's about a bite to eat?" Clabe said.

Hallie slammed the oven door shut and straightened up. "Clabe Sanderlin, you scairt the daylights out of me," she said.

"You sure are purty this mornin', Hallie," Clabe said.

Hallie snorted. She said, "Now you *git*. You can eat when the rest does." She patted her hair, pulled a kerchief out of her apron waist, shook it open and dabbed her face with it. She turned and stirred something on the stove.

Clabe stepped into the room. "Can't nobody between here and the Brazos cook up a meal good as you, Hallie," he said. "What's this here on the table?"

"That's my roast for tonight. You're in my way. I got cookin' to do." Hallie crossed to the table. Wherever she went her belly got there first. Hallie stuck her hands into a pan of sour-rising dough on the table, pulled off pieces the size of an egg, rolled them in a ball and put them in a greased bake pan alongside, turning each one over so that there was grease on top and bottom.

Clabe said, "Even Miz Steiber can't turn out a feed like you do. Ever'body says that."

"Oh, go 'way with you," Hallie said. She dusted flour on the tops of the biscuits and set the bake pan on a shelf above the stove. She opened the oven and fetched out another pan. Eight rows of tall, brown-crusted, smoking-hot biscuits. She set these above the stove, too, and began to slice big chunks of side meat.

The eight rows of biscuits stared at Clabe. "Goddammit, Hallie," he said, "I sure am hungry."

"Where on earth are your *boots?*" Hallie said. "I *thought* you looked queer."

"I'm toughenin' my feet for summer," Clabe said.

"Humpf," Hallie said. "More'n likely you've been in a scrape somewheres." She dredged chunks of side meat in flour and dropped them into a fry pan. "Leastways you could of wore spurs."

"On my naked feet?"

"They'd of been more decent."

"Aw, come on, Miss Hallie, give me my breakfast. I got to git."

"I expect you do. That or a hangin' party."

"Look," Clabe said, "here's two bits. Cash on the barrel-head." He put a quarter-dollar on the table.

Hallie glared at him. She sighed, put down the stir spoon. "You *could* pay me for last Thursday's breakfast, too," she said. "And the dinner b'fore."

"All right," Clabe said. He plunked a fifty-cent piece down beside the quarter. "Now we're square."

"Well," Hallie said, "them as does, gets."

"Does what?"

"You could fetch me in some more stove wood." Hallie broke several eggs into a fry pan.

Clabe was out and back with a turn of wood in two shakes. He kicked a couple of chickens on the way.

Hallie said, "Go wash your hands." Clabe stepped out onto the back gallery and rinsed his hands in the basin. "Use soap," she said.

Christa'mighty. Clabe washed and rinsed and wiped on the towel hanging on a nail. When he got back in, there was a plate and tin cup on the table.

Hallie said, "Pull up a cheer." Clabe sat to the table.

Hallie said, "Get your feet under the table, it don't look proper. I swear, it makes a body wonder, a cowboy walkin' about barefoot." She laughed. Clabe kept his mouth shut. His stomach felt like it was wrassling a wad of prickers.

Hallie poured coffee into the tin cup. She forked side meat off a platter and shoveled scrambled eggs out of the fry pan onto Clabe's plate and poured hot larrup syrup onto the plate. She broke off six biscuits and leaned them against the tin cup, then she turned out the rest of the biscuits and greased the pan.

Clabe loved the domed, burnt-flourdust tops of the biscuits. He licked at the top of one. Dry powdery bake taste. He bit into it, the crust crackled and chipped, the biscuit pulled apart into long light-bread threads, moist and hot and white. They were as close to bread as you could get and still be a biscuit. But not like baker's bread—wasp-nest bread. Hallie's biscuits chewed solid, with plenty of body against the roof of a man's mouth. Clabe sopped the biscuit in the larrup syrup, washed it down with hot coffee. He put a little salt in his coffee, which was how he liked it best. It was clear black Arbuckle coffee, strong-flavored. He drank three cups of it. The eggs were just right—juicy wet, the yellow streaked with white and here and there some cooked blood spots. He helped that down with coffee too. He put away big chunks of the chawy side meat. "You got any beans, Hallie?" he said.

Hallie was breaking eggs into a bowl, her hands sticky with raw egg and flour. "Do I got any brains," she said, "lettin' you in my kitchen while I'm tryin' to cook?" She wiped her hands on her apron. At the stove she shuffled a fry pan back and forth, gave the larrup a stir. "I got a damnfool weakness for red hair, that's what I got." She sighed. She took a plate down from the shelf above the stove and set it on the table. "Them's from last night," she said.

Clabe mashed the beans in the larrup and ate them. They put a good bottom on his stomach. "I sure would like to work for you for fifty cents a day and found," he said.

"I expect you would. Found only at eatin' time."

The mare out front whinnied. Somebody came riding up, out front. Clabe gulped down the last of his coffee. "I got to git," he said. He slipped the tin cup into his coat pocket. "Adios," he said.

"They're mighty flat feet," Hallie said.

Clabe stopped for a minute at the door. "Hallie," he said, "I'd marry you if you wasn't so damn fussy."

Hallie laughed. She shook all over.

Clabe grabbed a biscuit from the pile and went out. "Mornin', Ed. Mornin', Hollis." He didn't stop to talk to them. He climbed into the buggy and put his hat over his feet. The mare lit out for the stable.

At the livery stable Mr. Wittenberg, *Prop.*, said, "Jesus Christ, Clabe, what did you do, drive her through a mesquite thicket?" He looked at the mare's chest and forelegs. He walked around the buggy, his face getting redder and redder. A vein thumped in his temple. Clabe put three dollars on the buggy seat to help ease his troubles. In the wagon yard he gave Sam a ten-cent piece to saddle up Beel and feed him a measure of corn. Sam looked at Clabe's feet.

"Shut up," Clabe said. He walked across the yard and up the stairs to the bunkroom.

The first thing he did was to get into his boots, his beat-up ones. It felt like he had natural feet again. He took out his Henry rifle from under the mattress. He threw a box of cartridges, a can of tomatoes, a tin plate, Hallie's tin cup, a comb, a can of sardines, and a bottle of Hoyt's Cologne into his saddlebags. He stuffed his collar and his jacket and a shirt and Hallie's biscuit in it too. His slicker was on his saddle. He picked up the rifle and the saddlebags and his bedroll and went down into the yard.

Beel was in front of the feedhouse, his nose in a bucket. The horse lifted his head and stared at Clabe when he heard him coming. His ears went back. But he kept on chewing. He looked to be rested, his ornery self again. Clabe dropped the

gear onto the ground and walked up to him. The gelding's
eyes widened a mite. "Chuck, chuck, chuck," Clabe said. He
put his hand on Beel's neck, all the time rubbing and talking.
Pretty soon Beel had his nose back down into the bucket.
Clabe ran his hand along the neck, under the black mane
down to the withers. Blue roan. Blue hairs mixed with white.
A sound animal, lots of stay, a little narrow in the chest, but
with a good spread of ribs and a barrel belly. High withers and
long, sloping shoulders—puts plenty of horse in front of a
man when he's up. The only trouble was, Beel had spent too
many winters in the brush and he still had a few burrs under
his tail. Clabe rubbed the horse's shoulder, ran his hand along
the ribs and up the flank. Beel shifted. Clabe stuck his arm in,
way in under the blanket. It was clean. Sam had brushed him.
Clabe pulled his arm out and tightened the girt.

Clabe threw the saddlebags across the back jockey and
tied them on. He tied the bedroll behind the cantle and
stuffed an old tow sack between the bedroll and the cantle.
He slipped the Henry rifle into its leather under the fender.
The slicker and a hair rope were up front. Clabe walked Beel
around the yard and tightened the girt.

Harney and Sam were standing in a doorway, watching.

Clabe gathered the reins up to the apple, put a foot in
the stirrup and lit on up. It always came as an annoyance
to Beel when a man was up there. He took a step. Then he
humped his back and locked his knees and went to straight-
legging it around the yard like his hoofs were a set of springs.
The sun changed position several times. Clabe let him get his
licks out. It felt good. It felt good to have that wild between
his knees, prime horseflesh, the jolts hammering up through
Clabe's backbone, about to come out in a yahoo in his mouth.
When Beel looked to be about to quit, Clabe put a hand on
his hip near his tail and Beel took a few more jumps. That put
a piece of morning in Clabe's guts. Then Beel began to run.
Clabe circled him around the yard a couple of times and rode
out through the gate.

He rode out of town by the south way. A big, high wagon-load of salt pork was being unloaded in front of Blanchard's, the racket store.

The jail, the surveyor's office, two plank houses, a cow shed, a stretch of broken-down picket fence, and then the town petered out into the rough. The ground was still morning-wet. The air was cool and fresh and as tasty as branch water. All of a Monday morning! It was about an hour past sunup.

> *Rise up my dearest dear*
> *and present to me your hand*
> *we'll lead in the procession*
> *to a far and distant land.*
>
> *O the girls will knit and sew*
> *and the boys will plough and hoe*
> *and we'll rally in the cane brake*
> *and shoot the buffalo.*

Two wagon tracks for a way, rocky traces, with blue quail running in the brush and doves sounding yonder on both sides. The tracks turned west toward Corydon Mabry's place, but Clabe took a deer trail down-country, south. The sun on his left, white hot stove lid in the sky. That's spring in Texas: one day a norther, next day a summer sun. Already it was warming the morning air. Up over a rise through a stand of blackjack oaks down the slope to Dove Creek. The valley opened wide. Indian Hills on the left, Tobin's Knob on the right. Stone under the horse's hoofs, rock sound, slate sound, gravel sound, dirt sound. Brush scratched the horse's belly, an easy going, side to side, bunched or slack muscle, the bone shift. Beel was a pacer, not a trotter, and it felt good. The motion worked up through the leather into Clabe's hips. Hard, slick saddle under his ass: solid travel.

Spindles of cloud cotton drifted across the sky. Crows, tracks in the sky, and a ragged string of grackles heading north.

Clabe's shadow moved along the ground off to the right. It kinked its shape to move over bushes, slid flat as black silk on the clear spaces. He had twenty-five greenbacks in his pocket. Free! Like the time he'd quit home. Nine years old. His pa had chased him through the horse lot and caught him in the brush-pen corner. Pulled off a leather belt and strapped his legs until they were blue. It wasn't the first time. Clabe's legs had throbbed all night. The next morning, before anyone was up, he stole the plow horse and the old Enfield rifle and lit on out. He kept the Enfield cocked. The old man had better know better than to follow him (though if Clabe had had to fire the Enfield, as like as not it would have knocked him flat onto his back). He had ridden a long way through the morning dark. It had been so quiet. There was such a suppressed, fearful fret in him. Then the light had broke in the east. *Free!* The whole world lay out before him, bright and new. Free! Oh Christ, that had felt good!

Now it was rich bottomland and sandy loam as Clabe rode down through a valley between brush-covered hills, the sun higher now, smaller, more exact. Sweat on his back, sweaty hatband, leather reins sweaty in his hand. Sometimes a breeze, but mostly the grass was quiet. Smell of hot, dry winter grass, the new grass poking up through. New, red leaves on the brush. The mesquites in this section were leafing out, a bright, feathery green. A deer ran out of a clump of post oaks, its white flag up. Clabe rolled a six-inch cigarette from cut-plug tobacco. It lasted him four miles.

At noon they crossed the Llano. The water was fast, up above Beel's hocks. Clabe let Beel drink and took a drink his ownself. He wasn't hungry. Hallie's grub had stayed with him. He led Beel down the riverbed a way to a sycamore and took a piss, felt a deal better.

Something stank. A dead owl or hawk lay on the ground on the other side of the sycamore, mess of maggots and feathers. A crowd of midges shimmered above it. Clabe swung up into the saddle and rode on.

In the afternoon, he ate Hallie's biscuit. Overhead some crows were pestering a hawk. It would hold and they'd flutter above it, fussing, then drop down onto it in a rush, make it flap and screech and lift up higher, and then they'd fly back up above it. The hills began to close in. The country was roughening up again. Red-dirt country. Clabe let Beel pick his own way. He and his horse were all one thing, like their shadow on the ground there. Their bones moved together. Sometimes Clabe rode with one leg across the saddle or sat back against the cantle for a change. They went a long way. The sun moved west. The moon came up in broad daylight. Fat fingernail. They rode through some hills and down a stone gully and out onto an open flat. It looked like the grass was going to be good hereabouts, give it a few more weeks.

In the evening Clabe came to a farmhouse, a timber-and-mud cabin between a half-plowed cornfield and a patch of twiggy, dried-up cotton stalks. It was a one-door, windowless affair with swept yard and cedar-stake fence. Clothes of various shapes and colors and sizes, some mentionable and some not, were draped on the fence. Steam rose from a big black pot in the yard. A woman stood over it. "Halloo," Clabe shouted across the cottonpatch. A man perched on a tilted-back box next the doorway shoved forward. He stood up, slipped a jackknife and whittling-stick into his pocket, knocked the shavings off his britches and walked over to the fence. Children scatted out of sight—they looked to be as tame as wild deer. The woman was hurrying along the fence, pulling off every third or fourth piece of wash. She stashed an armful away someplace. Then she was back over her pot. She was a tall, bony, horse-faced woman with a thin nose and pinched lips. She wore a flour-sacking dress. "Howdy, ma'am," Clabe said. He tipped his hat as he rode up. She gave him a sour look. She picked up a paddle and went to battling a clump of laundry on a block. It smelled of strong lye soap. She went at it like she was clobbering a rattler. She dumped the remains into the pot. The family saddle-and-plow horse—a low-haunched, walleyed stick worth, Clabe figured, maybe a dollar and a half with the saddle thrown in—roamed loose in the dirt yard. There wasn't a stalk of grass in the yard for the horse to eat.

The man looked at Clabe. He had serious small blue eyes, tufts of hair sticking out of his nose, and a growth of stubble on his neck and chin. If you could call it a chin—he hadn't much more of a chin than a bird has. He said, "Light down, mister. Rest a spell."

Clabe said, "I got a ways to go."

"Fayette!" the woman yelled at her husband.

The man said, "How's the weather in your parts?"

"A plenty of fog."

"Well, it will put a good season in the ground."

"Fayette!" the woman said. She glared at her husband. The man picked up a slop jar that was hanging on the fence beside him and put it behind his back. The woman went back to pounding her laundry like she meant to pulverize the cloth or break the battling-stick, one. Faces peered out of the darkness in the cabin doorway.

The man said, "That's the cleanest woman I ever seen. All the time washin', all the time sweepin'. I don't know where I lost my foot off her neck. What kind of a piece is that in the case there?"

"A short rifle."

"Days, she sticks mesquite branches under the bed coverlid to keep a body off. I don't get no rest."

Clabe said, "You got any corn for my horse?"

"We hardly got enough to bread ourselves. None to sell. Where you headed?"

"San Antonio."

"Oh," the man said, "you don't want to go there. They got trouble there."

"How'd that?"

"Cholera. The whole damn town. Feller from Leon Springs on his way to look at some land up in Mason County told me that."

"When was it he came by?"

"Oh, a week—no, two weeks back. Folks don't even go out of their houses there. They keep their doors locked."

"Can you sell me a pone of cornbread?" Clabe said.

"Can we sell him a pone of cornbread, Tempe?" the man said.

The woman was jabbing a stick up and down in the pot. She looked at them both, missed a beat. Then she jabbed the stick up and down in the pot.

"Morris!" the man called toward the cabin.

A gawky, tow-headed boy slipped out of the cabin darkness. He pressed against the log front and stared at the ground. "Git over here," the man said. The boy shuffled through the dirt to him. The man said, "Fetch me a pone from the safe. On the top shelf. Right quick." He caught the boy by the elbow. "Here," he said, "put this in the house." The boy grabbed the slop jar and ran into the cabin. In a minute he was back with a stick of yellow cornbread. He didn't stay to witness the sale.

"Five cents a fair price?"

Clabe fished a dime from his pocket and gave it to him.

The man said, "Why don't you put up here? It's coming night on you."

"No," Clabe said. "Thanks anyways."

"You got any tobacco?" the man said.

Clabe offered him some plug tobacco. The man cut a little into a kerchief and stowed it in his pocket. Over in the yard the horse swung its nose above some chicks. Quick as a wink it gulped one down. "Mighty fine," the man said. He handed the tobacco back to Clabe.

"Goda'mighty!" Clabe said.

The man said, "She *is* a hardworkin' woman." He shook his head sadly. "It does beat all."

"No, I'm talkin' about your chicks," Clabe said. "Adios," he said. He jabbed Beel's belly with his boot heel.

"That's a mighty fine horse," the man called after him.

Clabe rode another hour. The sun was down low, orange-bodied and yellow-edged above the dark hills to the west. The whole sky was red, streaked with pink and black clouds. A high, scribbled line of birds. Stars showed. The moon held its own. A darkness was in the grass. The air seemed to press down close—Clabe rode through pockets of cool. It was awful still, that quiet stretch that comes just before deer time. Only Beel's hoofs and the *swick-swock* noise of the saddle.

Clabe stopped beside a creek, likely the Pedernales, a slow, slab-bottomed thing with mesquites and a few elms alongside. He let Beel drink. Then he got down and led him over to an elm tree. He unlaced the hull, dropped it and the rest of the gear to the ground. Beel snorted and switched his tail. His skin hitched and shivered where the saddle had left a sweat-mark shadow. Clabe pulled the tow sack from between the bedroll and the cantle. He made a hobble from the tow sack by pulling the stitching from the side and bottom, open-ing the sack and folding it into a triangle. He rolled this into a long hank, cut a four-inch slit lengthwise in the middle and passed the ends several times through the opening. He led Beel up a slope and hobbled him out, wrapping a piece of the tow sack around each foreleg and twisting and knotting it tight.

Clabe walked back down to the elm tree. He scraped some leaves into a pile under the tree and rolled his bedroll out on it. Got the sardines and the can of tomatoes from one of his saddlebags, ate them with the chunk of cornpone. Knifed the fishes from the tin and sopped cornpone in the oil. Drank the seedy tomato juice. Then he crawled into his bedroll. The saddle was as hard as a rock under his head.

It was dark enough to see by the moon, now. A wind moved across Clabe's face. Deer upwind moved to the creek, hoofs clicking against rocks. Some small thing skittered across Clabe's blanket. *What if I was to look at a tree right, like a hawk or a ringtail does? What all would it be? A whole other thing, likely, what I can't hardly guess at now.* Christ, he was bushed. Something pulled at the back of his head, yanking hard, dragging him by the hair backward through space. His brain blinked. Then he was slewing downward into sleep, like sliding down the twist of a greased auger.

A dog ran in the sun. *Here, Tick.*

She wore a small, black, piled-up hat, with a veil. She turned her face, puzzled-like, brushed back the black veil. Round, white face. *Do you think you can find me?*

Clabe woke. The moon was down low in the west. The Milky Way lay sprinkled like a track of lime dust through the sky. The Big Dipper was under the North Star. A bright, changeable star, sometimes green, sometimes red, snapped and kindled to the south.

A furry thing ran across Clabe's blankets and brushed against his neck. Before he could lift his hand it ran off. His body felt pasty wet. *Must of had a small fit.* He crawled out of his blankets, pulled on his boots, pushed the spur shanks down onto the heels and buttoned the leathers. His wet clothes stuck to his skin. *The thing is, to keep movin'.* He put on his coat and spooled the bedroll. He walked up the slope, the bridle in his hand. He clucked and talked, he held out a piece of cornpone in his hand. When Beel came to him he slipped the bit into his mouth and the headstall on. He gave Beel's back a short grooming, unhobbled him and led him down to the elm tree, flung the gear across and laced up. It looked to be a little past one by the Big Dipper. Clabe built himself a smoke and lit it. That tasted good. He swung up into the saddle. For a wonder Beel stepped right on out. He didn't even give his tail a hitch.

Splashed across the creek and climbed the limestone shelf and hit down-country. It was a different feel to the country now, long up-and-down slopes sprinkled with mesquites and live oaks. The trees weren't in motts, but one here and one there all to itself, like it'd been planted. Clabe followed the changeable star. The slopes broke and were hilly again. He rode up into the hills. The moon went down. Beel kept right on in the dark. He never stumbled over brush or rocks. He could have made his way at night down a bed of railroad ties.

The stars were down close, hundreds and hundreds of them. They gave a shadow light to the clots and blobs of earth, the bobbing horse's head, the dark curve of a ridge to the west.

Sharp smell of scrub cedar.

Clabe rode through a six-house town in the dark. Dogs barked. Somebody lit a lamp in a window. The window was a queer yellow square in the dark. They came to the Guadalupe River. The water was bank-full and fast, due to the melt-off from the norther. Cold, wet air came off it. Clabe could hardly see the river, but he could sure hear it. He lit down from Beel and loosened the saddle girt. He unlaced the saddle-bags and the rifle in its leather and slung the saddlebags over his shoulder. Then he swung back up, touched heel to Beel's belly. The horse picked its way between cypress stumps and roots and various trash and out into the smooth, slippery stones of the river bottom. Then they were in the water. Clabe held the rifle over his head. The water came up over the saddle. It was damn cold. For a minute Beel stood still, caught in the balance between the weight of their two bodies and the press of the current. Clabe roweled him hard. The horse struck out for the other side. When they came out on the other side Clabe's britches and boots and coattails were soaking. When they had gone a way he lit down and tightened the saddle girt again.

He rode through a rough, rocky country. The mountains

on both sides were built up of long layers of rock, as if somebody'd laid the world down here in slabs.

The sky began to lighten. Birds made their morning
noises. The same star Clabe had seen yesterday morning hung
in the sky to the east. It hung there all alone when everything
else went out. Then up came the Poor Man's Overcoat. The
birds really struck up then. It seemed like there were redbirds
everywhere, bright streaks in the brush. They chipped and
weet weeted and *wet year year yeared. Burty burty burty burty.*
And other birds too, scrub jays and such.

Steam lifted from Claiborne's britches.

He rode down into a valley and hit a road going south.
This looked to be a more settled-up section of Texas, painted
houses and plowed ten-acre fields. He met a passel of children carrying book satchels and dinner buckets in their fists.
They all had rosy cheeks. Most of them were yellow haired,
the girls' hair done up in thick, limber, straw-colored braids.
"*Guten morgen,*" they said.

Clabe lengthened the stirrup leathers to get the cramp
out of his legs. He rode down through the valley, good bottomland and then long stretches of mesquite grass with islands of
post oaks. A few scatter-dab flowers here and there, blues and
purples. Then more hills.

Clabe's hand was hurting again. The sore had come open.
He held the reins in his right hand.

He rode alongside a creek that ran in a draw below. Three
white cranes rose from the creek, flapping hard. They flew in
a widening circle. For a minute, crossing the sun, they were
black.

The road dropped down. Clabe forded the creek and
rode through more hills. He topped a rise and checked his
horse. About five miles below, on the edge of the South Texas
prairies, were the domes and white, clustered buildings of San
Antonio.

5

WHEN he woke, a dim orange light was slanting in through the shutters. It looked to be about three hours later than when he'd got in bed. A church bell clunked nearby. His bedroll, shirt, coat and jacket were scattered about the room. But he hadn't been able to get his boots off, they'd been so wet tight. He'd just crawled onto the bed and conked out. The boots were dry now. Clabe swung his feet down onto the floor and stood up. He rinsed his face in a basin, put on his shirt and the sack coat, combed his hair, fetched up his hat and stepped out into the long hallway. Yellow wallpaper. The rooms were on the right, the line of windows on the left looked down onto Dolorosa Street. He walked down the hallway and the stairs to the lobby of the hotel and went over to the desk.

"What's the time?" he said.

"Six-thirty, sir." The clerk, an old codger in a yellow and black vest, looked up. "*Wednesday*, sir," he said. "You ain't been atall sick, I hope," he said.

Twenty-seven hours!

"No," Claiborne said. "Just damn tired." Damned hungry, too.

In the Elite Restaurant on the north side of Main Plaza Clabe ate a supper of steak, fried potatoes, green food, coffee and stewed figs. Then he walked back across the plaza and past the old cathedral to the hotel. A street railway car pulled by two horses came by. It ran on steel tracks right across the plaza. It was a long, orange-painted affair with a platform at each end. In the middle of the plaza the car stopped. Some ladies got off. The conductor rang a bell and the horses pulled forward again. Clabe went on into the hotel.

Three men and two women—the men in three-button cutaway coats, the women in silk and taffeta—were coming down the stairs.

"So they got a license at the courthouse and sent a friend to the train to tell him his girl'd already married," one of the women said.

"Well I never!" the woman in a red walking skirt said. She looked at Clabe as they passed.

"Another state," one of the men said.

"That's what it ciphered up to."

"What of the cholera?" one of them said.

"Well, thank God we're clear of that. It was a terror while it lasted."

Claiborne went up the stairs and through the hallway to his room. He locked the door, pulled off his boots, dumped his clothes in a heap on a chair and crawled into bed. He was asleep in two winks.

The butchers were sharpening their cleavers in the market nearby. Clabe woke. It was already daylight. A pair of boot heels clacked on the sidewalk down below, walking fast. Voices from the street. A child hollered in Mexican. Horse hoofs—a wagon, rattle of iron rims in the street. Bright, morning sunlight came in through the shutters.

Clabe dressed and went down into the lobby. The woman of the red walking skirt was sitting on a settee near the lobby entrance. Today she had on a gray carriage dress and jacket. She looked up at Clabe, half-smiled as he walked past. Clabe went on out onto the plaza. There was a sweet, scorched smell in the air. The sun was already well up.

The first sound that hit Clabe's ears was a gunshot. He stepped right back up out of the street. But no one else was making for cover. A bosomy woman with a market basket kept right on walking, a boy on a stickhorse prancing along behind. Two bearded German shopkeepers, talking and gesturing, crossed the street. Riders on horseback trotted by. A hack with a fancy-dressed, parasol-toting lady in it rounded the corner and made across the plaza. A Mexican cart piled with blocks of fresh white uncut limestone clunked across the street railway tracks. A second gunshot rang out, echoing among the plaza buildings.

A line of ten or twelve Mexicans came out of Soledad Street onto the plaza. Four men carried a wooden coffin on their shoulders. An old woman, her face dark and wrinkled, her black shawl wrapped tight around her, followed, staring straight ahead. Behind her others walked two abreast, the women in white shifts and black shawls, the men in loose white cotton shirts and trousers. A Mexican with a revolver brought up the rear. The procession wound amongst the carts and wagons. Dogs ran alongside. There were more dogs than mourners. The Mexican pointed his gun into the air. Here, up close, it made a flat ca-*rack!* that seemed to slap against the building fronts and stick there. Claiborne blushed. At the corner the procession turned onto Dolorosa Street. Claiborne jammed his hat down tighter onto his head and crossed the plaza.

He walked east. The sidewalk, limestone brown-spattered with tobacco spit, was worn in ruts by many feet. A market house, a big stone building, took up the middle of the block. Ducks and rabbits hanging. Tongues and saddles and quarters of beef. German sausage rings in loops as big as washtubs. Barrels of pecans and rice and onions and dried fruit and coffee beans, dried red peppers on strings. Redbirds and finches in wicker cages. A Mexican woman brushed flies from her dark candies with a cow tail. Another sat hunched against the building, paper flowers in her lap. Women, Mexican and white, market baskets on their arms, wandered in and out of the building, bent over the stalls, poked at the meat and fingered the onions. On the sidewalk across the street, beneath a chinaberry tree, some white women sat at a table, eating rolls and drinking chocolate. Dogs were everywhere. A dog snatched a scrap of innards tossed out by a butcher. It made for the corner. Others ran after it. Suddenly there was a knot of teeth, backs, tails, legs, snarls, snaps and yelps. Claiborne walked to the next alley and turned up it.

Things were quieter in the alley. It was stone-paved and narrow, with a gutter up the center. An adobe wall ran along one side, and vines and the branches of mulberry trees hung over it. Clabe walked past an adobe house, blue-painted, its arched doorway one step up from the alley—thick oak doors, an iron balcony overhead. Near the end of the alley was a white clapboard frame house with pink window blinds. It was fronted with a picket fence and set back from the alley a way. Berry and vegetable patches between the front steps and the fence, the black dirt freshly turned. Pale, tender leaves were on the berry canes, darker, stiffer leaves on an apricot. A three-storied brick business building stood next to the clapboard house. Clabe stepped out onto Commerce Street.

The signs told you what was in each shop, but Clabe couldn't parse them. In a shop window little china dollheads. Trusses, crutches, feeders, and sponges in another shop. A wallpaper shop. A hardware shop. Shoes. Wooden awning— a barbershop. Clabe walked in.

"Well, it looks to be a fair day out. Come on in. We ain't all that busy. Charlie here's just visitin'." The barber jerked his green eyeshade toward the other person in the shop, a pot-bellied old fellow sitting on a bench against the wall. Tall-necked bottles, mirrors, marble sink, smell of lavender and bay rum. The barber tapped the back of the barber chair. "We'll have you fixed in two shakes," he said. "Lookin' like a new man. Feelin' like one, too."

Clabe hung his hat on the hat stand and sat in the chair. The barber flourished a big black-and-white-striped sheet.

"Looks like folks is startin' to come out of their shells again," he said. "Two weeks ago you wouldn't of seen nobody in the streets."

"Shave," Claiborne said.

The barber lowered the chair, slung the sheet across Clabe and pinned it up around his neck. He let the chair back so that Clabe was almost lying out straight. He put hot water into a mug and commenced to work up a lather. The brush handle knocked against the cup.

"So Gus Hofheinz is coming over tonight and they're going to see if they can settle it," the man called Charlie said in a deep-throated drawl.

"That so?" the barber said. He spread lather on Clabe's face and rubbed it in with his fingertips. "I take it you're in town on the go-by," he said to Clabe. "I don't think I've done you the tonsorial honors b'fore." The barber waited a moment. Then he turned and rinsed his hands at the sink.

"You can thank the good Lord you wasn't here, mister," the drawl said, "if you wasn't." He leaned toward Clabe, his belly piling up in front of him on spread-apart thighs. "Everything was closed excepting one or two saloons. The only sound you'd hear was somebody ridin' for a doctor or a hearse headed out East Commerce Street."

"Well," the barber said, "it's petered out. And that norther came along and cleared out the rest of it. But oh, before that, wasn't it a terrible warm winter? That's what let the cholera get out of hand." He put a hot steam towel under Clabe's chin and up over his face, with just the nose to show. He stropped his razor.

"Frank Mosley walked into Jack Harris's Corner," Charlie said, "ordered three fingers of bourbon. When they put it in front of him, there he was, propped up against the bar, dead and stiff as a board."

"Things are more back to normal now," the barber said. He removed the towel and put on another coat of lather.

"Thank the good Lord."

The barber leaned over Clabe. "Well, it's going to be a great town," he said. "We got a streetcar system just like the best of 'em. Telephone wires going up, got 'em right now at the waterworks. Business buildings going up." He wiped the razor blade on the heel of his hand and the hand on a towel and reached across, using a backhand stroke. His face was down close. A thin golden crack shone in the brown iris of his left eye. "'Course," he said, "we got to get a railroad through. There's the Sunset Road comes up from Houston, and they got track pushed out as far west as Ugalde. What they aim to do is hook up with El Paso."

"Southern Pacific," Charlie said. "*Then* it'll be a big to-do. Like the time they opened up the town to Moody and Sankey."

The barber gave Clabe's face a second turn, cross-grain. A woman in a white dress walked by the shop. She glanced through the window as she went past. Yellow hair and a small, dove-colored hat. A Mexican walked past. The barber pinched Clabe's lips and shaved around the corners of the mouth.

Charlie cleared his throat. He spat. "Odd Fellows is holdin' their first meetin' t'morrow night," he said. "Since."

"That so?" the barber said. He rubbed face cream into Clabe's face and put a hot towel over it.

"Jeff Nunley's the new Noble Grand."

"That's what I heard."

The barber removed the towel and rubbed on some smooth toilet water. He stood back and fanned Clabe's face with a towel. Lastly he dusted on some powder. He grinned. "There!" he said. "That ought to do you." The chair came up, the sheet off.

Clabe paid his fifteen cents. He walked back up the street to a restaurant. He had a plate of ham, eggs, grits and salted black coffee for breakfast.

Clabe's boots made a muffled, creaky noise in the sawdust—four inches deep of it on the floor. There was a big brass spittoon in the center of the floor, but the sawdust was stained with ambeer. Clabe walked over to the counter. "This the office of the County Clerk?" he said.

The small, hunched-over man at a rolltop desk on the other side of the counter swung around in his swivel chair. His head was bent to one side in a queer way. "I believe it is," he said. "That is the office I was so narrowly elected to." He smiled slightly. A newspaper was spread out on his lap. Without looking down he closed it, folded and creased it. With the two loose edges between the fingers of his right hand he tapped the crease on the palm of his left. Then he swung back to the desk and slipped the newspaper under a ledger. He turned back to Clabe. He had a close-trimmed salt-and-pepper mustache, cropped white hair and bristly eyebrows. He leaned back in the chair, pressing his fingertips together in front of his vest—fob in buttonhole, gold watch chain—and looked at Clabe. "Well, young man, what can I do for you?"

"I want to pin down a horse brand," Claiborne said.

"There's no skulduggery in it, I trust?" The clerk smiled.

"No. But I want to check it out. It was a **B** on the neck."

"Well, we don't brand a neck brand in Bexar County." The clerk tapped his thumbs together. "But maybe it was a sale. You find a counterbrand anywhere?"

"No, it's a clean brand."

The clerk stood up with a grunt from the chair. "What's it look like?" he said. He took a scratch pad from the desk and fetched it over to the counter, dropped it in front of Clabe and slid an inkwell across to him.

"It's fluidy mustard to me," Clabe said. "I can't make it out." He dipped the pen in the inkwell. "A three-fingered goose egg or a kicked-over milk stool or somethin'. Like this."

The penpoint caught in the scratch pad and a strip of ink spurted out, peppering one of the corners.

The clerk studied the mark. He shook his head. "It's nothin' I recollect, and I been puttin' 'em in the books sixteen years now." He frowned and pressed his fingers together. "There might be a one, though. Let me look it up."

He put a step stool up to the shelves of ledgers along the left wall and climbed up on it. He ran his hand along some ledger spines, stopped and tipped out a thin brown ledger. He dusted it with a kerchief, leafed through several pages and stopped. "No, that's not it," he said.

"Let's have a look," Clabe said.

The clerk stepped down and fetched the ledger to Clabe. "That's all there is," he said. He was gasping in short, quick breaths.

"No, that ain't it," Clabe said.

The clerk laughed gently. "Well, I *knew* that."

"Goddammit, whereabouts *is* it they register a **B** neck brand?"

The clerk laughed and shook his head. "Hell, son, that could be any one of twenty counties."

Clabe climbed the narrow, dimly-lit stairway between dark, varnished walls. At the top was a waiting room, a small parlor. Photographs were everywhere, propped up on a piano and on a table and hanging on the walls. Card pictures and cabinet pictures and pictures with frames tacked around them —round faces, bearded faces, wrinkled faces, scrubbed, faces of grandmas and grandpas done up to be handed down, soft-faced babies in fluff, little boys with a blank look, girls in their pretend, newlyweds, a pretty girl on a paper rock, a picnic basket in her hand. Clabe walked over to a door on the far side of the room and looked in. Camera. A chair with a head-stand behind it. A magnesium stand. "Anybody here?" he hollered.

"Von minute. Von minute," somebody said.

It smelled like a drugstore in there.

Knocking of billiards in the billiard hall downstairs.

A short, tubby man wearing a black rubber apron bounced out of one of the closet doors at the side. He blinked at Clabe. "Sitzenzie," he said. "Ach, but mit der hat not."

Clabe grinned and stayed in the doorway.

"You vant I should sit," the photographer said, "und you das picture taken?"

Clabe said, "I never did take right. What I want to know is, was this picture took here?" He pulled the photograph from his jacket pocket. There wasn't a gatepost anywhere in the shop.

The photographer bounced over to Clabe. He ran his thumbnail along the edge of the dress in the photo. "Nein," he said. "I don't the light so dark make."

"It wasn't took by you?" Clabe said.

"Nein. Nein."

Clabe turned the card over. "You don't back yours like this?" he said.

The photographer studied the print words. The billiards knocked in the billiard hall below. "Ya," he said, "everybody makes the same like dat."

Clabe turned the card back over. "I don't reckon you know who she is?"

"Could be, I tink, anybody," the man said.

It was the fourth photographer Clabe had been to today.

Three saddle shops. They weren't the same make of saddle.

The water carts were sprinkling the evening streets. Clabe watched some children playing. They pushed and chanted at the edge of a building shadow:

The moon and the morning stars!
The moon and the morning stars!
Who will step—O
into the shadow?

Then it was a scramble when one jumped across.

The street railway cars lit their lamps. In George Hoerner's Saloon Clabe tossed off a shot of whiskey. Outside it was getting dark. Clabe walked toward Main Plaza. The Mexican girls were promenading on the sidewalks, arm in arm, in threes and fours, talking, teasing one another, all the time looking to the left and right. In the doorways the men smoked their *cigarrillos*. Clabe ate at the Elite Restaurant again—redfish in fried hunks, potatoes and the rest of it. When he came back out there was a crowd of Mexicans on the plaza, laughing and talking, buying the food being sold there.

In the hotel lobby the gas jets in their china globes were lit. The clerk sat behind his desk reading a paper. He nodded. Clabe nodded and started up the stairs. He came smack up against the red walking skirt.

"Oh, excuse me," she said. "What a lovely day it's been out."

Clabe took off his hat. "Yes'm," he said.

"It's been awfully warm out. I'm so listless today. I think I've got spring fever." She smiled, brushed back a strand of hair from her face.

"It'll do a body thataway," Claiborne said. "Excuse me, ma'am," he said.

He went on past her up the stairs and through the yellow hallway to his room. Inside, the ceiling flickered with light from the lanterns above the chile tables in the plaza below. *Meskin talk—they'll be goin' all night.* And dogs yapping, all night, all over the place. Clabe closed the shutters. That helped some. He managed to wrangle his boots off his feet and got undressed and climbed into bed. Then he commenced to walk the streets of San Antonio.

The next morning Clabe went over to the stable to look at Beel. Beel had thrown a shoe. Clabe saddled him and worked the kinks out of him. He rode him east on Houston Street and then out Avenue C. It was another warm day. The sun was bright and the umbrella trees on each side threw a dark shade. Avenue C was a graded street with a set of rails— the street railway cars here were painted green. Clabe found a blacksmith's shop near the Sunset Road depot. A train was alongside the platform. Clabe led Beel into the shop.

Inside it was dark. Smell of metal and the bitter, burnt smell of hoof. The bellows bubbled. Kling *klang*, kling *klang* on the iron-nosed anvil. A cherry-red moon swung through the dark, *si-eest!* was doused in water. Then a second cherry moon. Now Clabe could see better. The blacksmith sighted a shoe against the light, checked it, dropped it onto the floor.

Clabe had Beel shoed all around. He eased Beel through the first pair. Then he went back outside. The sunlight was terrible bright. Up at the depot the train tolled its bell, about to leave. Clabe ambled over to the tracks to watch it. The whistle tooted and newsboys and sandwich-sellers got off. Steam hissed, sprouting from down among the wheels. An iron door slammed shut, a puff of black smoke boiled out of the stack. The great, black, iron, brass-trimmed boiler on wheels began to roll. It pulled loose of the wooden platform. Engine number 6, moving past Clabe, puffing a black smoke. Ripple of grunts between cars as it took up the slack. Odor of hot oil and burning wood. Cinders floated. The engineer in his bib overalls and kerchief and a broad-brimmed hat— leathery face and black mustache—saluted Clabe. Stack of cordwood on the tender. Three boxcars, a brakeman on the roof. Two passenger cars, yellow-painted, trimmed with black. The open windows slid slowly past.

Blue plush seats. Fancy woodwork. A face at a window. *Her face!* Same eyes, same black, pulled-back hair!

Fear dropped like a pudding through Clabe's guts. The

woman's gaze moved across him. A gray glove put a crisp handkerchief to her nose and mouth.

The back platform with its handbrake sticking up gave Clabe its rear.

"Out to Ugalde if it aims to follow track," the station-master said. "After that it'll have to grow feet and walk."

At the ticket window the ticket agent said, "Five to Ugalde, two to Hondo, two to Monday's Springs. Three of 'em gets off at Cantrell."

The blacksmith finished tarring Beel's hoofs. In half an hour Clabe was on his way out of town.

6

THE streets of Santone are like a skillet of snakes. Clabe worked his way west. He crossed the San Pedro stream, where Mexican women were washing and rinsing their family clothes on flat stones. The stream was clouded with soap. On the other side was Laredito, the Mexican section. Dirt yards and streets. Clabe rode past windowless Mexican shacks, huts of poles, mud, straw, sticks, flattened tin cans and any old drift, roofed with grass. Dogs and chickens were in the dirt yard. Pretty soon he was on a narrow road with mesquite trees on both sides. He passed a Mexican farm, a one-room adobe house beside a small field. The wall of mesquites closed back in for a ways, and then Clabe came to an open, grassy country. Strong new grass poking up through the flattened winter grass. Flowers, too, purple, yellow, white. Here and there on the rolling prairie a live oak spurted up: fountain of trunk and dark leaves. Clabe leaned forward, rubbed Beel's neck. Beel's ears went back. Claiborne laughed. *Oh, we'll find her*, he thought. *A man don't hurry. He just goes and he'll get there.*

He rode all morning. He crossed several creeks, all of them with water. The hills to the north went higher and higher until they ended in a blue mountain line. To the south, on Clabe's left, the land sloped down to the Medina River. The afternoon heat lifted the river trees, showed the Medina shaking like a silver string beneath them. Once Clabe rode by a stand of huisache bushes filled with humming, the smell so thick-sweet he could have cut it with a knife. Each flower—

yellow puff of light—bobbed with the weight of a black, native bee. The bees didn't offer to sting.

At five in the evening Clabe crossed the Medina. The water was hock-deep, about thirty yards wide here. It was as clear and clean as a sheet of glass, a touch green above the white limestone bed. Castroville was on the other side and Clabe rode through the town, a scattering of whitewashed cottages, two churches, a double-galleried hotel—not like Texas at all.

Here's where the San Antonio road ended. Past Castroville Clabe rode up into higher, more broken country. Plenty of open stretches, green as a wheat field, with motts of live oak and hackberry and elm. He rode an hour or so more, the sun directly in front, going down. About half an hour to sundown Clabe quit. There was a queer tiredness in his arms and legs. He unspooled his bedroll at the mouth of a draw where a seep spring came out of the ground. He fed Beel a ration of corn and hobbled him out. Clabe wasn't much hungry his ownself. He ate a handful of dried apples and some Borden's Biscuit and drank water from the seep spring. Then he slipped into his bedroll, already half on his way to sleep. It was going on dark. The ground under his pallet was still warm from the daytime heat. A cricket commenced chirping next his saddle pillow. Clabe smelled plum blossom and wild onion amongst his mind's scatterings. The last thing he heard was the long-drawn-out shriek of a train whistle a few miles off.

Not a dream all night. The ground was hard under Clabe. He felt his length stretched out on it, every bone in him with an ache, hurting in the marrow, kneebone and shinbone, the separate, breakable bones of his feet, thighbone bedded in flesh, connections in finger and wrist, crick of neck. There was a queer taste in his mouth, like it had been bruised. Dew was on his blanket. Various birds made first-light noises, like knives being sharpened, scissors snipping. Clabe sat up and pulled on his boots. He stood. When he walked he felt his bones swinging. They sort of hung in the meat, like cores just barely hooked together on the joint ends. It didn't feel right.

Clabe spread his bedding out on a bush. To the east the sky was lightening. He walked up the draw a ways and pulled apart a wood rat's nest, took the dry sticks and fetched them back. With a lucifer from the .38 cartridge he kept them in he started a fire. Stewed some evaporated apples in the tin cup and cooked strips of good, streaked sidemeat on a stick, but wasn't much hungry for either. He spooled his bedding and saddled up. Beel went through his usual morning she-nanigans. Clabe stuck him out. They were on their way before sunup.

The mornin' don't set right. Not to wear or taste. Grass soft and wet under: wellnigh no noise. A bird slid across, smacked into a bush. *Sun's up! Already hot, back of my ears and neck—it's a white one. Got a kind of weight to it. Hallie, what you bendin' over that stove for, all that ass up? Ass up. Sunup. Huh. Huh. Gug huh huh huh. That's who I miss.*

Miss, shit. I'm gonna ride out till I hit plumb off the edge of the world. Huh! Spurred the horse right off the shingle—stepped out, a good purchase on air like flying. And it felt clean, all the ragtag and truck and plunder behind, sometimes he could grieve.

Things change, so sudden slow you don't know. Look, that's a different leaf already. Shift in light? I take it there are different worlds. Take a tree, fr'instance. That live oak there. Ought to be brown like that all the way through, wouldn't you think? Ax flashed in the sun, sent out white chips. *See what I mean? How come that? Nor a white man white all through. Mex. No. Slide down slope out of sight. Face. No. Slide down slope. But* agarita, *for Christsake. Break a branch, it's yellow inside, ain't that a fact?*

But stones run true. Bust open a rock and what do you got—same color inside and out. It's only live *things wears an outward show?*

Let's see, can I think of a thing? Leather. A china crock.

Leona broke a new one once. Jesus, the smithereens! Picked up a splinter—smooth white out, white on through. *Huh. Well, but is there a live thing I can think of, same inside as out?* Not a man. Not my hand. I done said trees. Fish, flesh and fowl, no. No bug, neither: *squish:* yellow and green. *All right, you sonofabitch, how 'bout a leaf? Alive. Green all the way through.* I can't see that thin. *Ha, now I got you by the balls.* You're crowdin' me there, all right. *So how 'bout a leaf?* Hold off, hold off a minute! Tuna's a leaf—prickly pear, fat as my hand! Meaty inside, hard green out.

Talk's cheap, son. It takes money to buy whiskey.

A cedar bush drifted past.

Her face drifted by in the train window. *That's the same face. Is* that the same face? Clabe felt for the pasteboard-backed picture in his jacket pocket. *How come my stomick hurts?*

Peach ice cream. Smooth. *Settin' in the shade, crankin' the salty ice.* Pack it to harden, then lift off the burlap, open it up. Smooth. *Not the taste so much—the cold and the smooth. Somethin' to cool my damn stomick.*

Sun's got a new angle on my back. It's gonna be damn hot.

Clabe rode through a cross-timber of live oaks, which were getting smaller hereabouts. Stinging asps—a caterpillar—dropped from the trees. He brushed some off. Then he and Beel were out on an open stretch sprinkled with scrub brush and mesquites. Telegraph poles. He rode across a draw and hit some railroad tracks. He followed the rails westward from telegraph pole to telegraph pole, taking his time. The footing was rough underneath—loose caliche alongside the tracks. Four times he crossed creeks, all of them with water. Beel splashed across beneath the trestle bridges. Now the tracks went downgrade onto a rolling, brush-covered plain. Clabe could see a town a long way off, at the top of a rise. A road joined the tracks. Clabe rode down onto it. He came on a road crew putting in their five-days' tax. Two big steers and a road scraper, a team of mules and an earth-moving slip, pickaxes, shovels, rakes and sledgehammers. Sweat work, no doubt about it. The men wiped their faces and leaned on their shovels to watch Clabe as he rode up.

"Mornin'," a man with salt-and-pepper chin whiskers said. His shoes were split to make room for bunions.

Clabe checked Beel. He nodded. "Mighty hot," he said.

"It's a weather-breeder," a tall, lanky man with a rake in his hand said. Beel shifted. The men looked at Clabe.

A tree toad began shrilling in the bushes.

"You lookin' for Hondo, it's right on ahead," the man with chin whiskers said.

"Thanks," Clabe said.

"Two mile," another said.

"It's a weather-breeder all right," Clabe said, glancing toward the northwest. "Looks to be cloudin' up. Adios," he said. He touched his heel to Beel's belly.

In Hondo Clabe went directly to the railroad station. "Mornin'," he said to the man on the other side of the ticket window. "I wonder could you tell me, did anybody get off the train here yesterday from San Antone?" Telegraph keys were clicking away.

"It's due in in half an hour."

"No, I mean yesterday."

"Well, Mr. and Mrs. Chappel come back from a buyin' trip for her new dress shop. That's all there was. That who you're lookin' for?"

"Are they older folks?"

"You could say. But you'll never get her to own up to it."

"I reckon I come to the wrong town. This ain't Pearsall, Frio County?"

"Hell no," the man said. He stared at Clabe.

"Thanks anyways." Clabe smiled. He touched his hand to his hat brim, turned and walked out.

Rode through rolling, mesquite-dotted country. An anvil-headed cloud was rising in the north. About an hour out of Hondo the *Galveston, Harrisburg & San Antone*—same train as yesterday—went by, hauling yellow cars. In Monday's Springs Clabe sat on a bench at the back of a kitchen, amongst milk crocks and scrubbed gourds, and ate cornbread and buttermilk whilst the housewife who'd fed him busied herself inside. In the brush garden next the house cowpeas were coming up in neat rows, prizing the chunky dirt, tilting the clods. Clabe watched a sow bug founder in an ant lion's funnel under the bench. The bug tried to climb, but the sand shifted under its feet. It sank out of sight. Clabe put a dime on the bench for his dinner and rode over to the railroad station. A Mr. Guthrie and a Mr. Honeycutt had got off here yesterday.

Pink and white bindweed climbed the fences alongside the road outside Monday's Springs. The flowers reminded Clabe of morning glories. *Cherokee.* The sloped gallery, the rocker with the knothole under it. At each end of the gallery, morning glories ran up on strings. Nobody else in Cherokee could grow morning glories like that.

Mr. Sanderlin stood up from the fruit stock he was grafting. He was an old man. "Hello, young feller," he said, "where do you hail from?" Clabe sat his plow horse at the front gate. He held a dead blue quail in his hand. "I don't know how far you've come, young 'un, but you don't look thrifty." It was true. That damned plow horse had wellnigh shook Claiborne's kidneys loose. Clabe could feel it now. A pinpoint seed of pain sprouted under his ribs, widened through the small of his back and pounded, a dream pain. *"Leona," Mr. Sanderlin called into the house, "we got a caller."*

The Sanderlin house in Cherokee. Small plank house, up on posts. Boards weathered orange and honey-yellow, rust-colored knot holes. All those morning glories, climbing the strings.

"Leona," Mr. Sanderlin called again. Leona came out onto the gallery, her white hair—a braided ring of it—coiled atop her head. Like always. She was wearing the same blue dress and black apron that afterward he learned she always wore. "What you got

*there, child, a bird?" she said. "Come into the house and I'll cook it
for you." She picked up the blue quail, and later in the kitchen she
stewed it in a saucepan and fixed some greens and cornmeal dumplings to go with it. Meanwhile she prized out of him whereall he'd
come from. But not why. Clabe was too proud for that. She sent
him out onto the back stoop to wash his face and hands. He heard
her say "Mr. Sanderlin, did you see his legs? The little feller's been
beaten black and blue." When he came back in, Leona put a plate
on the table. Clabe was so hungry it hurt. After dinner Leona said,
"All our children are growed. But we've got a bed here for you. Till
you're rested up and set to get back on your journey." A week later
Mr. Sanderlin said, "I'll take the horse and gun back. I will also
speak to your pa."*

The plank house. Mr. Sanderlin's bees and fruit trees. *In
the house it's dark except for the bright doorways at each end. Cool,
scrubbed floor. Scrubbed and oiled furniture. Dark table with the
crystal centerpiece. The sideboard from Louisiana, Leona's best
dishes. "Go look on the table, son"—a peach on a saucer on the
lace tablecloth.* Clabe had stayed there two years. . . .

Too many deaths. The Mexican's eyes stared up at Clabe.
No, don't think on that!

One night after supper Mr. Sanderlin had started to get
up from the table. He had pitched back down. The next day
folks came to pay their respects, all their goddamned feet
shuffling through the house. *"Oh, Mr. Sanderlin!"* Leona cried.
"Oh, Mr. Sanderlin, Mr. Sanderlin!" It broke Clabe's heart. In
a month the rocker itself was empty, jogged back and forth by
a light breeze. . . .

A cloud shadow moved across the ground. Clabe slapped
Beel's rump. "Git along, old poke, there's a scab on the sun."
My stomick don't feel right.

In Cantrell yesterday three cowhands—friends—had
got off the train. Under their suit coats there wasn't a whole
shirt on a one of them. Their faces were puffy, blacked eyes
closed. One had two front teeth missing that'd been there the

day before, another an ear half torn off. "What the devil happened to *you* all?" the ticket agent had said. "Oh, we was just
havin' fun," one of them had said. "Just havin' fun," another
had said. "Nobody was at anytime even out of humor." They
had been put on the train by a deputy sheriff in San Antonio.

Clabe rode out of Cantrell under a lowering sky, the
clouds down close, flat as the underside of a table. They shut
the sun out—the air had a darkened, silverish look. Clabe
rode an hour longer. It felt like it ought to rain, like it was
pushing hard to rain, but couldn't. The clouds pressed down.
The air was packed and still. Clabe could feel it pressing
against his skin. It crowded his ears, sickened his innards.
Once in a while a pocket of wind stirred the brush. Clabe
could hardly breathe.

He felt a terrible pressure on his guts. His guts loosened.
Clabe lit down from Beel, snagged the reins in a bush, got his
britches down and squatted in the nick of time. Next a rock a
tumblebug was pushing its ball of dung, climbing it and rolling with it. Clabe hiked up his britches and walked over
to Beel. Next thing he knew he was down on his hands and
knees, his back arched like a cat's, his eyes tight shut, mouth
open, vomit splashing out of his nose and mouth. He gagged
on the sharp slop. Tears ran from his eyes. The fit knotted and
unknotted in his gut. Finally it left off. Clabe stood up and
caught hold of the saddle horn. *Well, that's done with. Now let's
git.* He jerked the reins out of the bush and pulled himself up
into the saddle. For a minute the world swung around. Clabe
pressed his legs hard to Beel's ribs. "Come on, Beel you sonofabitch." They jerked forward. It was darker now. The clouds
were down close. Clabe could see them boiling but they didn't
let down a drop. *Cool rain would help.* It felt like somebody
had put pieces of cracked glass into his head. Clabe rode
through a patch of flowers alongside the tracks. Way out on a
flat, about a quarter-mile off, a red light danced across the
top of the brush, like a lantern, sailing just above the bush

tops. Then it was gone. Clabe slid down from the saddle. He grabbed hold of a mesquite. The flat of a broadax swung through his guts, whacked the bottom of his stomach. It almost knocked him to the ground. Now and now: the hot, sick soup flooded from his mouth. It felt like his craw might come up with it. Clabe came up choking on the mess.

About as much time as it took to wipe his mouth and he was down on his hunkers, his britches down, rice-water pouring out of his ass end.

He got up and tried walking, leading Beel. Every once in a while he'd bend over and throw up. It gave him hiccups. His clothes were soaked with sweat. He'd never been so thirsty in his life. He began to founder, stumbling over rocks, lugging the hot pudding of his guts. *Why don't it let down a rain?* Of a sudden, rods of pain cramped his legs and feet. The arches of his feet bowed in their boots, it felt like his bones were about to crack. He was sweating like fury. *O Christ, I'm sick!* His back and arms cramped.

He managed to climb onto Beel. He rode through walls of air, wall after wall, burning inside, bloody and cold out, like a live, skinned fox let loose for a joke. He threw up again, barely keeping hold to the saddle. Clabe slid down, tied Beel to a telegraph pole. He fell to the ground, moaning and jerking . . .

Hail pounded on tin roofs. Clabe woke. In the glare of a yellow light Beel pulled at the telegraph pole. The train went by with a roar, runners pounding, stack belching sparks like a Roman candle. Lit windows. The people inside were like shadow pictures in the squares of light made by candles flickering in their round glass globes. Gone. The whistle shrieked. Comet tail of sparks died out. The rose glow of the firebox floated across the low-slung sky, was gone. Then it was as dark as a stack of black cats. Clabe shook. His teeth chattered. His clothes were soaked with a cold sweat.

A weight like a stone was on his chest. *I stay here like this I'm gonna die.* He pushed at the stone. He tipped it up over. It was nothing but air. He got onto his hands and knees, then stood up shaking onto his feet. Felt for Beel in the dark. "There, boy. Shoo, boy, shoo." Gentled him. "Shoo, boy, shoo." *It don't sound like me.* Clabe pulled himself into the saddle. "Come on, boy, git." Beel stalled. "I ain't gonna take no shit offa you. Git!"

They headed back toward Cantrell. Clabe gave Beel a free rein. A wind blew. It felt like it was going right through Clabe's bones.

Warm light shone from a window. It was a section house alongside the tracks. *Now who put that there?* Clabe didn't rec-ollect coming on that on his way out from Cantrell. He rode up to the stake-and-rider fence. "*Halloo,*" he called in a queer, froggy voice.

In a minute the door opened and a man came out. "Who is it?" he said.

"I'm sick," Clabe said.

"Just a minute," the man said. He went back into the house and came out with a lantern. He walked over to Clabe and held the lantern up between them. The light shone on his bald head. "You do look poorly," he said. He caught hold of the reins and led Beel into the yard. "Go on into the house," he said. "I'll take care of your horse."

Clabe managed to get over to the door. He stepped into a room where there was a nice, blazing fire. The walls were papered with newspapers. A canopy bed filled one quarter of the room. A woman sat in a hide-bottomed chair next the fire, sewing. She looked up at Clabe as he came in. She let out a screech that fetched her husband in on the double quick. "Cholera! Cholera!" she said.

The man looked at Clabe. "Are you from Santone?" he said.

"Yes," Claiborne said. He looked down at his hands.

They were blue, wrinkled, almost black under the fingernails. *Oh, Christ, I didn't think to have that.* He felt like he'd like to lie down and die right here.

"Well," the man said, "you have got it and I'm sorry we can't keep you here. I hate to turn a sick man out, but I got a wife and three children."

Outside, Claiborne hauled himself back up onto Beel. He got the horse out through the gate. The world tilted in the dark, it felt like Beel was walking straight up a wall. Clabe grabbed hold of the saddle horn to keep from falling.

The grave opened. The rocks began to lift and scatter.

A body lay in the hollow. Its nose and chin stuck up above the ground. That damn smile! *The saddle-colored face, white handlebar mustache. The old Mexican sat up in the grave.* "Here, you will touch this," *he said.* "You will put your hand here and touch this."

No. No no no.

The Mexican came toward Clabe. He came toward him so fast! The rim of the black sombrero flapped. The wet grass squeaked, kay-eesh! kay-eesh! *Dark, webbed face, shiny as a brown moon. The Mexican held open his bloody shirt front.* "You will touch this," *he said.* "Here is your cracked and bloody door."

"Damn you!" Claiborne said. "Yes, and damn the man that wouldn't damn you and damn the man that wouldn't burn up the shirt on his back to make a light at midnight to see by to damn you . . . !"

7

STARS disappear. *Ting.* A drop of water swelled at the tip end of a leaf, drooped, dangled by a thread.

Dropped. Just missed his eye. *Ting.*

Ting-ting.

The light of day. Day light, jelling. Stalks, branches climbed up through the clear jelly and the light held them. Leaves lay flat in the jelly or caught at an angle in it.

Slurg nearby of river talk.

Feet. A double face hove in from the edge of his eyes, blocking the sky. Woman face. Bent down to him. He heard the movement of her dress. She must have touched him somewhere.

She stood up. *Switch switch* of the dress, hurrying away of feet. *Ting.* The bush shook. Water drops shook off. They likely wet his face. A mouth tugged at the bush. Sheep. Belled. *Ting.* Ting-*tang*-ting. The sheep stopped. It stood over him, rattling its breath, dripping sheep snot from its nose. Then it shook its head, *tang tang tang tang tang,* and commenced to pull grass alongside. And other sheep were around about, drifting past, browsing or cropping grass. A streak of fleece shone on the bush above him.

The sheep scattered. The woman tucked a blanket around Clabe.

She rubbed the backs of his wrists. She lifted his feet and beat the bottoms with a stick. Clabe heard the whacks. *Huh.* It did make his heart catch. The woman bent over him. She had one face now. "That's better," she said. She propped up his head and he could see a good deal more world, mostly particular.

The woman squatted beside him, watching him. She stayed there a long time, maybe years. Her face was sunburnt and she was sandy-haired. She wore a dirty, short-waisted, twill cotton dress with an overskirt held up by suspenders. The sun went over, shifting through the jelly, making it swell and at midday flattening it out toward the edges. The woman pulled a slat bonnet onto her head. It shaded her face so that all Clabe could see was her mouth and chin. Sometimes she went away, but she always came back. Once she fetched a goat from amongst the sheep and milked it. The milk splatted onto the bottom of a tin cup, sizzled into its own liquid. The woman fed him a dribble. He could almost taste it.

Toward evening she was gone for a spell. She came back driving an old wagon with busted wagon bows and a torn wagon sheet. A bony, dried-up man with a red kerchief on his head and long arms and a neck like a sand crane was on the seat beside her. "Well now, doddammit, I cain't he'p it," the man said in a high-pitched voice. "The doddamn tree fell right acrost it." He looked like sticks hanging together when he climbed down from the wagon.

He came over to Clabe. "Oh," he said, "it don't look good. It don't look like it's gonna do us no good atall. Yeezus help us, Zena, lookit his face. I ain't seen a color blue like that sinct Airs Wilbarger got hit by a thunderbolt. Broke his neck and melted his spurs, put a blue welt down his back. Oh, I wisht he'd of gone and done it somewheres else, whatever all it is. It ain't gonna do us no good. You notice he's got red hair? Like Eaf Baggett's nigger was—a red-headed nigger, the one that went hog-wild. Charlie Fisher has red hair, and he's a hog-stealing thief. You say he was laying there just like that? Ain't that our blanket? How come him to be here? Ever'thing always has to happen to us."

"Maybe he crawled out from under a rock," the woman said.

"I'm always comin' out the little end of the horn. Like that bay I traded for last fall. Come to find out he had bishoped teeth. Traded him off and got a horse with glanders. Sonofab'ditch. But Magruder down the river swaps his blind mule for an old dry sow and she farrows twelve. Doddamn brastard lives off the top of the pot. And he ain't even a Baptist."

"Pick up his feet," the woman said.

"I reluct to touch him."

They hefted Clabe up. Branches and bushes fell down out of sight. He felt so nothing, so light, like he'd been gutted and air had scrubbed the hull out and only a little piece of heart was left, alive, up under his gullet. They lugged him, grunting hard as he swung from side to side. Then he was on the bed of the wagon. Sky through a ripped-open wagon sheet. The wheel hubs croaked, the wagon bounced. Busted wagon bows slid through an evening, strawberry sky. When the creaking quit and the wagon-sheet tatters hung stock still, they hefted him up and carried him into a cabin.

A smoky light sputtered in the dark. Clabe tried to talk but he couldn't move his lips, couldn't force air through his talk box either. He felt light-headed. An edge tilted. He started to slide, scrambling and clawing, slid off head first, dropping through air. The light got smaller, farther off, something pinched it out. *"Claiborne, boy," Leona said, "I sit here and I sit here. Oh, dear child, how'm I ever gonna live?"*

When Clabe opened his eyes, a fierce morning light shone through the open doorway. The strong, greasy smell of sheep jolted his nostrils. It made his eyes water. He took a deep breath. A prickly, tingling feeling ran all through him.

"I says, 'I didn't come out here all this ways to tote rocks.'" It was the bony, dried-up man talking. "'Well,' he says, 'it's you the one's got the wagon. You was suppose to be here'" *wuf wuf wuf* "'four months ago. I got a son down sick with cramp colic,' he says, 'and one gone to the devil, and a wife that's poorly and I'm tryin' to get my plantin' in the ground. If you want the work you'll have to fetch the rocks your ownself.'" *wuf* "'May I be packed off to sell hot peppers in hell b'fore I'll do that,' I says. 'Why then,' he says, 'they can just set here.' 'I ain't gonna haul them stones,' I says. I told him I'd not do it." *wuf*

"So how'd you work it out?" the woman said.

"I had to do it anyways."

"Can't you blow that fire no higher?" the woman said.

"I already feel like I got gills from blowin' it so hard," the man said. *wuf wufuuuuuu* . . . "There!" A slip of fire popped into life. "We ought not to of let it go out."

"It'd help if you was to leave me some wood," the woman said. "Not this mess of brush. I can't cook on trash like that."

"My ax heft is still broke."

"I wisht it'd grow itself two feet and walk out and fit itself to a new ax heft."

"It's another one of them headache days," the man said. A pan clattered. "Oh, Zena, don't do that," he said.

"Shut up," the woman said. "I think he's awake." She came over to Clabe.

The man fidgeted around behind her like a shadow ghost. "What's the matter?" he said. The woman knelt down beside Clabe. "What's the matter?" the man said.

"Ain't nothin' the matter," the woman said. "Fetch me that bottle of bitters." She tucked the blanket around Clabe. She felt his forehead. "You all right?" she said to Clabe. "Here, take some of this," she said.

"Don't . . . touch me," Claiborne said.

"You got to get well," the woman said. She propped him up and made him take some bitters.

Clabe had a hard time swallowing it, but it did stay down. "You ought . . . not . . . to touch . . . me," he said.

"Don't touch him, Zena!" the man said.

"Shut up," the woman said. "Now you lay back and sleep," she said to Clabe.

The man and the woman moved about in the cabin or sometimes outside, at one chore or another. It was a one-room, cedar-picket cabin, with rags and cedar bark stuffed between the pickets. Light showed between some of the logs. The only other place that let in light was the open doorway. Sacks hung from the rafters. A box was on one of the walls, with tin cups and crockery and a fry pan and two white Dresden plates in it. A table and some boxes for chairs. A one-legged bed. Tow sacks were spread out on the dirt floor. A thready, curly, cream-white vine grew out of the corner near Clabe's pallet, headed for a light chink.

A lark was singing in a tree outside.

"I reckon I ought to kill a goat," the woman said. She began to sharpen a knife on a whetrock.

"Why don't that bird out there quit?" the man said. "Zena, quit scritchin' that knife acrost that stone like that."

"Did you fetch me some more water?" the woman said.

"I'm fixin' to," the man said. "I cain't stand that knife a-scritchin'," he said.

"Go out and fetch me some water then."

"I'm headed in that direction. Is the bucket handle fixed?"

"I can't do ever' damn thing, Rome Pirtle," the woman said.

"Where do you reckon I put it?" the man said.

"Put what?"

"That doddamn bucket."

"How'm I suppose to know?"

"Oh that tuckin', sonofab'ditchin', corruptive, ace-hole bird!" the man said. He ran out. Clabe heard him yelling and pitching stones into the tree. The woman moved around in the cabin, humming "Chicken in the Bread Pan."

Where's my horse, my . . . gear? But Clabe was too fagged-out to ask or to keep worrying on it. Sometimes he slept. Once he turned over to piss into a crock.

The afternoon sunlight shifted across the floor. Whenever Clabe woke the sunlight was in a different place on the floor. Toward dark Zena built up the fire and lit the plaited greasewick in a tin can on the table.

She fed Claiborne some soup. "Looks like you just might pull through, mister," she said. Her stringy, gopher-colored hair was caught up now in a tucking comb. Thin furrow lines ran across her cheeks and from the corners of her eyes, like on an old woman's face.

"You feed . . . my horse?" Claiborne said.

"It'll take catchin' him first. He'll show up somewheres."

Christa'mighty yes, down in Piedras Negras, under some greaser's ass. Sonofabitch.

"That all you're gonna eat?" Zena said.

Yessir, all you own now's on your back or in your belly, one. Shit. Clabe turned his head aside and closed his eyes.

In the evening, at the supper table, Rome said, "What I aim to do is put up a stake-'n'-rider fence from here to that there dead cedar elm and then on down to them sycamores and back up and acrost. I been thinkin' on it. Cut out that cedar section at the bottom of the slope and them'll do for posts. Run it into a shearin' pen. It'll make a good-sized trap."

"I wish you'd fix my spin treadle where I can use it," Zena said.

So God-awful tired.

". . . ain't what Magruder said that got me all riled up," Rome said, "it's the way he . . ."

A mouse skittered up the wall. Sheep moved together close by. Their smell, their restlessness. Could hear the wether bell. *Ting.* Like his fork—before grace—to Leona's crystal centerpiece.

Two weeks later they put him out on a bench in the sun. Zena wrapped a blanket around his legs. Clabe closed his eyes and felt the sun onto his face. Heat came out of the ground and out of the logs behind him. He soaked it up like a lizard. Flies buzzed and sunned themselves on an old deerhide tacked to the logs. A dirt dauber built its nest, a mud tunnel, up under the shakes. It hauled mud in its back legs and packed it in dabs onto the nest.

A mite breeze shifted the air some—smell of a river off somewheres. An open space covered with sheep droppings and rocks and stubble grass stretched between the cabin and a brush pen where the sheep were kept at night. Pieces of rotted leather and warped barrel staves and crockery bits and old wagon parts were scattered across the open ground. A gray, weathered, nearly spokeless wagon wheel leaned over its broken axle like a ghost over its gone life.

Rome Pirtle came walking up across the open space, his head pulled back like he was shying away from something, his legs, each swing forward, dropping down just short of their full reach so that it looked when he walked like he was picking his way through a nest of scorpions. He came out from below the brush pen and saw Clabe. He walked up to him. He was a small, birdlike man, jerky and nervous. He broke off a piece of grass from a clump that grew in a chink of the cabin and sat on the ground near Clabe, his back against the logs, chewing the straw. A cool, rotten-leaf smell came up from the river. "Things're beginnin' to green up some," Rome Pirtle said.

Here came the dirt dauber on its long haul up from the river, a black speck that grew out of nothing in the air, then got bigger to be itself, *zzzzzzzsp*—caught at the mud nest, satisfied.

"Seems like a body just cain't get ahead," Rome said. "I work two weeks puttin' up a fireplace and chimney and it don't hardly pay for molasses. Last month I was three weeks to Acklen's, over on Difference Creek, layin' up the stones for him. You cain't get nowheres like that."

"Why don't you build up your stock?"

"Well, I'll tell you. Wool sold for seventeen cents a pound last year and that's as low as you can get."

Claiborne laughed. "I've hit rock bottom my ownself," he said. He fished around in the pockets of his coat and smoked out two ten-cent pieces. The cabinet picture was in one of the pockets. "Well, no," he said, "I ain't broke. Just pretty bad bent. No feet, neither."

"Oh, your horse'll turn up. Next time I'm in Privilege I'll ask around."

Clabe said, "I know that thin-eared sonofabitch. He's took off for the brush." He said, "I can't figure it. I been here two weeks already and you-all ain't took sick yet."

Rome said, "Oh, we'll get it. Whatever it is, if it's bad enough we'll get it." When he talked his Adam's apple looked like it was pumping the air in and the talk out. A small scab like a tobacco stain was stuck to his lower lip. "I been walkin' off the ground for a stake-'n'-rider fence," he said. "It'll take a power of cedar posts. Wouldn't be so bad if it was some young'uns about. A man wants help." Out in the open space between the brush pen and the cabin the trash and rocks and droppings shimmered in the heat. Rome said, "Wisht I'd stayed back in East Texas." After a while he said, "Wisht I'd stayed out of sheep."

In another week Clabe was up and about. At the supper table Rome Pirtle said, "I mean to put in that stake-'n'-rider fence. It's a chore, I know it. A man ought not to have to do it by hisself."

Clabe put a little salt into his coffee. He said, "I might can help out."

Lopped off an ash limb with a borrowed ax. Worked it down to an ax heft. It wanted seasoning but would have to do. Split the shoulder of it. Burnt the old shoulder out of Rome's axhead and forced the new one into the eye. Pounded in a wedge—a night's soaking made it tight. The new ax had

a deal of spring and was a mite overheavy in the handle, but
seasoning would firm and balance it. Clabe sharpened the
double blades until they bearded: a clean bite, both bits.
Down in the cedar brake the fat chips flew.

The blades sliced into the ropy, muscular cedar trunks.
Gray moths flew out of the cedars. The ax cut through the
shredded bark, through the live, white wood to the heart
cedar, brown and tender as the dark meat in a fish. Fat wedges
popped out. Cedar needles fell onto Clabe's neck and shoulders. Each *thunk* knocked dust from the cedar branches.
Clabe's face was plastered with dust and sweat.

Rome said, "Why you always got that kerchief on your
hand?"

"I got to keep it wrapped," Claiborne said. The sore on
his hand had come open again.

Clabe swung the ax into the tree. Sweat ran down
Clabe's face, it fell in drops from his chin. He could smell his
self, the sourness of his armpits, sweat smell of his body as he
swung the ax. Smell of fresh cedar chips. He felt the power in
his rump. It went up through his backbone. It spread like
quicksilver through his arms. *Oh, Christ, that feels good.* He
came down hard—*umf*—into the cut and fetched the cedar
down. He lopped off the branches.

Rome talked. "I layed up the chimney," he said in his
screeky voice. He gave a chop at the cedar trunk he was working at. "I layed it up straight and high. Two flues to it. It's
a two-story house and he wanted a fireplace in the upstairs
room. They ain't no other like it hereabouts. I wanted nine-
teen dollars for the job. We was agreed on that. So when he
come to pay me, he pays me off in greenbacks. Now that ain't
right. You go into Privilege, you go into any store anywheres
in Texas and put a greenback on the counter—they discount
'em fifteen per cent. You know that, Red. It ain't right, doddammit. It ain't right." He said, "How come a man works so
hard?" He looked at Clabe with his little-boy's eyes. "Puts in
all his prime days follerin' the hind end of a mule and all

he's finally got to show for it's a piece of scrabble ground he couldn't raise careless weed on? Swaps a good horse for a better'un and directly it dies of the heaves on him? Marries a civil, purty womern and she takes to snappin' his head off, like as not?"

"I don't know," Clabe said. "Maybe it's what all he was headed for in the first place."

"Sometimes I think I was bornt bass-ackwards, like gettin' up on the wrong side of the bed, and I cain't get right," Rome said.

Noontimes they sat by the river and ate their dinners—beans and johnnycake and strong, boiled coffee that Zena fetched them. In eight days they had the slope cleared and the posts stacked at the foot of it. They loaded the posts onto the wagon and hauled them to the fence line. For five days they dug post holes and sunk the posts in pairs. Then they commenced to lay the rails. They laid them on the slant, overlapping the butt and tip ends. "That looks fine to me, Red," Rome said. When the sheep trap was done, they built a brush arbor in the center of it. "That looks fine to me," Rome said. They made a new coupling tongue for the wagon. Hewed it from a felled hackberry and fitted it into the hounds. Burned holes in the tongue for the pins to go in. They split oak laths and soaked them in the river, bowed them to replace the broken wagon bows. "The doddamn elm tree fell right acrost it," Rome said. "It weren't much of a wind, but it come down anyways. I was so dum mad I just layed there and let it rain." Clabe laughed. Zena put their plates on the table. Rome and Clabe built a lean-to against the north side of the cabin. They hammered wedges and stuffed cedar bark into the washed-out chinks between the cabin pickets. They found an auger bit wrapped in a piece of tow sacking and stashed away in one of the chinks where Rome had put it so he'd remember. He'd been looking for it for the past four days. "Rice a'mighty, here's my auger bit!" he said.

□

One day they rode into Privilege, a dirt street with a general store, a blacksmith shop and four or five plank houses. A pair of railroad tracks ran across the brush flat nearby. Zena and Rome and Clabe went into the store. "This place's got a little bit of ever'thing and not much of that," Rome said. Oil-brown saddles hung in a row by single stirrups from the ceiling.

Off in the brush, the saddle slung under his belly, or down in Piedras Negras, under some greaser's ass! Beel trailed flags of yellow slicker. A tin of tomatoes dropped off the saddle. The back housing rotted, rain wet the rifle barrel. The leather headstall rotted from Beel's head. *Sonofabitch.* Beel ran with a herd of mustangs through the brush, not a strap on him. *Sonofabitch.*

Rome sold some wool and cedar posts in trade. Zena bought herself some thread and a card of pins.

Sometimes when Rome was away to build a chimney, Clabe helped with the sheep. There were sixty or seventy of the smelly, greasy-hanked, drippy-eyed, drippy-nosed things. A few Spanish goats were run with the bunch, to keep out sheep scab, Zena said. The sheep grazed into the wind, each cropping the ground on one side and then on the other and then moving forward a step. Clabe went up to look at the ground.

"What the devil do they eat?" he said.

"Oh, we're lucky here," Zena said. "It rains. Things get a chance to green up. They ain't had no rain atall up on the Plateau."

When the sun got hot the sheep strung down to the river. They drank their fill. Then one sheep would stick its head into the shade of a cedar bush and another into the shade of that one's belly and so on until the whole caboodle was packed tight as cotton in a mattress, heaving and panting, smack out under the hot sun. There was a big sycamore down by the river but the damnfool sheep wouldn't move into the shade of it to save their lives. They were the damnedest, stupidest things. "A sheep's always lookin' for a place to flop down and die," Rome said. Sure enough, one would get onto its back, legs in the air, gas ballooning its guts, and lay there as useless as you please. *What the hell am I doin' messin' around with sheep? It ain't white man's work.*

In the evenings the sheep drifted back to the cabin, following each other, dropping their little pokey droppings, nosing here and there, each one like it was looking for a piece of pie.

What the hell am I doin' messin' around with sheep?

Zena put supper on the table. Cornbread. Coffee. Sonofabitch stew: various odds and innards. She'd killed a goat today.

Rome said, "So what the b'deezus was I suppose to do? Shirt-fire. He'd waited all winter for me to get there. I was way late. 'I ain't got no cash,' he says, 'will you take it in trade?' His wife was standin' there. She'd been cookin' all winter under a live oak. What could I do? 'I expect I got to,' I says. 'Well,' he says, 'I can spare this Avery middlebuster and gear. It ain't hardly been used.' He must of fetched it all the way from Rolling Fork, Mississippi. It was leanin' against a tree. 'I reckon I got to,' I says. We got it onto the wagon bed. 'That's a first-rate piece of machinery,' he says, 'if a man can use it.' Doddamn. Now what'm I gonna do with a batwing cotton plow and a mess of mule harness?"

Zena said, "You might wear it into town and trade yourself off for a burro and a bushel of horse shit."

Rome tightened the kerchief on his head. "It's another one of them headache days," he said.

Zena picked greens by the river—poke salad, lamb's quarters, sour dock. "I crave greens," she said. "I got a terrible cravin' for greens." She fetched them to the cabin in her bonnet, picked the leaves off the stems and put them in a pot of water with a chunk of side meat. "For a tonic," she said. Everyday she took a spoonful of Chamberlain's Remedy.

She had dry, scaly elbows. She was all the time shading her eyes with her hands. She wore a twill cotton dress, white once, that looked like it'd been pulled through a stovepipe in the spring. Once she lifted her arm and the sleeve tore apart at the armpit. "Oh," she said. "I ain't seen the cloth for a new dress in three whole years." She ran out weeping. Later she pieced the tear together with cross-stitches.

Whenever Zena was working sheep she wore a black overskirt held up by old suspenders. Her hands were small. It always surprised Clabe to look at them. She had a worried, animal look about her. Thin, pinched lips. Crow's-feet wrinkles at the edges of her eyes. Two deep creases between her eyebrows. Thirty years old, come next July, no older than that—it might have been a pretty face if it wasn't so pinched-looking. She had a small, pretty nose. Small ears. A rounded chin. Zena always talked slow and quiet, like she was letting out threads from some big, dark ball in her mind. Dark threads. Only when she was angry did the threads get bright. Then she would snap them right and left in the air. Other times she tended to her chores, and wound and rewound the ball in her mind like a woman might ball yarn in her closed parlor. She was small-boned, small-waisted. Clabe could see she'd always been a slight woman, and only held out by perverseness. Her teeth were tight and hurt her sometimes, she said. She parched coffee and hauled water and butchered goats, wore the patched-up dress, all the time trying to keep a little space between her chores and her womanness. It looked to be a losing battle. One evening she put her white Dresden plates on the table. "Them's the only good things I have," she said. Zena's eyes had a way of turning blue or green or violet according to what she was wearing or what was behind her. Right now they were gray. "Ain't even a window in the wall to put curtains to. Might's well be livin' in a goat shed," she said. "That's what it comes to anyways."

She and Clabe ate their supper. "I notice you're left-handed," Zena said.

Clabe said, "I guess I was born that way."

"That shit-ass Rome," Zena said. "A stonemason, and we ain't got a stone fireplace here yet. Looky that. A stack of mud and sticks not fit to fart in. Oh, sometimes I want to flat quit. Sometimes I just want to climb up the chimney and go up with the smoke."

She coughed. "I crave somethin'," she said. She touched the threadbare pleats of her shirtwaist. She said, "I all the time hurt here."

Once she came on Clabe naked, washing in the river. He plopped down under. She said, "Oh, it don't make no more difference to me than a horse or a goat." But after that her dress looked whiter. She washed her hair in rainwater and dried it in the sun. Now mostly she didn't talk or look at Clabe. Went about her work as mute as an animal. "Acts like she's done lost her bite," Rome said. Zena put a plate down in silence, touched a lid like she was dabbing at feathers, swept and stooped and straightened and turned and walked through a cotton air. Was quiet long times to herself like an arm in a sleeve. A piece of sunlight on the floor could make her start. At the supper table, between spoon sounds, Clabe heard the catches in her breath. He saw her looking at him. Her face was different. It had the same wrinkles and lines that work had put there, but was softer and rounder and more private now. A kind of shining had come into it. Her eyes were deeper, more dark. Gray, green, blue, violet. She smiled at Clabe.

She coughed in the night and the blankets rustled.

One morning when breakfast was over Rome went down to the sheep trap. Clabe was washing his face in the basin outside the cabin door. He looked up to see Zena standing in the doorway. She leaned against the door frame, a shoulder and hip to the weathered frame. Gray eyes, color of the shadow of the door lintel. "Don't just stand there dripping," she said. She laughed. Of a sudden her face darkened. "I got work to do," she said. Then she was gone into the cabin.

In the dark in the cabin after supper, after the beans and the johnnycake and the talk, when Rome had gone outside, they brushed against each other. Their hands touched. Their lips touched. "Oh my God, my God," she said.

8

WHAT he was waiting for, all roused up for. Softly blankets were slid back. Corn shucks creaked in a tick. Clabe heard the cloth-against-skin of her standing up. It was pitch dark. She walked across to the door. He heard it open quietly.

He was quiet, too, finding his way to her. Came up against the door frame and stepped out. His blood followed the going of her, moving in the blind dark of her. Sound of her breaths. The solid of her in the dark. He touched her. Her heart was thumping hard. She caught hold of his hand. Into the black night. Not even stars. Stopped. Lips. She laughed, low, damping it against his throat. Led him through the dark. A tree trunk fetched them up short. Center of nowhere. Axle of night. He shoved her up against it.

Oh my dear. Mouth stuck to mouth. Knee and hipbone knocked. He had a hand on her rump. She pulled her mouth free, jerked her head aside. Yes. Oh my God yes. He browsed on her neck, nuzzled her breasts under the thin cloth shift. They weren't flat and dangling like they might've been if she'd had babies to suck—their nudge softness held up, their points lifted. Clabe sank to the ground, grabbed hold of her knees. She held his head tight against her belly. Such wide, terrible softness. She pulled him up. Her shift lifted. That was fat. She kept her face turned aside, her loud breaths. He hunted for her on her neck and in her ear. Ah, she said. Her legs were around his hips. He held her up. Oh my sweet, my sweet, she said. He eased into her and it was a hot, tight caught. She gasped. Perched light as a bird on his hickory limb, fast-hearted as a bird thing. Tip and swing, tip and swing. Sweet. He could have gone on all night. But the black grabbed hold of his legs, climbed on up, curdled in his balls, knocked at the upper door. Fingers scraped his back, heels banged the backs of his legs. There there there there there. Off. *Uff!* Light crossed. Oh heart. He shattered. The tree they were up against shattered. Clabe's body trembled. He staggered, shaking as if with the chills. His tailbone ached.

The next morning Zena said, "I feel like I've been scrubbed fresh."

A breeze moved the leaves next his shoulder. She lay on the ground, her face half in the shade. They had spread her overskirt on the ground for her to lie on. Her hair lay loose on the selvage of it and partly on the ground, where it was caught in some dried, same-color grass. Her eyes, wide open, were violet now, and she smiled. Her dress was bunched up under her chin. The two brown eyes of her breasts looked out from under it. Her face and arms and hands were tanned from the weather, but the rest of her, naked from under the dress, was a queer white. Her wiry, reddish thatch glistened in the sunlight. She reached for him and he covered her with his shadow. Her rump bounced. She had her eyes closed, her head bent back, churning from side to side, her mouth half open like a laugh. Could see the strainings in her neck, the pale, stretched-open wrinkles. The hot sun burnt down onto Clabe's bare ass. He was getting there, getting there, right on up the steps, and the top step stalled. He held. Every little mouth in him opened, dribbled a drop: the drops rolled in from his fingertips and the balls of his feet and his heart and his back muscles and his legs and swarmed together into his balls. Zena rocked and screeched. His rooster really had its neck caught. Its wattles shook. It crowed and crowed.

"That was as good as venison and honey," Zena said. Her mouth tasted of Chamberlain's Remedy.

"I'm so God-awful lonesome," she said. "I been all the time lonesome. Got married when I was fourteen. Thought I just *had* to get hitched. He's twenty years older'n me. 'Course, my folks wouldn't of heard of such a thing if they'd knowed anything about it. Rome went into Clarksville on a borrowed horse and got a license. Then he come out one night and picked me up onto his horse and we went lickety-split for the justice of the peace in Mabry. I didn't know no better. I was runnin' away from ever'thing. Into a worse loneliness. Oh, Red," she said, "take care of me. Be good to me."

The tick creaked. The one-legged bed rocked. She was pushing up against him, her chin up, her head straining back. She let out a long-drawn-out, tight-throated yell that like to busted his eardrum.

Clabe pressed her against the cabin wall, the unbarked cedar pickets. A big red moon to the east swelled out of the earth like a balloon. "*Th-th-th-th-th-th-th*," Zena said.

The sun poured down. "Touch me there, touch me there," she said. His hand rinsed along her hip, crossed her belly, moved amongst the hairs. Zena rolled on the ground. She never put a damp sponge in or made him wear sheep gut. He hunched over her and put the soft nubbin to it and pushed on in. "Look at that sky up there," she said. "That blue just scatters your mind. I use to look at it when I was a little girl. It kept pullin' at my eyes. And I thought, how does God ever get a toehold? There ain't no place to *step*. Some people think like there's one layer, and up above that that's heaven. I don't know. You look real hard and it gets farther and farther and it hurts to look." She shivered. Clabe nuzzled her neck. "Oh," she said. "I feel so sleepy when we're done."

She came up from the river with a bucket on her shoulder. Her head was bent to one side, her eyes on the ground. She crossed under the shade of a live oak, its leaves new green. Now she was out in the sunlight again. Her body from the waist up leaned to the left. She was so slight from the waist up. How come women are so slight? Each step pulled the hip forward. Her foot touched the ground and the weight of her body went onto it and her hip slumped as the other leg swung forward.

Between her legs, at the tight crotch tendon, crushing the kinked hairs, pounding the bone. The two bones knocked, he was pushing hard. She fought him with her belly and her breasts. Her rump bumped the wagon bed. Divide. Divide. Divide.

Moths circled the greasewick light. Zena tossed her shirt into a corner. Naked in the greasewick light. Her body was so girl-like and slight. It always surprised him, the slight shoulders, the thin arms and narrowing body to her waist. *I ain't never gonna leave here.* The tucking comb had come out and her hair fell down onto her shoulders.

"Do you think I'm pretty?" she said. "Look at me," she said, "gettin' thinner and thinner. Look at my hands, all work-lookin'. And my face never did look pretty."

"You got a fine, pretty nose. The prettiest eyes." He liked her eyes. They had long, soft lashes. Greenish-blue irises, gray-brown streaks coming out from the centers.

Her head was on his shoulder. He touched her face, caressed her cheek and her chin. It was a pretty chin. The lines on her face had softened. Her lips had softened. He kissed her on the lips. His hand touched her belly.

"Zena, you pretty thing," he said.

"Oh," she said, "I love your red, curly hair. *Oh!* I can't *breathe!*" she said.

He lay on her with his forehead on the ground. He was almost asleep. She was almost asleep. A ladybug lit onto his hand.

Zena spread her legs and pulled him into her.

It was getting small. "No, don't go yet," she said.

They lay stark naked in the spring rain and laughed. Her face tightened, her limbs tightened, her back arched, lifting them both off the pallet.

The sun bore down onto his back. Their bellies were

slick with sweat between them, her wet neck tasted salty. His heart thudded like a drunkard. A grasshopper flew across, rasping its wings. Clabe listened to the river. He heard sycamore burrs dropping.

"I'm tired of sneakin' around him. I hate it," Zena said.

Zena pushed against him. She was breathing fast. Her mouth opened and a low moan came out of it. Of a sudden it broke and jerked. She was crying. Her whole body jerked in short, quick hitches.

He looked at her. "Zena, Zena, what's the matter?" he said.

Tears spilled from her eyes. They streaked down her temple and pooled in her ear. Her shoulders shook. "I can't have no childern! I never had no childern! I never will have no childern!" she said.

"There, there, there, there, there!" he said. He kissed her.

"I just crave a little one about."

She shivered. Clabe held her close and rocked her from side to side. After a while she quieted. Clabe got stiffer and Zena smiled and her breath caught and he fetched her up again.

An ant ran across the back of Clabe's hand. It woke him out of his half-sleep. He rolled off Zena. The air was warm and smelled of scrub cedar. The whole slope was covered with the same warm, dead brown needles Clabe and Zena were lying on. Over to the left, almost where Clabe could touch it, an old, split-open cocoon dangled from a scaly, blue-green twig. One of those queer cedar-needle cocoons that you find in scrub cedars.

Clabe propped the photograph against a rock. He stared at it. The round, white face. The white dress. *Do you think you can find me?* she said.

□

A walkingstick stalked up the door frame. Flies buzzed. Sand sifted down an ant lion's funnel.

The body lay in the hollow, amongst the rocks.

Zena stared up at Claiborne something fierce. Her mouth was partway open and she made *s* and *th* sounds between her teeth. She looked like she was about to yell or something, like she was trying hard. Her face tightened. It got redder, more clotted with wrinkles. Her eyes squeezed shut. Her lips pulled back from her teeth. The strings got tighter in her neck. She lifted him up. She clawed his back, pushed against him, scraping at the root, thrashing under him like a trapped animal. Clabe rolled off her. They lay on the old pecan leaves, the new-leaved tree up overhead. Flies buzzed. *The Mexican climbed down from his horse and walked over to the fire. He walked stiff and slow, like it was too much weight. He smiled. The wrinkles tightened at the edges of his eyes.* Clabe pressed his head back against the pecan leaves. *Get away from me! Git.* He took a deep breath. *Zena, you know what I done? I have killed a man.*

Enough blood to paint a house, Red.

"Oh, darlin', what're we gonna *do?*" Zena said. "It's got to where I can't stand him. I can't stand him to open his mouth. Nighttimes he climbs in bed with me. Don't that bother you? Not that there's any ginger in him, but don't it bother you?" A light breeze moved the tops of the pecan trees. Zena turned to Clabe, propped herself up onto her elbow. "What're we gonna *do*, darlin'?" she said. "Oh, I must of been deaf, dumb and blind when I married him. He had me thinkin' I was about to put my left foot in Paradise. It's been stuck in the mud ever since. And then to cook for him. To put that plate down in front of him and have to set there listenin' to him chaw. Even the way he gets into his clothes of a mornin': first his hat, then his britches, then his boots. It gets my back up."

The sun was a smashed pomegranate in the sky.

Clabe felt it coming on him. He felt it pulling at the back of his head. He stepped under the brush arbor and the ground slanted, the cornerposts moved apart. He grabbed hold of air.

"What's the matter, Red?" Rome said.

"Nothin'. Nothin'. Leave me be." Clabe put a sack of stock salt on the ground, or almost on the ground. He managed to get back out from under the arbor. The sunlight came down in splinters. He staggered off up the slope and leaned against a slant of sunlight.

Later he said, "I'm all right. I get them spells sometimes. Where d'ya want this stock salt put?"

A cloud crossed the sun. The black sombrero flapped. The old man smiled and nodded, the web of wrinkles tightened around his eyes. Clabe grabbed him by the shoulders. He shook him hard. *Who are you?* he said. Something pulled at the back of his head. Light welled up. He looked out of a window onto a great, white light. His eyes jerked open. He fell.

The sun's massive boulders tumbled down. Clabe lay on the ground, looking up. A few feet off, a scrub cedar stood up into the air. Bark trunk and scaly needles. It grew up out of the hard ground. Sunlight was all around it. It stood up into the light. It was like it was watching him.

The old Mexican came toward Clabe.

"*I hate you! I hate you!*" Claiborne said.

Clabe waded into the Agua Fria River. He reached down into the water. It bubbled around his elbows. Cool, flowing fast. He loosened a rock from the bottom and fetched it up. It was a big one, all its edges rubbed smooth by the water. It was twice as heavy when he lifted it out of the water. He sloshed out of the river and up onto the drift-and-pebble shore.

"Christ, this is heavy," he said.

"You want help?" Rome said.

"No, I can get it." Clabe lugged it to the wagon and set it on the endgate.

"There. That was a bastard. We got enough?"

"Prett' near," Rome said. "A couple-three more big'uns and we'll be done."

Clabe waded back out into the river. He felt around on the bottom with his hands. Here was a big one, if he could work it loose. Clabe said, "Where's all this water come from? There ain't been no rain atall this spring that you could call it that."

"Up in the canyons. It comes out from under the Plateau. I don't know how it does it. They ain't had rain up on the Plateau in nigh two years. That's what I hear tell, anyways."

"Where's that?"

"Alto Springs. Balcones County. Up on the Divide."

B neck brand.

The blood welled through the bloody tucks. "Ah . . . Alto," *the old Mexican said.*

Alto Springs?

"Don't know why they call it that—Alto Springs," Rome said. "Ain't nothin' but a couple seep springs up there."

The river pressed and bubbled around Clabe's knees. Water dripped from the rock he was holding.

Zena said to Clabe, "Take me away from here. If you don't take me away I'll kill him. I can't stand to look at him. I'd like to wrap him in a backless shroud. Under the ground. Under the dirt ground where I don't got to think on him no more. Oh, I can't keep on like this. *I want to be with you!* I'm goin' crazy the way things are—I'll stick him with a pair of hand shears if I got to. *Goddamn you, help me,*" she said.

That night Clabe rolled up the blanket from his pallet, a box of cartridges and a slab of bacon in the center of it. He took Rome's old Sharps rifle from the mantel. It was pitch dark in the cabin. He stood still a minute and heard Rome and Zena breathing soft and regular in the corner. Clabe didn't make any noise. On the way out he grabbed the coffee-pot. Up on the slope he slapped a twine on one of Rome's culls. He knew the animal, a shad-bellied, low-haunched mare with gotched ears and white spots from tick bites on her chest and shoulders. She wasn't much, but she'd have to do. Slipped a curb bit into her mouth. Clabe led her down to the sheep trap, where he'd left his gear. He threw a sheepskin and an old kak saddle onto her back and laced up. Tied on his bedroll, the Sharps rifle and the coffeepot. An owl hooted. Nighthawks crossed in the dark overhead. A scant, thin new moon hung in the sky to the west like a fine silk thread. Clabe led the mare into a stand of pecan trees alongside the river. Then he lit on up and headed up toward the canyons.

9

THE birds were edgy, but it was too dark yet for them to stir from the branches. Here and there a nervous peep. The mare pushed her way through chest- and fender-high bushes. Her hoofs clacked on rocks. An iron-gray sky in the east. About an hour to sunup. The stars were dulling there. Chill, fresh, early-morning air scraped past Clabe's face. He liked the moist freshness of it on his neck and face.

Clabe followed the river north. The mare was slow, damned slow—a regular creeping Moses. Low in the withers and short-gaited, not the kind of horse you fall in love with. The light grew pale in the east. The river, a dull, tarnished silver, riffled and coughed over its rocks nearby. Scrub-covered hills to the left and right of Clabe. The more the sky lightened, the closer the darkness seemed to hunch down onto the earth. The mare pushed through a stand of broom willows. The mountains to the north were flat-topped or gently mounded, dotted with scrub. They were taller now that he was close.

Here a small bluff came down to the river, and Clabe rode onto a gravel bar and through some slow water and came out amongst box elders and broom willows. The sky eastward was yellow, the color of the skin on cream. *Wakin' up now. Rome hawking and snuffing. Spits into the fireplace. "Where's my rifle?"*

The empty pallet. *Comes into the open doorway. "Zena, my saddle's gone! Zena, he's took Sukey!"* Zena with the darkness in her heart.

But they won't never try to come after me.

Clabe touched the saddle. It was an old shank of a saddle, a slickfork with pecan stirrups and wrecked, sour, rawhide housing. All that held it together was habit and a few whang strings. *Zena lay on the ground next to Clabe. The wiry, reddish thatch glistened in the sunlight. He kissed her face. He kissed her breasts, the grainy nipples. There was a hurt in Zena's eyes. He kissed her eyes. He kissed the furrow lines on her face, the years that had been, the years that were ahead of her. Why did he do that? What was in him to do that? Christ, this world hurts.*

The mare's head pumped up and down in front of him.

The sun came up. Clabe kept on upriver. What he needed was a smoke. He'd forgot that. *Shit. Not the makings of a thing.* He broke off a stick from a bush and chewed it. He left the river for a spell and cut across a flat to where it looped on back. There was a gap up ahead, about six miles off. By mid-morning Clabe rode into the mouth of a canyon. *Don't know whereall I'm headed, but it looks like the hard way to get there. Already way out from any settlement.*

The canyon was an opening about a quarter of a mile wide between bluffs. The river ran with a milky-green color over rocks, shallow and fast, between stands of box elders and hackberries. Clabe rode a long way up it. The sun climbed higher. Smell of early plum blossom, heavy and draggy in the heat. Toward noon the mare had begun to stumble. The river looped under a limestone bluff. Clabe crossed over to a flat opposite, a small, grassy place with one mesquite tree and a hawthorn. He let the mare drink, then rode over to the mesquite and lit down. The ground felt queer, it was so solid, and he walked stiffly on it. He unlaced the saddle and dropped it to the ground under the mesquite. He roped the mare out to graze in the open space. It looked to be about eleven o'clock of the morning, according to the sun. Clabe pulled some dry flood trash from its stashings in the broom willows next the

river and built a fire. He unspooled his bedroll and cut a
chunk off the piece of side meat he'd stashed in it. He stuck
the side meat on a stick and propped it out over the coals.

He picked up the coffeepot and started toward the river.
He stopped. *He'd forgot to fetch coffee too.* The sack of coffee
beans hung from a rafter in the cabin. *Yes, you damn fool—
fetch up your bedroll, latch onto the coffeepot and light on out. And
not a coffee bean, one. You ain't got brains enough to fry an egg in.*
Clabe walked back to the fire and tossed the pot onto the bedding in disgust. The grease from the bacon sputtered and
smoked on the coals. Clabe sat by the fire. While the meat
was cooking he broke open the Sharps rifle and breeched a
cartridge. It was a single-shot breechloader. He put several
cartridges into his jacket pocket. He ate the side meat and
drank water from the river. At least it put a bottom on his
stomach.

The sun was hot. Clabe lay on his bedding in the thin
shade of the mesquite, his head on the saddle dish. He pulled
his hat down over his face. A beetle clicked. The mare moved
a step and pulled grass. Clabe's body loosened and sank
against the ground. He thought cool. *A milk well. The cool,
dark of Leona's kitchen. Sitting on the spindle chair and eating one
of Leona's big, cool, peeled turnips, sweet as an apple.*

A piece of sunlight was on Clabe's hand, a small, burning flake. He moved his hand. It fell to the ground beside
him.

Clabe woke. Some cowbirds were gossiping, tinkling and
bubbly, in the top of the hawthorn, carrying on like a Women's
Auxiliary Sewing Circle. Clabe got up and went to the river
and rinsed his face. The mare was dozing on three legs. Clabe
bridled her, flung the wood and leather onto her back and
girted up. Tied on his gear. Then he rode up the canyon five
or six more hours until it got on toward dark. When he came
to a camping place—a clearing in the brush by the river—he
roped out the horse, cooked some more side meat and bedded
down.

The next afternoon Clabe shot a turkey. He had been riding along thinking about the time he and Dolph Tomlinson had rolled the barrel down on Emmitt. He and Dolph had put some rocks in an iron barrel and hefted it up the outside staircase of Blanchard's racket store. Blanchard's was the only two-story business building in Cherokee. A dance hall was on the second floor. They got the barrel up onto the landing—balanced it at the edge there—and Dolph hunkered down behind it. There wasn't a sign of life anywhere except for a pigeon—that just then lit down onto the wooden awning of the Equity Saloon—and Clabe, who stood waiting at the foot of the stairs. Pretty soon a cloud of dust showed, up the street, and a man came riding up. Happened it was Emmitt.

"Emmitt, I been wantin' to talk to you," Claiborne said.

Emmitt nodded and lit down at the hitch rack, tied on and came on over. "This here is strictly private," Clabe said. He motioned toward the staircase. He went up about six steps and sat on the outside edge.

Emmitt followed him and sat next him, curious as all get-out. "Well, what's up?" he said.

Clabe lowered his voice. Their hat brims touched. "I just think somebody oughter tell you . . ."

About that time Dolph shoved the barrel. It bumped and thundered down the steps like all hell had broke loose. Clabe jumped over the railing to the ground. Emmitt started to get up, slipped, skidded down the stairs, got up onto his feet and took off like all forty down the street. Men poured out of doors and stuck their heads out of windows to cheer him on.

When Emmitt came back he had a hangdog look on his face. "Aw, Red, why'd you have to go and do that for?" he said.

Clabe chuckled. He scratched a bug bite on his back.

That's when he heard the turkeys yelping. He lit down from the mare, caught the reins in a bush, pulled the rifle free

and cocked the hammer. In the nick of time—a flock of turkeys came trotting down the river bank. Clabe fired into the
bunch. They scattered. Wing-thunder, squawks. One lay
flapping on the rocks. Clabe ran over to it. It thrashed its
wings, splotching the rocks red. The 40-caliber bullet had
knocked its back off. It opened its beak and tried to make a
noise. Its eye blinked, then closed, its feathers loosened and it
lay still. Clabe cut a slit in its belly and gutted it and stuffed
the hollow with wet grass. He tied its feet together with a slip
of willow and hung it from the saddle horn. Then he recommenced his ride up the canyon.

The turkey swung at Claiborne's knees.

Sometimes the river was just a thimble-deep show over
rocks. Other times it deepened into ponds of milky-green
water. Once it went down underground clean out of sight and
Clabe rode up a dry riverbed. A hundred yards farther up, the
water was running over rocks again. Once Clabe came on a
set of the most God-awful big tracks sunk in the limestone
rock of the riverbed. A washtub could have been set in any
one of them. The giant toes were pointed up-canyon.

A great, white underbelly thundered past. Claiborne
laughed. *Christ, I'd hate to meet up with a critter like that.*

There was Slotty McGonigal, McAllister and O'Burke,
A Scandinavian fisherman, Norwegian and a Turk
The ladies, the babies were cryin' all the time.
Ever' man in bed at eight or locked out after nine,

he sang as he rode up the canyon.

Across the river from Clabe the canyon side lifted up
from the water like a wall. It was built up of layer on layer of
rock, like a deck of cards—some world-changing shuffle a
long time back. A little farther up the canyon Clabe came on
a bunch of javelinas browsing on prickly pear. He came on
them from downwind so that he was right up to them before
they smoked him out. They quit their browsing and snuffed

the air with flat, hog snouts. One popped its tusks. They took off quick as a wink into the brush.

The sun shifted west. The canyon wall slowly darkened, a wedge of shade spreading out from its foot. Toward night Clabe came on a pond. Cliff swallows twittered above it. Clabe unsaddled the horse and hobbled her with a clog, a two-foot-long forked stick lashed to a foreleg, and turned her loose to graze. He broke some dead branches from a mesquite tree and built a fire.

He felt for the photograph in his jacket pocket. *No, don't look at it. Not now.* Instead, he watched her face in lamplight as she turned up the wick. She bent over a table, next the lamp Clabe's mind had put there.

Somewheres. Oh Christ, there's just the ground to cross over, the creeks to pass, wherever all she is. And I'm gonna get there.

Clabe cut the head off the turkey. He cut the legs and wings off at the joints. Then he made a slit across the breast and stuck his fingers in and pulled off the pelt.

> *We've give him up for good,*
> *He's layin' in the lane*
> *And just about ever'body knows*
> *The old man's drunk again.*

He rinsed the carcass in the pond. *Ain't it queer how in dreams there ain't no stars or sky? Not that I can recollect. And when anybody talks, their chins move, you know whatall they're sayin' but there ain't a word, one. Don't know as I've ever heard a word in a dream. More like the different colors of words. Now what got me thinkin' on that?* He spitted the turkey on a shaft of green mesquite and put it out over the fire. *Wish I'd brung some salt.* Three hours later, by campfire light, he ate a sizable chunk of the turkey.

He spread his blanket down next the fire and looped the hair rope around it. *Scorpions and centipedes and snakes and such won't cross a hair rope.* He lay on his pallet and watched the stars. The cooling embers of the fire clicked. The mare cropped grass. Crickets cricked. Frogs croaked back and forth, back and forth. A fish leapt and plopped out on the pond. A hoot owl sounded. The dark canyon wall lifted up toward the stars.

In his dream Clabe was chopping at a tree. Blood ran from the tree when he struck it.

The next morning Clabe took a dip. He crawled out of his bedroll and stripped off his shirt and britches and string drawers and walked through the cool morning air to the pond. A thin sliver of moon hung in the east above the bluff, a crisp, bright star above a tip of it. Clabe stepped into the water. *Uh!* Cold as a welldigger's elbow. He waded out past pads and pods and other weeds until he was up to his particulars in it. He plumped down under and the caul of cold like to knocked his wits loose. Then it felt better. He paddled around some and waded out of the pond. He put his clothes on without drying. He liked the feel of cool, damp clothes next his skin. Just like in the heat of day he liked the feel of sweat worked from his pores by the sun, though sometimes he got a headache from the difference between the cold sweat and the hot blood it was wrung from.

He pulled on his boots. The mare was cropping grass. She looked like she needed rest and fattening. Her rib bones and hipbones showed. Clabe walked over to the campfire and pulled a piece of breast meat off the turkey. He sat on his blanket and chewed it. *It wants salt.* The mouths of fishes made rings on the pond surface. The paler the sky grew, the lazier Clabe got. He watched Mr. Sanderlin's hands graft apricot to plum. Cramped, arthritic hands. The notch in the plum, the slip of apricot. The hands waxed the union. They wrapped strips of white cloth around it for bandages. Clabe lay on the blanket and pulled part of it across him. When he woke again sunlight was onto the blanket and flies lit onto it or lifted from it and buzzed.

Clabe lay on his back with his hands behind his head. He watched a hawk make circles way up in the white, bleached sky. *What's a hawk think? Not a word that's for sure. What's he light down onto? Not a "rock" or a "branch." Christ, ever'body I ever knew had a word for ever'thing, till you can't see the things for the words. Might's well be livin' in a fuckin' schoolbook. Some one of these days somethin's gonna tear a few pages out, make us look at what's there . . .*

"Claiborne," Clabe's ma said, "promise me. Whatever you do, be honest and truthful." She lay propped up on a sacking pillow on the one-legged bed, her face white and fleshless on the eggshell bone, her blue eyes large and shining, her dark brown hair, that seemed too rich now for the face, combed and spread out on the pillow. Her thin hands lay on the counterpane. She hardly ever lifted them anymore, or moved her head or any other. Clabe stood at the foot of the bed, grabbed hold of the tattered counterpane and nodded his head. Six years old. Many's the time his ma had stood by, her eyes angry and lips tight, while his pa had whipped him. Then when his pa had gone out she would take him to a dark corner of the cabin and comfort him. But after she was gone there was nobody left to take his part. His pa beat horses. He was a horsebreaker and a cowhand, off and on. He would whip a horse and holler at it till it looked like it couldn't stand it anymore. One time he whipped a horse until it dropped. He had the horse snubbed down, and it couldn't stand it any-more. He whipped Clabe and his brothers too. Clabe was the next to youngest. Once when Clabe had a chance to go fish-ing with Johnnie Hollins he ran to his ma. "Ma, can I go fishin'?" he said. "Ask your pa." Couldn't find his pa any-where. So he told his ma his pa had said it was all right. Knew it was wrong, but he wanted to go so bad and for sure his pa wouldn't let him. All the time he was fishing he had a fretty feeling, but they caught a good string and it was a fine day.

His pa didn't whip him that night. But the next morning some little old thing Clabe did riled him and he said he'd just whip him for all of it, in particular for going fishing yesterday. He beat Clabe like he did his horses, on the head, across the chest, down his back, on his legs. Clabe lay on his back and saw the strap come down, he rolled over onto his belly, he rolled over onto his back, he scrunched and doubled up, he pissed in his britches. His screams were one blind holler. The strap banged down . . . *shit on that!*

Clabe sat up and shook his head. He got up and walked over to a mesquite tree and took a piss. Then he commenced to walk around the edge of the pond. Frogs jumped in ahead of him. Thick stands of weeds grew along the edge and out into the water. Weed pods floated on the pond. When Clabe got over to the other side, along the foot of the bluff, he stepped from stone slab to stone slab. Some dead bees were floating on the water. Up overhead two big black honeycombs hung down like a pair of lungs, and bees shimmered around them. Clabe worked his way down to the foot of the pond, flipped some stones over with his boot. A hellgrammite big as a finger wiggled in the socket under one of them. Clabe put the stone back in place and put another stone on top of it. Over near his camp he cut the head from a sotol plant. He sat in the shade next his campfire.

Clabe piled sticks on last night's ashes and built up a fire. He hacked the saw-edged leaves off the sotol with a knife, leaving a head about the size of a cabbage. When the fire had burnt down to a pile of coals he poked them aside, put the hunk of sotol in, heaped ashes over it and covered the ashes with hot coals.

Out on the pond the glare light pressed down. Blue snake doctors hung over the water or balanced on the tips of weed. They looked like splinters of fire. A mite breeze rippled the surface, slashes of light shimmered on the rock wall. It was too bright to look at for long.

Clabe spent the morning making a fishline from the fibers of the sotol leaves. He made a make-do hook from the turkey pully bone.

In the afternoon he slipped a cartridge into the Sharps rifle and shot a slab of honey from the bluff. The comb fell into the water. Later, when the bees had gone off, he walked on around and fetched out the chunk.

He lay on his back and watched birds fly across. He lay on his belly and watched the mare rub her rump against a mesquite. He dozed a mite.

Toward evening he cut a sycamore sapling for a fish-pole. The sun was to the west now, the pond shaded. Clabe trimmed the twigs from the sapling and tied his hook and line on. He walked to the foot of the pond, turned up the stone and got the hellgrammite. He turned up some more stones and found another. Also caught a couple bitty frogs on his way back, stashed them all in his shirt pocket.

Here was a likely-looking place. Clabe fished out one of the hellgrammites and ran the bone hook under its collar. Clabe swung the bait out onto the water—*plop!* The hell-grammite sank slowly down. Directly the line started moving to one side. Clabe gave the hook a jerk. The line swung in the other direction. Clabe didn't waste any time playing the fish but worked it right up to the surface and flipped it up through the air and onto the shore. It was a good thing he did, too, on account of halfway there the hook came out of its mouth. Clabe ran over to it and kicked it farther up onto the rocks. It was a sun perch, about the size of his hand. Its gills gaped. It flopped and flopped. Clabe wiped his hands in some dirt and caught hold of the fish and ran a stringer of broom willow through its gills. The perch's belly was yellow. It had blue on its gills with a black spot at the tip of each gill. Clabe tied the stringer to some weeds and left the fish in the water.

The hellgrammite was half torn off. All that was left were some tag ends of bug gut and collar. Clabe pulled them off and tossed them into the pond. Mouths came up and popped the pieces out of sight. Clabe baited his hook with the second hellgrammite. He lost his bait on the first strike: mouths and a splash of back, the line went down, he pulled up on it, the hook sprang naked as a pin into the air.

Clabe put a frog on the hook and swung it as far out onto the pond as he could. It floated on top of the water. Then it went down, and the line went down with it. When the line pulled tight, the fish didn't stop going. It was a big one. Clabe feared it would break the line. He stepped into the water. The line wove back and forth like a kite on a string. Whatever was onto it must have swallowed the bait whole or it would have shucked the hook by now. Clabe kept just enough heft on the line to have the pull of the fish and give it slack when he had to. He followed that fish all over the pond. Half the time he was sitting in the water, the rest of the time he was trying to get up onto his feet. Finally the fish made for a patch of weeds. The line caught in the weeds. Clabe ran over to it. He fell down several times before he got to it. He grabbed hold of the line, ran his fingers down it. Here was the thick, quick flesh, thrash and fins and spines. It was hampered by the weeds. Clabe scooped up weeds and mud and the fish to his chest. It slapped against his belly. Clabe got three of his fingers into its gills and lifted it up into the air. It was a bass. Its tail reached to his elbow. It slapped and banged against his arm.

Clabe was breathing hard. He stumbled ashore and flung the fish onto the rocks. It slapped the rocks—a big, bulge-bellied, white-bellied bass with a mouth big enough to stick your fist into. The frog was still in its mouth, the broken line hung from its lip. Clabe let the fish flop. He was too tuckered to give a damn. He sat on the ground, water streaming from his shirt and britches. Pieces of mud and weed dribbled with the water. He picked some of the weeds off. Christa'mighty, he'd lost the other frog from his pocket! Of a sudden he laughed. *Shit, a body's got to have some fun once in a while.*

Clabe rested. The pond was quiet. The leaves in the trees were quiet. Just the sound of water dripping and the lessening slapping of the fish. He pulled his boots off and poured water out of them. After a spell he waded out into the pond and rinsed himself off. He came back out and put the bass on the stringer and slogged on back to camp.

He gutted and scaled the fish. Built a fire. Filled the coffeepot with water and stuffed some dewberry leaves into it and set it on the fire to boil. When he had a good heap of coals he spread them out and laid the bass and the perch onto them. After a spell he turned the fish over. The cooked sides were charred, the burnt skin bubbly, with chunks of coals stuck to them. When the fish were done Clabe brushed off the coals and set the fish aside. He poked around in the ashes with a stick and worked out the charred chunk of sotol. It was piping hot. He cut it in half with his knife. Its core was yellow-brown, with layers of stalk tight around it like an onion. He tore off the burnt outer layers, slapping his fingers against his thighs to cool them. He ate the stringy center. It had a scorched, sweet taste to it, like the burnt, stringy part just under the skin of a baked sweet potato. Clabe ate the fish. The flesh, laced with thready, black veins, was so moist and tender it came right off the bones. He ate all of it, even thumbed out the little cup of meat under the cheek of the bass. He drank the dewberry-leaf tea. He ate honey for his sweetfood.

It was chilly toward dark. Clabe rolled up in his blanket. He wished he had a smoke. Cut plug—*Rosebud* or *Albion*. He turned it over in his mind. Rolled a shuck and lit it, the blue smoke curled upward in front of him. *Well, shit.* He turned over onto his side and thought of the woman in the red walking skirt in the lobby. In a few minutes he was asleep.

The next morning it was a red sky. Clabe ate a sparse breakfast. He slapped a twine on the mare and led her back to camp. She had a little vinegar in her this morning. He flung on his gear and laced up and she tried to kick him, which was a good sign. Not that there was any *real* show in her—Clabe lit on up, the mare humped her back and took a couple of stiff steps like she had a broomhandle up her ass. That was about the size of it. Clabe put his heel to her belly and they headed up the canyon.

The canyon narrowed. Clabe rode up one last, thready stretch of water. After that it was dry creek bottom. In an hour or so the draw forked and he took the left fork, which went in a westerly direction. The air was hot and sticky, the sky a queer, bourbon color. Clabe's shirt was soaked with sweat. All morning long as he rode up the canyon the sky got darker. The wind lay. Great rags of cloud began to pile up overhead. They came from the southwest. By noon they had built into dark green thunderheads. In between the bundles of clouds Clabe could see that queer, bourbon sky.

He rode through some of the roughest, rockiest country he'd ever set eyes on. Cherokee was bottomland compared to this. Clabe had to lead the mare up the worst parts of the draw. Here were the breaks and headers of the canyon behind him—deep, rambling ravines between cedar-splotched hills. Lime-rock country. Agarita and prickly pear and deer laurel. It looked like he was getting plumb out of the world.

The sky was all blacked up. The clouds were in a turmoil. Gusts of wind scuttled down, shaking the brush. It was going to be mean weather, he could tell that. Raindrops struck the ground for a moment—that sweet smell that comes from rain on dry dirt.

Up overhead, meshes of sheet lightning spread through the clouds like lacework but didn't make a sound. The clouds were boiling. They were greenish-black under. It was as dark now as the shank end of evening excepting for the thin, bourbon skyline all around. And not a damned place to take cover.

The canyon was close to topping out.

A round, flat cactus, its crown covered with pink, wax-like flowers, bloomed in the half-light. Clabe had never smelled such a pretty smell before. More so than honeysuckle. He checked the mare to smell of it.

Fat drops of rain hit the ground. Clabe rode up the draw. The sky was boiling like molasses candy. Next thing Clabe knew he was in a hard rain that turned to hail. The hail stung Clabe's thighs and shoulders, raised blood blisters on the backs of his hands. The mare squealed. Clabe lit down and grabbed hold of the curb strap. He backed the mare into some brush. She reared and squealed. The hail was bouncing on the ground like marbles. Then it quit. Clabe heard a buzzing like ten million bees, a roar of a thousand trains crossing trestles, booming across trestles from every direction. Smelled sulphur. Could hardly breathe. The air screamed overhead. Clabe looked up into the funnel of Hell.

Great, ragged mouth of swirling clouds, black as blackest night, lit up inside with lightning flashes. Could see half a mile or more up into it. The funnel swirled. Green and blue and yellow lightning zigzagged from side to side. Swiveling cloud-stuff spun loose, writhing around the rim, making a hissing noise. In the mile-high hollow center one small cloud floated up and down.

The twister roared. Clabe's ears hurt. His scalp ached, his lungs felt stiff, as if he hadn't breathed in hours. He had a crave to go up into the twister, up into the twist and rage of it. It went on over. It touched down, then lifted again, sucking dust and brush into the air. It hung in the air, swinging back and forth like an elephant's trunk. Then it moved off toward the southeast, drawing up into the clouds. *There you go, god-damn you, meaner than you come.* Its snout poked down for a minute and as suddenly disappeared.

Clouds boiled overhead. Clabe rode the mare up the hail-whitened draw. The great black storm line moved toward the southeast. The hail had stripped leaves and branches from agarita and smashed whole clumps of cactus.

A little farther up the draw, in a patch of sunlight, Clabe checked the mare. A horse had slid down the side of the draw. It had slid down in a hurry, that was for sure. Two long furrows showed where it had come down, likely on its hocks. Shod all around, number two size—a big horse. Some dirt was on top of the hail but there were whole, uncrushed hail-stones in the hoofmarks.

"*Halloo! Halloo!*" Clabe called. He listened and waited but got no reply.

Clabe jabbed spurs at the mare's belly. She lumbered up the slope and topped the rise.

Another country. Gently rolling limestone plains, like ocean swells, under fresh, bright sunlight. And the trash of the twister: melting hail, dead birds stripped of their feathers, sheared-off brush, a crumpled sheet of iron roofing, scraps of splintered lumber, a slew of dead rabbits. That house-lifter had cleared a track a quarter-mile wide through the brush.

10

CLABE followed the track of the tor-
nado. The rolling tableland lifted and fell monotonously, the
ground rocky and broken, with here and there stands of scrub
cedar and half-dead, snake-branched live oaks that looked
like some ghost hand had twisted the juice out of them. The
grass was sparse and shallow-rooted. A hardpan, drouth country. The mare perked her ears and strained to see ahead,
hoping to get to *some* place. Great piled-up clumps of
laundry-white clouds moved from the southwest, hauling
their dark floors, and the sun bore down between. A hawk
circled overhead. Toward evening a breeze came up, cool and
sweet, gentle and fresh and steady as a sea breeze. Clabe made
camp where some pot rocks had caught water from the
twister. He lay on his blanket and smelled the dry cedar and
grass smells in the breeze. The stars moved overhead.

He rode all the next morning, in a cantankerous mood.
He'd spent a bad night on the flint rocks that had littered the
ground. He'd shifted from one place to another. He'd tried to
work the rocks out from under him. He'd tried to fit himself to
the rocks. When he woke he'd felt like he'd been beaten with
a stick. Then, taking up the saddle girt, he'd got his fingers
caught in the dee ring, no reason why. He'd lit up into the
saddle, hoping to light up out of his mean disposition. *Shit.*
He hadn't even liked the feel of the hull, a bunch of Mexican
fuste and asshole leather slapped together.

He followed the track of the twister. Snapped mesquite
trunks stuck up at him. Branches littered the torn ground.

Outside the path of the twister it was bald country, too—
bleached grass, black limestone dirt, catclaw and scrub oak
and prickly pear. As lonesome as the edges of time.

The sun got hotter. Clabe's mouth was so dry he could
spit cotton.

Shadows lay on the ground under things. They didn't
seem part of the things. Color broke things apart. Dead
brown slashed across stone, cactus green crashed against rock,
white leaked out of the splintered ends of branches.

The front of Clabe's head pounded. He stared at the
ground. Many's the time he'd gone over the ears of a horse
and made an impression there. But the worst time was when
he'd got thrown by that big, glass-eyed, hog-backed claybank
with the stripe down its back, out at Bradford's when he was
sixteen or so. He'd had to tie the sonofabitch's hind foot up to
its neck so's he could get up on. That horse had pitched! It
had turned its pack. Clabe lay on the ground with a little
blood coming out of his mouth. He hadn't felt like he was
really hurt. But after that he had a mean feeling in him. Not
just that old feeling he'd always had of being lost or kicked
out, but fretfulness. Talk coming across the lot irked him. It
irked him to hear a chair scrape or a meal get belched or a
knife drop onto a plate. And at night, lying in his bunk with
an arm under his head, every place his skin touched hurt.
There was a terrible, cramped feeling in him of grief or rage.

A bird chirped in a bush. Bright new blood color on its
breast, brown, dried-blood color on top. The bloodsprinkle in
the photograph, the white dress.

The brown face looked up at him, shiny with sweat. The
eye stared. The mustache quivered and the teeth grinned.
No. "*No no no!*" Clabe said out loud.

A rock squirrel skittered over some rocks, its black tail
flicking.

It is so goddamn hot.

Once, when he was batching it with Cotton Tucker and
Frank Allison up in Brown County, about a year after he'd

been pitched by that horse, he'd come in from bedding down his string. It was after dark. Frank was frying a batch of steak and potatoes for supper. Clabe had walked over to the table and washed in the basin. A coal-oil lamp was on the table, next the basin, its bright flame flaring inside the smoky chimney. Clabe rinsed his face in the basin. Some drops of water spattered on the chimney. The chimney exploded like a firecracker. A windowshade snapped up. Black night was over everything. The night was heavy and thick as dough, and the ground cracked under the weight of it. Grass cracked. Trees shivered. Beasts ran with their flesh split apart as if they'd been cleavered. The world came flat apart. Everything was in pieces. When Clabe finally came to, Frank and Cotton were standing up over him. They were pure strangers.

The ground moved under Clabe. The mare's hoofs clicked on the rocks. *Oh, Christa'mighty, travel this whole world over, plumb lost.*

"Spider in your dumpling, Red."

Nobody knows who I am. And it's a damn good thing.

Here was a piece of front gallery, no house to it, sitting in the middle of nowhere, put down here by the twister.

A small, splintered shipping box with print words on its side.

Some tin roofing.

The noontime sun bounced up from the rocks. Clabe looked up. Off in the distance, toward the southwest, the roofless top of a courthouse.

Clabe brushed his boots and straightened his hat and rode into town. It looked like several acres of kindling. Four or five stone buildings were around the square, every one without roofs and all the windowlights out. Clabe rode through a mess of timbers and signboards, broken glass, tin roofing. Folks wandered through the litter, pulling this and that out of it. They didn't even look at him. On the square, which was more cleared off, men were loading timbers onto a wagon.

Teams stood about, their wagons loaded with trash or waiting to be loaded. Plenty of saddle horses on the square—Texas slickfork saddles, and Mexican saddles with big *tapaderos*. Several women were unwinding bolts of yard goods, stretching them out to dry on a plank-littered lot next a store. Tents were pitched behind the store and in other places, with clothes spread out to dry on their canvas sides. A chest of drawers was in the street, with dishes stacked on it. An old, almost bald woman stood next it, wiping and wiping a dish on the folds of her skirt. A windmill lay toppled over a cedar cistern on the courthouse "lawn" and some men were working to salvage it (a divided privy on the opposite, southeast, corner of the lawn had got through whole). Other men and boys, whites and Mexicans, worked to clear the trash off the lawn, and others carried files, desks and suchlike plunder from the courthouse. The big roofless limestone building loomed over everything, a blind stone thing, blue sky through its upstairs window casings.

On a corner of the square a crew of men was lugging wreckage from the stone hull of another building. Clabe lit down from the mare and tied her to a leafless tree. He slipped the spurs from his boots, hung them to the saddle horn, walked over and pitched in.

These men looked so brown Claiborne thought at first they were Mexicans, though he saw in a minute that most of them weren't. It was just they'd soaked up a deal of weather up here on the Plateau. They'd most of them got so much in the habit of squinting they squinted even in the shade. Their faces were grimy with sweat and dirt. They'd likely been working without letup since the twister hit. They didn't say a word to Clabe and hardly looked at him. Didn't waste any breath amongst themselves, either. Once in a while somebody'd say, "Boys, put a hand to this" or "Grab a holt of that" or something in Mexican, and that was the size of it.

It had been a harness and saddle shop, with a feed store in the rear. The roof had collapsed. The place was half-filled

with trash—tin roofing, building stone and timbers. Clabe
hefted stones and helped knock apart a wooden partition—
dark, varnished wood, a calendar still tacked onto it. He
dragged sacks of wet feed out of the trash. After a couple of
hours a woman came around with a pot of black coffee. The
men sat on a stack of timbers and drank coffee. The woman
handed Clabe a cup. "Can I get some water for my horse?"
Clabe said.

"I'll tend to it," the woman said. "You come up from
Ugalde?" she said.

"No'm," Claiborne said.

"Ain't this just terrible?" she said, her voice shaking. She
swept an arm to indicate the scattered wreckage. "I don't
think we're gonna ever get over it."

"How's Miz Bennett?" one of the men said.

"She's all right," the woman said. "We lost little Bennett, though."

"Oh no."

"We ain't told her. She don't know about it yet."

"Oh, Lord." "Oh, Jesus Christ," some of the men said.

"I tell you it feels like the end of the world," the woman
said. She started toward the courthouse. "I'll see your horse
gets some water," she said to Clabe.

The men drank their coffee. It was good coffee. After a
spell a boy fetched water to Clabe's horse. The men rolled
cigarettes and commenced to smoke. One of them offered his
makings to Clabe. "Thanks," Claiborne said. He shook tobacco onto a shuck, rolled it and twisted both ends. He lit up
and tasted the blue smoke. That smoke felt like the first meal
he'd had in a month of Sundays.

"You come from Krugerville way?" the one who gave
him the makings, a tall, quiet man with a brown mustache,
said.

"More or less," Clabe said.

"Then maybe you seen that twister."

"It went right on over me. Sounded like a dozen railroad trains."

"Evening b'fore last all hell broke loose here," the man said.

Another man leaned forward, a slight, lightweight, nervous sort of fellow about thirty years old, with long, thin, delicate, almost woman's fingers. He was the only one whose hands and face weren't sun-browned. In fact, it looked like he'd been kept under a bushel all his life. His skin was pale except for one big rising on his nose, which gave it a raw look. His ears stuck out like jug handles. His eyes were dark and sunken. A clerk or some such. He said, "Twenty-seven people were killed. Mr. Blackwell was killed. Mr. Lacey was killed."

Claiborne said, "I'm sure sorry to hear it."

The man cracked his knuckles. He said, "Both the Castellanos were killed. The whole Mayfield family was killed. And hurt people everywhere. It just came down on us from out of nowhere. We had a few plank houses but they all went."

The man with the brown mustache said, "It turned a few iron kettles wrongside out."

"Folks are sleeping under wagons and in tents. It just flat blew the town square away."

"It wouldn't of been so bad," another man said, "exceptin' half the town was at the schoolhouse for a program, and *it* was the hardest hit."

The men finished their smokes and got up and dusted off their britches. Clabe took one last puff on his cigarette and tossed the butt onto the ground. They recommenced to work. Somebody backed a wagon up and they loaded it with trash.

Later in the day a dark cloud came up from the southwest and the wind rose, a sudden freshening. Folks stared up scared to death of it. The cloud let down a sharp, quick rain. Everyone made for cover. Then it was over. It moved on toward the east. Clabe came out from under the wagon he'd sheltered under. The man with the long, delicate fingers— whose name, he'd told Clabe, looking at him with sad, pea- ked-looking eyes, was Wash Delong—and another man were under it with him. The other man, a sun-browned, Mormon- whiskered fellow with big, knuckly hands, said, "We got more rain right then and evening b'fore last than the whole damn last fourteen months put together."

The wagons began to rumble off to dump their loads. The teams' hoofs splashed through puddles. Wheels rinsed with a hiss. It was getting on towards the tag end of the day. The men quit their work. Some went to their tents or what- ever all it was they'd rigged up to sleep their families in, others mounted their horses and rode out of town. A few men kept on working on the courthouse lawn, unbolting the timbers of the fallen windmill. But daylight was frittering down to a shirttail of orange and then lavender to the west. Some black scatterings of birds flew across.

Clabe and the whiskered fellow and Wash Delong talked for a spell. *Alto Springs, Balcones County, the county seat, what's left of it. No rain here for fourteen months. Clouded up and begun not raining. Foxes and skunks went mad. Hydrophobic stal- lion in a lot, screamin' in its madness—chased a steer all over the lot and when he caught up to it bit chunks out of its side.* "That twister like to wiped us off the map."

Then the man with the chin whiskers said his good night, *buenas noches.* "I'd put you up, but I got a woman and eight tykes and we're all sleepin' under a plank," he said.

"That's all right. Thanks anyways," Claiborne said.

Wash Delong said to Clabe, "Where do you aim to spend the night?"

"I reckon in the brush."

"No need to do that. You can put up at my place. Plenty of room to lay down a pallet. Corn for your horse, too."

"I've run out of somethin' to use for money."

"Right now money don't count for much here. We'll feed your horse and cook up some grub."

"I don't want to put you out," Claiborne said.

"I got to cook it for myself. It's no chore to 'cut fodder' for one more."

Clabe looked at him. "Well, all right," he said. "I *am* damn hungry."

"Lead your horse," Wash said.

Clabe followed Wash and led the mare. They walked on around the square. Wash pointed to a bare plank floor. "What's left of Lacey's Saloon," he said. The dirt street was still wet, splotched with puddles. A cool evening breeze came up. "We get that breeze every night," Wash said. "It's a comfort."

Various cooking fires were around about. The canvas tents were chines of white from the candles and lamps inside, like light through new beeswax. Tucked the shirttail under the west—the night sky was pinpricked with stars. Wash and Clabe stopped in front of a tent.

"Stake your horse out over there," Wash said. He went on inside and lit a candle. Clabe unlaced his tree and dropped the gear to the ground. He staked the mare out. Wash came out of the tent and shook some ears of corn onto a towsack he spread on the ground in front of the mare. He walked over to a campfire. "Rest your hat and coat," he said, pointing to a place on the ground near the campfire. He raked aside a heap of coals with a stick and lifted a spider out of the ashes. "As it happens, it's already cooked. I put this in this morning. Here's a couple plates," he said. With his hat he brushed the ashes from the spider lid. He lifted the lid off with the stick. Steam billowed up. Wash dished the contents onto the plates and he and Clabe sat together and ate. It was some of the best beef stew Clabe had ever greased his chin with.

Wash had come out here from Krugerville a year and a half ago, "when the ground was wet and the boys were drinking whiskey." Hadn't been headed for any place in particular and what notion had taken him to put down here he'd never known. "This country promises more and gives less than any place I've ever seen," he said. Set up a faro table in Lacey's Saloon. "Do you go for the spotted cards?" he said.

"Not in particular," Clabe said.

Then came the drouth. Dust where grass ought to be. "And we're in a pickle if they don't get that windmill fixed. Water's so scarce the Baptists have taken to sprinkling. What brings *you* out here?" Wash said.

"I don't know. I reckon like you I'm just *here*. I ain't got no more idea where I'm goin' than the man in the moon."

After they'd eaten, Wash and Clabe went into the tent. Clabe fetched in his gear. It was a big wall tent and had a wooden floor. Clabe stomped the floor. "How'd you latch onto this?" he said.

"Door from Valdez' and Nance's blacksmith shop."

A cot was along a wall, with a rumpled comfort on it. There were boxes filled with canned goods and plates and skillets and such. A ham hung from the ridgepole.

Claiborne said, "I call this livin' off the top of the pot."

"Well, I'll tell you," Wash said, "right after the twister I done a little quick thinking and rounded up a few things before anyone else did."

He pulled a bottle of whiskey out from under the cot. "How about a shot of forty rod?" Wash set two cups on a crate and poured three fingers' worth of whiskey into each. It was smooth whiskey. It went down Clabe's gullet and spread like a fever through his chest.

"This beats a hen a-scratchin'," Claiborne said.

Wash sniggered. "Don't it though?"

They had several. In a while Wash was half drunk. "Yessir, if I could just get up the cash I'd set up in Schramkrug's in Austin," he said. "Or in the Bluebonnet Hotel." Clabe spread a blanket down on the plank floor, with his saddle for a pillow. "Keno, faro and a monte bank," Wash said, "the whole line. It is terrible to be a failure. They stripped me like a fruit tree in Krugerville. And I ain't never broke more than even here." Clabe helped him lie out on his cot. "You're a prince," Wash said. He hiccuped. Clabe blew out the candle and lay down on his blanket.

Night breeze. The tent seemed to breathe. Of a sudden Wash sat bolt upright. "Sometimes I walk in my sleep." He sat there in the dark a minute like he was thinking on it. Then he flopped back down. In a few minutes they were both asleep.

The white dress . . .

Claiborne woke. Something was moving in the dark. The breeze had stopped and the tent was still. Over at the front of the tent a dark figure slowly lifted an arm and made noises with its thumb and fingers like it was sprinkling salt or seeds. "Wash," Clabe said. "Wash!" he said. The figure took two or three steps toward the left side of the tent, still sprinkling the seeds. Clabe got up onto his feet. He landed a hard left on Wash's jaw and Wash went down without a sound. Clabe carried him to his cot and laid him down and straightened him out comfortable and tucked the comfort up under his chin. Then he crawled back between his own covers and shifted around to get settled. He had a good night's sleep.

The next morning Wash sat on the edge of the cot, holding the left side of his face. "Christ, what happened last night? I feel like I've been hit up the side of my head with a plank."

"I'm feelin' a little bone sore my ownself," Claiborne said.

After Wash had cooked breakfast—fried ham and Borden's Biscuit and coffee—he and Clabe went over to the square, Clabe on his horse and Wash walking alongside.

White sunlight flooded down. The morning air tasted moun-
tain-fresh and cool.

It looked like the windmill workers had been working all
night. The wooden tower was up, but the vanes and rotor
hadn't been mounted yet. Clabe tied to a picket fence, a short
section left standing by the twister. Several other horses were
alongside. **B** neck brand on the roan next to him. *Balcones*
County? Some had Mexican saddles—flat, dinner-plate horns,
sloping cantles, *tapaderos*. One had conchoed skirts.

"Where do them rigs come from?" Clabe said.

"They make 'em here. That is, till the day b'fore yesterday."

The man with the brown mustache of the day before
came riding up on a buckskin horse. "You two lookin' for
work?" he said. "They need help out to the schoolhouse."

"Suits me," Claiborne said.

Wash cracked his knuckles. He said, "I sure would like
to oblige you, O. W., but I've plenty cut out for me right
here."

The man said, "Pickin' up the spotted cards, I reckon."

Clabe unhitched the mare and lit on up. He said to
Wash, "Ma, hold supper for me. I may not get back from the
dance till late."

Wash grinned. "Don't wear out your shoe soles, son," he
said. He turned and walked toward the courthouse. Clabe
rode alongside the man on the buckskin, whose name, it
turned out, was Moore. They rode toward the south side of
town. "That Wash Delong does nothin' in particular and does
it mighty well," Moore said.

The schoolhouse was a large, rock building at the edge of
town. The tin roof had been lifted off. Desks and bluebacks
and papers were scattered for miles toward the southeast. The
schoolbell had ended up in a live oak somewhere.

Clabe worked all morning helping clean out the schoolhouse and the schoolyard around about. Folks told him how
much they "'preciated his help." *Shit.* But he kept himself at

it, sweat dripping from his eyebrows and chin. In the afternoon a light carry-all wagon went by with two bodies on it
wrapped in muslin, their feet sticking out off the endgate,
headed for the little brush-rimmed cemetery nearby. Some
men and women in buggies and hacks followed after. Not a
lick of breeze. Bugs scraped, cricked, shrilled, buzzed and
ticked in the brush. It made all one noise, like water. And the
gently rolling, brush-covered plateau spread out from the
town in all directions like an ocean sea.

Late in the evening Clabe rode back into town. Wash
was sitting on the steps in front of the racket store. Clabe rode
over to him. A Haynes buggy with a pair of fine, matched
bays was drawn up in front of the store. Up on the roof men
were tacking on new tin roofing. It hurt the eyes to look at it.

"Christ," Wash said, "they had me working all day!"

"What you been doin'," Clabe said, "sortin' out clothes
buttons?" He grinned. He put his left leg across the saddle
dish and leaned forward onto the nubbin to make himself
comfortable.

"—looking much better now. But I'll fetch some more
tarps and blankets into town," a voice said inside the store. A
young woman dressed in black stepped out onto the gallery.
She wore a small, black, piled-up hat with a veil thrown back.
Clabe's horse startled at his shift.

"¡Vamonos!" the woman said, half under her breath. She
hurried across the gallery as if she were angry. A little old
Mexican woman in a dark brown dress with white collar and
cuffs hobbled after her. At the top of the steps the girl stopped
and looked at Clabe. She brushed back a piece of veil from
her face.

Black hair, rounded chin. She was a smaller woman than
she'd looked to be in the, looked to be in the. *That dark window in the air.*

Claiborne grabbed hold of the saddle nubbin. A stone-
cold chill went through him. There was something fierce in
the girl's eyes, a caged-in anger and hurt. It was like if she'd

had a knife in her fist she'd have jumped Clabe then and there. And yet she wasn't really looking at Claiborne at all. It was something she saw beyond him that was making her eyes burn through him like that.

The veil slipped from the rim of her hat and with a flip of her wrist she brushed it back again. She went on down the steps. "¡Ándale, Tía!" she said.

She climbed into the buggy and reached out to pull the old woman up beside her.

Flicked the reins at the horses' rumps. The buggy bounced toward a corner of the square and disappeared behind the courthouse.

"Who was that?" Clabe said. His blood was frozen in his guts.

Wash said, "Soledad."

That night, sitting by a fire in front of the tent, Claiborne said, "Who was that—what'd you call her? Soledad? That we saw today."

Wash said, "Ain't she a pert little bundle?"

"Shit on you. What's her name?"

"Now what're you mad at?"

"What's her name?"

"Soledad. She's the niece or granddaughter or some such of don Reyes. From out to the Tres Coronas."

"Don Reyes? That's a Meskin?"

"I don't know what else you'd call him. He's a big man hereabouts. There wouldn't be no Alto Springs without him. He squared off one of his sections, sunk that deep well here, even built the courthouse. Then he offered the whole she-bang for a county seat."

"I don't know as I've seen him about."

"You're not likely to."

"How come that?"

"Oh, the town passed a resolution back in February call-ing on the state legislature to provide a relief appropriation.

On account of the drouth. He rode up into Crockett and Tom Green counties to get backing for it. Then come that blue norther. He just disappeared."

The black sombrero flapped. The hawk flapped in Clabe's head.

He said, "What's she got to do with him?"

"I told you. She's his kin."

"She ain't Meskin."

"*Part* Mexican."

Clabe felt a headache coming on. After a while he said, "What's he look like?"

"Who? Reyes?"

"Yes, goddammit."

"Tall, dark-complected. Had a big white handlebar mustache. I only saw him twice. Folks here thought he hung the moon and the stars."

"She ain't got nothin' to do with him."

"She's his *kin*. She's been runnin' that ranch out there ever since he left."

Clabe jumped to his feet. "*She ain't got nothin' to do with him!*"

"What the hell's got into you, Red?" Wash said. "They must of had you out there workin' in the sun with your hat off."

Clabe laughed. "Let's have a swig of that rotgut," he said.

Later the front of his head hurt so bad he could hardly sleep.

Rocks moved. The top of the pile lifted, a head pushed up through it. Black, laughing eyes, white mustache above dirt-brown lips. The rocks scattered as the body lifted, wet and slick as a newborn babe or a skinned rabbit or a pulled stalk of rain lily . . .

Clabe saw the one called Soledad off and on around the square, in the buggy with matched bays. Sometimes she'd stop to talk to folks. She'd lean out of the buggy, nodding or shaking her head. The little old Mexican woman was always with her.

"Who's that?" Clabe would say, jerking his head toward the girl in the black dress.

Some said Reyes. Some said Kincaid. *Soledad.*

One evening, down on the courthouse lawn, the rotor of the windmill was oiled and the tower heisted up like a sweep. The vanes turned in the wind.

"Looky that," the man standing next to Claiborne said. "Ain't that thing a wonder?"

"I seen a few up in San Sebastian County," Clabe said.

"That contraption was put up eight-ten years ago. There weren't nothin' like it then."

"Mebbe."

"He fetched a feller down here clean from Chicago to get that built. An uppity-lookin' feller full of crazy notions about windmills. But they worked."

"Who did?"

"Don Reyes. El Señor."

"Sounds bass-ackwards to me, to put a town where it ain't no water."

"They had to sink that well two hundred eighty feet."

"To hell with it. I don't want to talk about it," Claiborne said.

One morning the girl named Soledad drove by the courthouse in her buggy.

"What's she *do* in town here?" Claiborne said.

"B'fore the twister we hardly ever seen her," somebody said. "She's set up a camp about two miles out to take care of hurt folks. Feedin' a few families. Too damn uppity to suit me. We don't need charity. Christ. Some folks seems to like her. *I* ain't one. Her grandpa was all right, for all he was a Meskin. But there's somethin' off-horse about *her.*"

"How come she always wears black?"

She'd been wearing it for months now. "Some say it's on account of a brother or cousin or something that died of the cholera in San Antonio. Some say it's on account of don Reyes."

The Sunday following, after a brief, late-morning rain, Clabe rode out to the camp. He hadn't seen the girl in town for four or five days. The camp was on a flat, under some live oak trees—a brush arbor, two big, high-peaked tents that looked like pecan camp tents, their sides tied up to let in whatever breeze, and a cook wagon with a tarp stretched out from its sides. Smoke rose from some cookfires near the wagon.

Clabe rode up to the tents. Children were playing under the live oaks. They ran over to Clabe. They were clean, though barefoot and dressed in ragtags. They stared at him out of small, open faces. Two women came out of one of the tents, one of them with a baby in her arms. "Howdy, ma'am. Howdy, ma'am," Claiborne said. They shaded their eyes and nodded.

Clabe didn't see the buggy or the matched bays anywhere about. He rode over to the cook wagon, where a white man in a long apron was up to his elbows in a sack of flour. The man looked up at Clabe. He was as big a man as Clabe had ever seen and looked like he ought to be a prizefighter. He had a heavy-boned face and a neck like an ox. His forearms were sticky with flour paste. "I know you," the man said. "You're the stranger here in town. Light down and rest your bones."

"It looks like you're mighty busy," Claiborne said.

They talked for a spell. It turned out that Miss Kincaid had gone out to the ranch three days back.

"Do they got any kind of work out there?" Clabe said.

"Not as I know of," the cook said.

After a while Clabe said, "I reckon I better be moseyin' on along."

"No need to rush off."

"No, but I got things needs tendin' to."

"Adios," the cook said.

Clabe rode back by the tents. "Hello, mister," a voice called from the dark of one of the tents. A white, skin-and-bone arm reached out toward him. Clabe checked his horse. "I ain't gonna bite you," the voice cackled. Clabe rode up between the tent ropes. He could make out an old woman lying on a cot at the edge of the tent, her face sunk into a bolster, in a nest of white hair. The face was whiter than the hair or the bolster. The parchment skin and delicate bone seemed to shine in the dark of the tent. She was dressed in some sort of blue, flimsy stuff. One hand lay on her belly. The other, liver-splotched and clawlike, had a hold like a bird foot to one of the tent ropes. The loose-skinned underside of her arm was as white as a fish's belly.

She said, "Oh you look good up there. I wisht I was up and about."

Clabe said, "How are you?" She minded him of Leona.

"Poor. Poor. I can't move. And my back and the backs of my legs is so sore. You see, I've broke my hip."

"That's no good. I'm sorry to hear that."

"I'm so sweaty and my head's so sweaty on this bolster."

"It ain't so cool out here."

"No, but you're up and about. I feel like if I could just set up I'd be some better."

"Did you tangle with that twister?"

"It never come near me. I heared it pass by toward the south and went out and stepped on one of my chickens and fell back. I don't think I know you," she said.

"No'm. I just come here."

She stared at him a moment. She said, "You see that dead branch yonder?" She pointed to a tree behind Clabe.

"Can you break that cussed thing off?" It was a lower branch
with a hunk of ball moss on it.

"I reckon I can."

"It's drivin' me loco. I keep seein' a face in it, the way it
crosses that other branch. That moss is the chin."

Clabe backed the mare up to it. The branch came off
with a snap. White ants dropped out of the punky center.
Clabe tossed it to the ground.

"That's a blessin'," the woman said.

"You get well now," Claiborne said. "Adios."

"Good-bye. I do wish I was up and about."

In town Clabe got his gear together. It was hot in the
tent. Sunlight glared through the white, cotton weave. Clabe
put what he owned into his bedroll. It didn't amount to
much—that Sharps rifle, his jacket, a box of cartridges and
the coffeepot. He felt in the jacket pocket for the photograph.
It wasn't there. He felt in the other pocket. He looked around
on the floor. He felt along the edge between the tent footing
and the blacksmith door. *Where in hell did I put that thing?*

Well, she's here. I done found her. I don't need it no more.

He spooled the bedroll and went out and tied it on behind the cantle. He tied the rifle where it would ride up under
his knee. Then he lit up and headed out to the Tres Coronas.

A pair of hawks pinned their rings up under the sun. The
land rose and fell. Clabe followed a wagon track in a northerly
direction. The mesquites were all leaved-out. The squatty live
oaks held out dark, waxy green leaves that threw back the
light like mirrors. The sun pressed down its naked hand onto
the Divide.

Here came a rider toward Clabe along the track, a long
way off. The figure topped a rise then fell down out of sight
then topped another rise. Horse and rider got bigger as they
came closer. They shimmered in the heat.

Black coat and britches, black hat, white shirt. It was Wash Delong. He trotted up on a fat bay.

"Howdy," Claiborne said. "What're you doin' out here?"

"Out riding. I got tired of being cooped up in town. Besides, they were about to put me to work again."

"Whose horse is that?"

"Jim Tate's. He gave me the loan of it. Where're you headed?"

"Out to the Tres Coronas."

"Whatall for?" Wash Delong said.

"Lookin' for work."

Wash gave a queer laugh.

Clabe said, "I ain't got a single greenback in my pocket."

Wash took off his hat and wiped his face with a kerchief. He said, "Lord, it's hot. Reckon you'll be coming back?"

"Not as I know of."

Wash shook his head. "You sure are a queer one, Clabe."

"How so?"

"I don't know. Maybe it's on account of the red hair."

"I can't help that. I'll tell you, though. I was born half wild and when I went to walkin' the other half went wild."

Wash laughed. "As like as not."

A fly was on the back of Clabe's hand. He brushed it off. The horses switched their tails.

"What the devil do you want to go out *there* for, Red?"

"Work."

Wash looked at him a minute. "Well," he said, "*buena suerte*." He jabbed his heel at his horse's belly.

"What's that mean?" Clabe said.

"Good luck," Wash said.

Clabe said, "I don't hold by luck." Of a sudden he didn't like Wash any more.

"Adios," he said. He put spurs to the mare.

"Adios."

TWO

11

THE sunlight made a white square on the floor. It flared along the edges of the window frame and burnt on the sill. The air was motionless in the room. It had an immense silence to it.

Speckles of sweat were on Soledad's forehead, a dampness beneath her collar. Her breasts felt oppressed in their binding cloth. Her bed was too big for the room—the hand-worked *sobrecama*, the six pyramided, lace-trimmed pillows—and it seemed to push her toward the window. Her hand was on a brass knob. Her other hand stuck out in front of her in its black sleeve, pale and clawlike as it held the cabinet picture, the stiff pasteboard with its queer, blackened sprinkles in one corner—*What are those spots? They weren't there three months ago when Grandpapa had taken this photograph with him to Santa Angela*—the thumb-smudged hem of her white dress.

That morning Soledad had got up in darkness and put on the black dress that Tía Lupita had laid out for her the night before. "O *corazón, mi vida*," Guadalupe had said, "why must you always wear this? Your brother has been dead five months now and all the mirrors are *still* to the wall." *I shall wear black until Granpapá comes back.*

"You're too young to wear black," Lupita had said. *Lupita may stop wearing black, but I shan't.*

Lupita had knocked on the door and come in with a candle and done up her hair. It was beginning to gray outside when she and Soledad had gone downstairs to the small dining room where Angelina had put a plate of *pan dulce* and two blue-figured cups on the table. Angelina came in with a pot of coffee and a pot of hot milk. "*Buenos días, Cholita. Buenos días, Lupita,*" she said. She poured milk and coffee into Soledad's cup.

"*Buenos días, Angelita.*"

"I think it will rain again today."

"It won't do us any good," Tía Lupita said. "Yesterday a hen crowed, and I do not think that is a good omen." Soledad ate a roll and drank the milk and coffee. Tía Lupita drank sugared black coffee. Then Moro was led up to the front of the house and Tía Lupita went to her sewing. "Bring me back some leaves of *albácar,*" she said.

Soledad mounted Moro and rode around the drive past the garden with bean and tomato plants poking up and past the row of bee gums and the orchard and out through the north gate. The morning air was moist and fresh, the only time of day when things were cool. Soledad rode sidesaddle, her knee up around the double horn, her long riding skirt reaching down to Moro's knees.

Moro was feeling frisky. He trotted on the hard, stony ground. The sun was up but the sky was overcast, a *cielo* of sheeted gray, the light soft and diffused. After so many blare, white mornings, three rains in five days! Soledad crossed Contrary Creek. She rode up the slope and over an open flat toward a stand of live oaks at the foot of a low hill. Two men were sitting under a live oak by a fire on which a pot of beans and a pot of coffee were boiling. Some sheep were in a pen at the foot of the hill.

"*Buenos días, Patrona. Buenos días,*" the two men said as Soledad rode up. They got up onto their feet.

"*Buenos días, Santos. Buenos días, Brígido,*" Soledad said. "*¿Cómo están?*"

"*Bien, gracias.*"

"Are the sheep ready?"

"*Sí, Patroncita,* come and see."

Brígido helped her down from Moro. Soledad took off
her riding skirt and flung it over the saddle. She walked to the
fire. "Finish your breakfast," she said. The two men sat and
ate their beans and drank their coffee and told her all the
news. A letter from Mexico: it is thought Tomás will take a
new wife. We saw Raúl yesterday and he says they have found
the good bull. In the Cañon de los Lobos.

Soledad was impatient to get to work. The three of them
walked up to the pens.

About two hundred ewes, recently weaned of their
lambs and with a twelve-month fleece, were in the largest
pen. Because of the drouth the lambs hadn't come as growthy
as Soledad wished, though she had ordered oak brush to be
cut and prickly pear leaves singed to feed the ewes. But the
dry winter *had* made a good fleece—all in all Grandpapa
would have been pleased.

Santos opened the gate for her and they walked across
the pounded dirt of one of the empty pens. "Give me your
stick," she said to Brígido. He handed her his shepherd's
crook. She walked over to the head of the chute.

The two men went through a gate into the larger pen.
Santos drove the sheep into the chute and Brígido stood
thigh-deep among the creamy yellow backs, bending down to
them, checking the length and fineness of their fleece. "*Esta,
sí*" or "*Esta, no,*" he would say, and a ewe would come scut-
tling down the narrow chute, wide-eyed and bleating, toward
Soledad. "*Now that,*" her grandfather said, reaching into the
chute and grabbing a hank of wiry fleece, "*won't ever do. Too
much yolk, Cholita*" or "*Too much wool blindness,*" and Soledad
prodded the ewe into the small pen if it was a cull or pushed
open the gate on the opposite side of the chute if it was a good
ewe. She meant to shear in three or four days, provided it
stayed hot.

The air suddenly brightened, whitened the backs of the
sheep, made the silvery weather-beaten cedar fence glow.
Soledad looked up and saw a pale, white sun, but a film of

cloud was pulled back over and the light flattened out again.

Soledad had stayed at the chute most of the morning. Then, when she was satisfied that Brígido was selecting properly, she mounted Moro and rode back toward the house. At Contrary Creek she stopped to pick some herbs for Tía Lupita—green stems and leaves with small white flowers. She rode through scrub brush and cedar to the house. It looked as if it might rain again, in fact. The bees as she rode past them seemed to be staying close to the hives.

In the house she had hung her riding skirt on a hook in the hallway and put her hat on the calling-card table. She went into the parlor, where Tía Lupita, wearing sewing glasses, was sitting on the *sofacita* embroidering scallops and eyelets on a chemise yoke. Lupita was as small as a bird, smaller than Soledad herself even. Her knotty fingers had the queerest way of holding a needle, but she could still sew. In the mornings, she loved to put her hands around a cup of hot coffee, her fingers hurt so, or to lay them in sunlight on her lap, but she insisted on doing all the things she had ever done, though Soledad had told her so often, *Dear Pita, mi vida, you mustn't push yourself so.* Lupita was old but that didn't keep her from looking after her *niña*, her "child." Now she stared up at Soledad with that surprised look on her face she always had when something was advancing toward her, whether it was a person or a cup of *atole*.

Soledad kissed Lupita on her cheek. "*¿Traeme algunas yerbas, hijita?*" Lupita said. Her head shook a little as she spoke.

"Here they are—*aquí están*," Soledad said. She put the kerchief with the herbs in it on the sofa beside Tía Lupita.

"*Gracias,* Cholita," Lupita said, peering up at Soledad through her glasses. She got up and walked over to a window and spread out the green leaves and stems on the sill to dry. Soledad sat to a small table where her grandfather's account books, flock and herd records and correspondence were spread out.

She pushed back some account books and tally sheets and flattened out a piece of paper on the cleared space. "Dear Miss Lita," it said. "We were so surprised and grieved to hear that your grandfather . . ." Anger flushed through Soledad's chest. She crumpled the letter and flung it to the floor. She spread out another letter, from California. "Dear Miss Kincaid . . . your letter of the fourteenth . . . a good angora buck . . . good stock out of Mr. Davis's buck . . . will ship by way of . . . your remittance of $20.00 per doe and $300.00 for the one buck . . . freight rates to . . . a good South African buck . . ." Soledad spread out a fresh sheet and dipped her pen in the ink. *Twenty-third of May, Tres Coronas.* Her handwriting looked almost like her grandfather's. "Dear Mr. Landrum," she wrote, "I have your letter of the twenty-sixth, and the description is agreeable. I think you must ship them to San Antonio by way of Fort Worth—it seems the better route—and then out to Ugalde. They can be driven up from there. You had better send a man with them and I will pay his transport. However, you must forgive me, but I will pay upon receipt of the stock in good condition. I could not have it otherwise, as you will understand. This must be a sound buck goat, good chest and girth, of good size, bright flat-lock fleece as described in your previous letter, shearing close on sixty pounds the year, the does all as good. I shall expect . . ."

"*¡Patrona!*" Ramón called from the front steps. In a moment Angelina came in.

"*Perdóneme, Patroncita,*" Angelina said, "a man is here."

Soledad said, "Do you know who it is?"

"I don't remember his name."

Soledad put down her pen and stood up from the accounts and papers.

"What is it, Cholita?" Tía Lupita said.

"Someone has ridden up."

Angelina went back to her kitchen. Lupita put aside her sewing and her glasses and followed Soledad into the hallway.

Probably somebody from town. Soledad walked through

the hallway and the front room and out onto the gallery. *It's that slack-off Wash Delong, sitting Mr. Tate's bay horse.* Lupita walked to the end of the gallery and sat in her willow chair.

"Mornin', Ma'm," Wash Delong said. "I hope I'm not intruding on . . ."

"What do you want?"

"Mind if I light down?"

He lit down from the bay, tied the reins to a post and came to the steps. He had a dangling way of walking, as if he were hung from a clothes hanger. He took off his hat as he came up the steps.

A few drops of rain spotted the steps. "Now ain't that the darndest thing," he said. "It looks like the weather has turned over for sure."

"I'd say it's about time."

"I believe that twister must have knocked it loose, don't you think?" He talked like an old woman visiting. Soledad pressed the palms of her hands against the front of her dress.

There were several chairs at the top of the steps. "Mind if I sit?" Wash said.

"You might as well," Soledad said.

Wash laughed. He sat on one of the chairs, with, of all things, his hat wedged between his knees.

After a moment Soledad sat. "And so how are things in town?" she said.

"As good as can be expected under the circumstances. It looks poor." Wash stared at her, pinched his hat brim between his spinet-player fingers.

"Well," Soledad said finally. "I don't suppose you came out here just to chat."

Wash cracked his knuckles. "Well, no," he said, "I fetched you this." He reached inside his coat and felt around. He reached into the other side. He poked around on the left side again, lifted the lapel and stuck his nose in like a turkey buzzard tucking its head under its wing.

He fished out a pasteboard-backed cabinet picture and handed it to her.

Cold rushed to the back of Soledad's head. She managed to get back her breath. She turned the photograph over and laid it on her lap. She cleared her throat. "Angelita," she called into the house, "bring Señor Delong a cup of coffee."

It didn't sound like her own voice. She turned to Wash and said in English, "Would you like a cup of coffee?"

"Don't mind if I do," he said.

Her fingers traced the edge of the photograph. "*It is a fine retrato,*" *her grandfather said,* "*and I will put it here beside María.*" *Her grandfather had put the photograph on the bureau beside that of her grandmother upon which, written in the lower left-hand corner,* "María, su digna esposa," *pulsed and flowed like a thin, blood line.* And sometimes her grandpapa would say before one of his trips (had said before going to Santa Angela), "*I'm taking you and María with me,*" stashing the two photographs inside his riding jacket.

A few heavier drops spattered the steps.

And where is the photograph of my abuelita?

Angelita fetched a cup of coffee in one of the blue-figured cups. Wash took a folded kerchief from his coat pocket and put it on his thigh and set the cup of coffee on that, pinching the handle between a thumb and finger. Of a sudden a conflux of rain beat down as if somebody had knocked the bottom out of a bucket. The raindrops smashed onto the steps, disintegrated into fierce circlets of wet drops, smacked with a leaden, birdshot sound onto the ground, making a carpet of dust-brown mist an inch or so high above the riddled surface. For one brief moment there was some hail mixed with the rain.

"Will you look at that!" Wash Delong said.

The photograph lay on Soledad's lap.

SAN ANTONIO

—Her sixteenth birthday. The buggy rolled through sunlight, clattered across the newly-laid street crossings. Up in the studio, sunlight flooded down through a skylight overhead. Had a feeling of wanting to stick out her tongue at the ridiculous, accordion-nosed camera. What is it Papa's saying? But must be serious. Her father and her brother Edward stood at the back of the studio . . .

Abruptly the rain quit. "If that ain't the darndest . . ." Wash said. He supped his coffee, wiped a trickle from the edge of the cup with his thumb. "Didn't that twister come through town like a train through a stack of chicken coops?" He sucked air in across his teeth.

Soledad said, "I hope we never see the likes of it again." She said, "I suppose you found this in the street."

She touched the photograph that lay on her lap.

Wash cleared his throat. "Well, no, not exactly."

Soledad's fingers traced the edge of the photograph.

"That there's—ah—off an acquaintance of mine," Wash said. "New here, the twister sort of blew him in. I don't know *what* his name is. He's got red hair."

"I believe I've seen him. Rides a tick-spotted brown mare say ten, twelve years old?"

Wash nodded.

Soledad said, "I believe the sun's coming out." Bright drops dripped from the edge of the gallery roof. Wetnesses sparkled in the sycamore in front of the house. Soledad and Wash sat a moment in silence. It seemed to Soledad as if the wet sycamore and the rain-darkened drive and the hunched, glistening orchard trees beyond it were in another country. There was a kind of hum of distance upon it. Wash set his cup on the floor beside his chair. "I'd better git," he said. He wrapped his left hand around the fingers of his right and cracked his knuckles. He stood up.

Soledad said, "It was good of you to come out."

Wash said, "Oh, I had a notion that . . ."

"So considerate."

"Well, yes'm," Wash said. He backed and shuffled down the steps.

Soledad said, "Thank you so much."

Wash stood at the bottom of the steps, his limp brown hat pressed against his chest. Then he chunked the hat onto his head. "I must say your persimmons and plums look thrifty," he said.

"Yes. We have water here."

"Well, *adiós*," Wash said. "*Adiós, señora*," he called to Tía Lupita.

"*Adiós*," Lupita said.

Wash Delong turned abruptly and walked to his horse. He put his foot into the stirrup and swung on up, shifted and jerked his coattails out from under. "*Hasta luego*," he said.

He rode out through the gate.

The sycamore went up, flaked and spotted, into the mass and separation of its leaves—wet leaves that loosed their drops to feed the root. Its silence and selfhood were terrible. Light crowded down around it as though to confirm its solitude, welled down onto the ranked orchard trees, every single one. Soledad stood more certainly than ever in her own separation. She felt lightheaded.

"Lupita," she said, "I am going to my room."

Inside the house Soledad climbed the stairs to the second floor. On the landing she felt as if every hand that had built this house was pressing against the back of her head. She walked up the hall past the three closed bedrooms to her room.

She sat on the bed. She kept rubbing the edge of the photo with her finger. She started to rock back and forth on the bed.

Tía Lupita knocked softly on the door. "Cholita, are you all right?"

"Yes, *corazón*, go back downstairs. I'll be down in a moment."

Lupita's footsteps diminished down the hallway. *What are these black spots? Who put this thumb spot here?*

The white dress. A rush of bitterness came over her. *Grandpapa is not ever going to come back.*

No! He is! I know it!

Soledad got up abruptly. She left the cabinet picture on the bed and walked across the hall to her grandfather's study.

The room was kept closed, the windows shuttered. Bars of light lay on the floor. It was an intrusion when Soledad's dress rustled. She sat on the settee upholstered in bluish-black horsehair, and the hair stuffing crackled. Grandpapa's writing desk, brass oil lamp with the milk-glass shade, walnut chairs, the settee—*meubles* from the house in San Antonio. Abuelita María's and Tía Lupita's laces and tattings lay on the seats of the chairs and on the back and arms of the settee. At the windows the lace curtains caught the silence in their heavy folds. Grandpapa's bass viol leaned in a corner in its closed, locked case. His books, with stamped, leather bindings, were on their shelves. Some were in Spanish or English, some in Latin and Greek. A plaster Madonna in a blue mantilla, to the left above the bookcase, inclined her forehead outward from the wall, as if leaning against the silence.

The faint sounds of Angelita working in the kitchen came up through the parlor floor. *No, Grandpapa isn't dead. He'll come back. He isn't dead. Not until I know it.*

"*You fuss too much, Cholita,*" her grandfather said. He wore his black vest and, of course, one of his bleached, starched shirts, like the one he'd worn three months ago when he'd gone to Santa Angela. His face commenced to disintegrate in front of her. The skin was drying on the bones. He walked over to a window and said, "*I think it is going to snow.*"

Yes, I am that cold.

O Granpapá, come back to me! I want the door to open as if he'd just come home. I want him to walk into this room!

Edward, too, the wax face on the bolster!
Open the windows and let the spring air in!
Sunlight, the day two years ago her grandfather had met
her in Alto Springs. She had said goodbye to her father and
her brothers Edward and Ian, come a long dusty journey,
come up through the canyon from Ugalde, sitting on her
trunk in the bed of the wagon. In town folks watched her
from the shade of Van Zandt's storefront. The men tipped
their hats. *But I don't trust them. I didn't even trust them then.
Grandpapa's a* Mexican—*"Meskin" to them.* Her grandfather
put her trunk in the buggy. He spoke to her in Spanish and
was pleased when she answered in it. He wore a black arm-
band. "These are my neighbors," he said to Soledad. He in-
troduced her to them. "My granddaughter Soledad." Men in
shirt sleeves and vests. Mr. Van Zandt wiping his hands on his
canvas apron. Six or seven women in their summer dresses,
some with parasols. Mrs. Haby wore a slat bonnet. "My, you
must be tired, dear." "So good of you to come." *Do you think I
believe that? I'm part "Meskin" myself.* Some groceries were in a
box at their feet in the buggy. She and Grandpapa rode past
the courthouse and saloon, past the corner house with the
white picket fence and out the north street onto the rolling,
grass-covered, mesquite- and cedar-splotched Divide. "Your
grandmother was very patient," Grandpapa said in Spanish.
"She hadn't either longing or grief, though she spoke often of
you. Lupita and Angelina and I tended her, she didn't have
any pain. She was sweet and gentle. She died very quietly in
the afternoon—'I am so happy, so happy,' she said." *¡Estoy
Feliz!*
They rode along the rocky, rutty track. It had been
nearly nine years since she had seen her grandpapa last, except for his one short visit to San Antonio three or four years
back. Soledad had been a child then. Now she was grown.
They should have been strangers but they weren't. Soledad
felt as if she were coming to her real home after the years of

waiting in San Antonio, after her grandfather and her *abuelita* María had moved away and her father had come back from the war and taken her and Ian and Edward back again.

Grandmother. María. Castrejon de Reyes. The huge, fine house in San Antonio, on the San Pedro stream, where when Soledad's mother had died and her father had gone to fight in the war, she and her two brothers had spent so many years. Her grandmother Reyes picking quinces in the orchard. She was a small, delicate woman, a little plump—a plumpness that fines down to delicate wrists. Abuelita María had been beautiful as a young girl, everyone said. Black hair, black eyes. Her long braids, as she reached her hands amongst the quince branches, were streaked now with white and wound like a crown around her head, on which she wore a small silk cap to prevent aire en la cabeza.

The buggy bumped along the rocky track. Soledad was struck more than ever by the sense of strength in her grandfather. He hardly seemed changed at all. The same long, dark, handsome face she remembered so well from her childhood, the same gentleness in his hands and his voice. Don Reyes. Alvaro Reyes Ibarra. He asked about the family and his son-in-law's business and Soledad's own doings in San Antonio. Though he could speak English, they talked in Spanish. It was Soledad's preference as well. Her grandfather talked quietly about Abuelita María and Tía Lupita and the ranch and the town. At the ranch house Tía Lupita wept and embraced Soledad, calling her "Cholita," her "nena," her "niña." Tía Lupita seemed not to have gotten older at all but simply smaller and brisker, a winter sparrow.

The riding jacket. Very tall on his horse Águila. Mr. Blackwell and Mr. Peterson were sitting their horses nearby, waiting to go to Santa Angela, up in Tom Green County. It was a warm February day, not at all a thought of the blizzard that would come six days later. The horse was nervous, shifting on its quarter-stockinged feet—such a powerful animal, black as mud, except for the blaze on his nose and the white, quarter-stockinged feet. By El Grillo out of Satterwhite's Valentina. Not like Moro. Moro is all black. Don

*Alvaro kissed Soledad goodbye. He took the napkin-wrapped din-
ner that she handed up to him. "We will be back in fifteen days," he
had said. Then he had ridden off with Mr. Peterson and Mr.
Blackwell.*

The bars of sunlight striped the study floor. The Madonna
listened in silence. Soledad's grandfather walked back and
forth, a ghost. He said, *"You mustn't sit here like this, you'll make
yourself ill."* He said, *"You've got a mind like a quail,* corazón, *apt
to break cover when the foot's close. You must keep a calm mind."*

But there had been other, happier days. *"This is what we
sheared today,"* her grandpapa would say, shuffling papers on
the dropleaf of the desk. *"I think they had better be moved up to
the north pasture."* Sometimes he spoke in English and sometimes in Spanish. Soledad had loved to work with him, to
check his account books and business papers, to work in the
orchard with him or ride beside him, he on Águila, herself
on Moro.

Suddenly Soledad became aware that her hands were
without feeling. In fact, there was no sense of touch or inter-
nal organs or heat or cold at all. She could not even feel the
settee she was sitting on. She rubbed the horsehair weave.
She had the sense of weight and motion in her arm, but
nothing happened in her fingertips.

She heard the faint, bustling noise of Angelina working
in the kitchen below. Don Alvaro said, *"I know you are afraid.
Do we know him? A red-haired man? A brown tick mare?"*

I have seen that face before. Somewhere! When I was
. . . moving past?

"You're too nervous, corazón. *He may have* found *the photograph somewhere. Wait! He'll be there. Two or three days, a week,
then we'll go into town. Time to think. Now you have work . . ."*

The bars of sunlight had grown straw-thin on the floor.
"Andrés will be working in the orchard," her grandfather said. *"It
is time to go down. Though I shall want to come back later and
tend to these papers."*

Soledad had closed her eyes and rested in the silence for

awhile. Then she had stood up and closed the study doors and gone down the stairs. She put on an old straw hat that was under the calling-card table in the hall and went out onto the gallery and down the steps. Most of the wetness had dried off. She walked across the drive and among the rows of slim, whitewashed trunks. Andrés was pruning dead branches from a plum tree.

Soledad said in Spanish, "How is the work, Andrés?"

"Very difficult, *Patrona*," he said. These were branches that ought to have been removed last fall, but her grandfather had sent Andrés out with the others to cut brush and burn prickly pear to winter-feed the stock. Now Andrés was cutting the dead branches out with his *podadora*. "These are very dry." He threw a branch onto the ground. Andrés was a short, plump, bald-headed man who—so Soledad had been told— even when he slept wore his soft, narrow-brimmed hat. He had been gardener to don Alvaro for twenty years, here and in San Antonio. Now what he wanted most of all was to go home to his ninety-year-old mother in Mexico. His face glistened with sweat. He wore a blue kerchief wrapped around his hand because the plum branches had sharp spurs on them. The tree was filled with hard green bead-sized plums.

Soledad had worked with Andrés for a while. Often she had the sense of her grandfather at her side, inspecting this or that tree, advising on a pruning. Often her hand moved as his did. The pruned branches littered the ground. A shallow, weed-filled irrigation ditch ran from tree to tree.

"Tonight we shall want to open the *puertas*," Soledad said.

"*Sí, Patroncita*. The trees want water."

Soledad had talked about the pruning. She spoke with Andrés about some new plantings. Then the bell had rung for dinner. At the table Lupita had said the *bendición* and rung the small silver bell. Lupita was tiny and wizened, dark as a parched coffee bean. Her head was frail, the bones thinned and sculpted by age. Upon her neck it nodded and shook like a dry weed. Angelina had come in and set a *sopa* on the table. But Soledad had hardly eaten.

After dinner she had gone back up to the bedroom, where the photograph lay on the bed.

What are these dark spots? Who put this thumb smudge here?
The air in the bedroom was hot and motionless. A fly flew in through a window and circled loudly. Outside, the sun beat down onto the brush and rocks like a white, muffled noise. The three hills to the west—the *tres coronas*—were bare, blank humps, denuded by light. A man was riding up the track. His horse made a little wake of dust. A brown or dark bay mare. *A brown tick mare.*

He rode past the house. He glanced up toward her window and she stepped back from it.

Soledad did not wait for Angelina to come up for her but went directly from her room and down the stairs. Angelina was at the foot of the stairs. She had just waked Lupita from her afternoon siesta.

"Why did you do that, Angelita?"

"I didn't know where you were."

Tía Lupita stood in the parlor doorway, staring into space and vaguely pushing some escaped hairs back from her face. "It makes me cross not to sleep," she said.

"*Corazón*, go finish your nap."

"I'm awake now."

Soledad walked through the front room and out onto the gallery. Lupita followed her. Soledad heard her gasp as the sunlight struck her eyes.

The man was sitting his horse under the sycamore tree. A bedroll was tied behind the cantle. "Evenin'," he said. He spoke in a soft, restrained voice. Lupita crossed to her chair.

Who is this man? What has he to do with my grandfather?
Soledad put a hand to her throat, pressed her fingers against her collar. She said, "Do you come from town?"

"Yes'm."

"Light on down," Soledad said.

The man swung down from the mare. The yoke of his jacket and the back of his britches were dark with sweat. His wet shirt stuck to his skin. He dropped the reins to the ground and let the mare nose around for a little grass. He was of ordinary height and build, and his bones—his wrist resting a moment on the saddlehorn—seemed in some way delicate. He said, "I seen when I crossed the river there's water."

"Yes, there are some springs up above."

He crossed to the steps but did not come up them. Soledad felt as if the heat or her dark, hot dress were smothering her.

"You've got a nice place here."

He pushed his hat back from his forehead. He looked about twenty-four or twenty-five years old. He had coppery red hair and orange eyebrows and eyelashes, and his face, slick with sweat, was covered with freckles so that it looked as if it was set behind a layer of rusty flakes. Suddenly he blushed— but she must have imagined that. His mouth was womanish, almost pretty, but the chin was strong and cleft. He wore a faded brown ducking jacket and worsted britches tucked into the tops of a pair of old mule-ear boots.

Soledad said, "Are you passing through?"

"Well, I don't know," he said. "I thought you might have work."

She looked at him. The heat and light between them were like a solid thing that seemed to connect them. She didn't like it at all. And yet there was something altogether innocent about him—whether it was in the whiteness behind his freckles or in the lightness of his frame and bones or in the green, unassuming eyes she couldn't make out.

She said, "I'm pretty much filled up now. My man Andrés wants to go back to Mexico. Do you know anything about keeping yard and tending fruit trees?"

"Tending *fruit trees*? You don't run stock?"

"Yes. But I have all the hands I need."

He looked mighty downcast. "Well, I don't know," he said. "I got a horse and rig." The shadow of a bird slid across the ground at his feet.

"I haven't anything else to offer."

He kicked at the dirt a little. He flipped a hand toward the orchard. "You mean that over there?"

"Keeping yard and tending fruit trees and keeping bees. Do you know anything about that sort of work?"

"A mite."

"Do you want it?"

"It'll hold me a spell."

"There's an empty cabin down by the water lot. You can sleep there. I'll send you some food and cooking things. Do you speak Spanish?"

"No."

"We all talk Spanish here."

"I'll make out."

Soledad felt lightheaded. She closed her eyes against the light. The stranger's blood-orange form floated in the blue dark surrounding it. She opened her eyes. He was looking up at her. A flushed, tingling feeling went through her. Her lungs seemed to collapse in her chest, as if some terrible longing had sucked the breath out of her.

I don't like you!

He said, "Can I have a drink of water?" The look he gave her ticked at the back of her head.

Soledad called into the house, "Angelina, *trae una taza de agua.*"

"*¿Qué?*" Lupita said. "*¿Qué?*" She sat upright.

"I think she's been to sleep," the man said, jerking his head toward Tía Lupita.

"What's your name?"

"Claiborne—Arnett."

"Where do you come from?"

"San Sebastian County."

Angelina came out of the house with a cup of water. She went down the steps and handed it to the stranger.

"Thanks," he said.

"¡María Santísima!" Lupita said, fanning her face and shaking the sleep from her head.

The man drank. A trickle of sweat ran down his throat and the wet skin there looked pale and vulnerable. He handed the cup back to Angelina.

Soledad said, "You go out that other gate and head north until you reach the bluff. The cabin's out there. It's just a short way."

"Do you have any feed for my horse?"

"There's some hay in one of the sheds."

"That'll do."

He walked back to his horse and took up the reins and mounted. It wasn't much of a horse. It looked as if it might have kept company once with a plow. Claiborne Arnett tipped his hat and nodded. He jabbed the mare's belly and trotted around the curve of the drive and out the north gate.

Tía Lupita lay back in her chair, flapping her large linen collar at her neck and chin. "¡Ay!" she said, "it is so hot!"

Soledad felt as weak as a newborn calf. She said, "I am going upstairs. But I will be down to finish my accounts later. Please open the window by my desk, dear."

She went into the house. Blood thudded in her ears. She went up the stairs and to her room.

The fly buzzed at the windowpane. It circled when she entered the room and bumped again against the pane.

White dress. The thumb-smudged photograph lay on the *sobrecama.* Soledad did not look at it. She picked it up and propped it on the chiffonier, with its face to the wall.

HE was weeding in the garden, she knew.

Earlier that morning, while it was still cool, three men—Mr. Peterson, Mr. Haines and Mr. Green—had ridden up to the ranch. They tied their horses in the shade of the sycamore in front of the house. "Come on business," they said. Soledad invited them into the parlor, where Lupita was sitting on the *sofacita* with her sewing. Lupita rose and carried her work-basket to the rocking chair by the window.

"Why don't you sit?" Soledad said. She was impatient for them to be gone but made a special effort to be polite. "What we want to do is get your help, Miss Kincaid," Mr. Peterson said. It was Mr. Peterson who, four months earlier, had fetched her grandfather's belongings to Soledad: the saddlebags, bill-fold, money and watch that her grandfather had left in his room in the hotel in Brady City where the delegation—Mr. Peterson and Mr. Blackwell and *Granpapá*—had stopped to spend the night on their way down from Santa Angela with their relief petition to the state legislature in Austin. In the evening her grandfather had ridden out when no one had known about it, just before the blizzard, with no more care against the weather than a yellow slicker. *It was like he'd left all his things on a bridge and jumped off,* Mr. Peterson had said. I don't *believe that,* Soledad had thought—*I don't want to hear what you have to say about it. For two or three days he hadn't been sayin' much,* Mr. Peterson had said. *It was like he was gone into hisself. Just leave his things here and let me be,* Soledad had thought. "What we want to do, Miss Kincaid," Mr. Green, sitting uncomfortably against the cotton pillows on the *sofacita*, said, "is get you to underwrite a piece of financing."

Soledad had coffee and *bizcochos* served. As the three men explained it, the whole south side of the square, as Miss Kincaid well knew, had been blown away. It was a complete loss. Now was the time . . . take advantage of . . . reconstruct the whole south side. Put up some fine new buildings. State help from Austin. A committee.

"Now, Mr. Beecroft suffered a big loss when his own ranch was hit but he is backing us for twelve thousand," Mr. Green said.

Soledad would have liked to have given them two figs. *They are almost all white people in town, what do they care about Grandpapa?* But it was her grandfather's town, he would have wanted her to do it. Soledad had questioned them closely and agreed to make herself liable for twenty thousand dollars, to be drawn if necessary upon her grandfather's account in the Diehl Bank in Krugerville. "But I shall want to be on that committee." "You're on it now," Mr. Peterson said, "and I yield you the gavel."

They had discussed other aspects of the business. Then the men had left. Soledad was glad to see them go. She called for Moro to be led to the front steps. She put on her riding skirt and her black pill hat, tucked a kerchief into her waistband and went out onto the gallery . . .

Soledad rode around the curve of the drive. *Yes, there he is in the garden.* Claiborne Arnett looked up from weeding tomato plants as she rode past. Soledad wanted to look at him, wanted to stare at his eyes and nose and mouth as if that would tell her who he was, as if the color of his eyes or hair could tell her what he had to do with her grandfather. But she did not let herself turn her head in his direction at all. *Let him drift a while longer—as he has the past few days.*

Apparently Claiborne Arnett couldn't stand to drift. He had come up to the house and commenced to weed the garden on his own. Soledad felt his look bore into her back.

Moro's hoofs crunched the dry caliche. The bleached, half-powdery drive threw up a glare light. Sunlight plastered black patches onto the ground under the orchard trees. Soledad rode out through the north gate.

She rode across the rocky, brush-dotted slope to the shearing pens. A cloud of dust hung over the pens. The unsheared ewes crowded together and panted for breath, their smooth, silky noses on each other's backs looked like fish stranded in shoal water. It was the third day of shearing. Soledad spent the morning watching the shearers or walking among the flocks to check their condition. The sheep did not appear to have been too badly shrunk by the dry winter. All they needed was a little fattening and she would have them bred. The sun went on past its height. Blat of sheep, crisp bite of the shearing blades. The last sheep was sheared and Soledad rode back to the house.

Claiborne Arnett was still bent over the tomato plants in the garden as she rode up the drive. He was tying up the plants. *Where had he got the cloth?* He did not look up.

In her room Soledad changed from the heavy black alpaca to a cooler black tamise. At the washstand she poured water from a pitcher into a porcelain basin. She wet her face and her throat and the back of her neck and her wrists. White porcelain—*white rags with which he is tying.*

The pasteboard-backed cabinet picture still leaned, its face to the wall, upon the chiffonier. Its stiffness, its blankness, its rebuke. *Her brother Edward's face on the white bolster—no!* The letter had arrived the day after Grandpapa had left for Santa Angela. "It would be better if you did not come." Soledad had gone anyway, riding down through the canyon in the night with Ramón and Vicente to accompany her as far as Ugalde. When she had got to San Antonio the next afternoon, Edward was dead. He had died early that morning. He lay on the settee in the parlor, his face shiny as wax, his head on the white bolster, his blue hands bound together with a kerchief, his mouth tied shut with a piece of gauze bound up under his chin as if it had been the mumps he'd died of instead of the cholera. *No, no, those things are not him!* Soledad's whole body shook. She took a deep breath. She dried her face and her neck and hands with a napkin. *And Ian and Papa had been so ill she'd had to stay and care for them.*

All the objects in the room waited in silence. Soledad put her hair up a bit tighter and walked across the hall to her grandfather's study.

In the study she crossed to a window. She held back a curtain. He was still in the garden, between two slats of the shutter—far enough away not to hear the sounds of his movements except for the faint, delayed *thonk thonk* of the stone with which he was pounding a stake into the ground. *Yes, he is left-handed.* He threw the stone aside. He stood up. *Not the working ways of a man who has his chores, who uses the hours easily, tying one moment to the next with a motion of his hand and a patient, urging intent.* He wiped a sleeve across his face. He took off his hat and ran his fingers through his hair. His hair glared in the sunlight like carroty copper. The back of his neck was white. *He likely has chalk-white shoulders.* He didn't look as if he belonged in this country.

He brushed his sleeve across his face again. He stared at his hat a minute, turned it around, pinched and poked the crown into several sorts of shapes. Then he punched the crown in, turned it over and punched it back out and put it on his head. There were some strips of white cloth hanging from his britches pocket. He pulled one out and bent over— his legs widespraddled—and commenced to tie a tomato plant. The sun beat down onto his back, onto the brown jacket and faded britches. His black smidgin of a shadow swung back and forth across the top of the tomato plant.

Why had Grandpapa been so strangely quiet those last few days before he had gone to Santa Angela? "Like he was gone into hisself." Soledad had noticed it. It wasn't the trip to Santa Angela—he had seemed to welcome that. But some letters and the usual newspapers had come three or four days before.

Papa and Ian and Edward were well—"Thank God the epidemic appears to be over. For five days now there have been no deaths." That was a week before Edward had taken sick—Esperanza and Olivia and their families were well. But for two or three days Grandpapa had hardly spoken. Not as though he were worried or angry but as if he had gotten away to some locked room with a high, closed window that mostly he had elected not to look out of.

Suddenly Soledad felt her grandfather standing behind her, over by the door somewhere. Grief pounded in her throat. She did not turn around. She felt that by not looking she might hold him there. *Oh, Grandpapa, don't go back. Don't leave me here.* She closed her eyes for a moment and felt him riding beside her on his horse Águila—proud and wise, master of his house and lands and of her too, almost.

She heard her grandfather clear his throat. She felt him coming toward her, she turned to him with a breathless joy. The desk and the chair and the settee stared at her in silence . . .

When she had got control of herself she looked out the window again. Claiborne Arnett stood up from his work and turned toward the house. Abruptly Soledad let the lace curtain drop. *But he can't see you through these shutters.* He hiked up his britches, picked up the stone, moved down the row a way and commenced to drive another stake into the ground.

Who is he? What has he to do with Grandpapa? How did he get that photo?

He was tying up a plant. *Wrap those white strips about his wrists. I will drag you from here to yonder until you talk.*

I can hardly breathe! This room is so close! The books with black and brown bindings shimmered on the shelves. Grandpapa's desk loomed upward from the floor on its four spindly legs like some strange, delicate, dark-brown animal. The stuffed blue horsehair settee seemed about to explode with silence. The bass viol, in its black, locked case, waited in the corner.

Soledad went down the stairs and through the downstairs hall, through the front room and out onto the gallery. She stood for a moment at the top of the steps until her heart beat less fiercely. Then she went down the steps and toward the garden, where Claiborne Arnett was bent over the tomato plants, his shoulders bobbing slightly. A yellow butterfly, dab of sulphur or chip of sun, flew across in front of her. The sun felt as if it was right above her head. Its heat worked like fingers into her hair. She grew a *mostacho* of sweat.

Claiborne heard her coming and stood up to face her. He wiped his hands on his britches. Soledad dabbed the sweat from her upper lip. "How are you?" she said.

He said, "I'm makin' out." His freckles seemed to float on his wet face.

"Where did you manage to get the cloth?"

"I went up to the house and asked for it. There's a woman up there."

"I expect that was Angelina. But you don't speak Spanish."

"I made noises and used my hands."

"Whatever did you say your name was?"

"Claiborne Arnett." He spoke with a kind of hurt sullenness. He stared at the ground and kicked at a chunk of black limestone dirt with his boot.

"I expect they call you Clabe."

"That's what I'm called sometimes."

"Or Red. Have you been finding enough work to keep yourself busy?"

He looked up at her again. "I got fed up with waitin' and come up here and done this."

"You do a good job."

"I ought to be on a horse."

"I'll send Andrés this afternoon to work with you. There are some trees to be put in."

"If that's the kind of work you mean to have me do."

Soledad felt a stab of anger in her breast. "I think you'll

do what work I tell you." Claiborne blushed. His face reddened behind the flakes of rusty freckles and a confused look
came into his eyes. Soledad's palms were suddenly prickly and
sweaty. She wiped them against the front of her dress as if
smoothing out a pleat. The sun beat down onto the top of her
head. She said, "You say you're from San Sebastian County?"

"Is that what I said?"

She felt the stab of anger again. But she said, "How does
the dirt work?"

"It works real good."

"My grandfather had the garden dug out and compost
laid underneath."

"Things ought to grow real good."

She said, "I've been busy with the shearing or I'd have
had a talk with you sooner." The bell rang for dinner. She
said, "Andrés is heading back to Mexico in another week.
Then I'll come down and we'll decide on the rest of the
work." She turned to go to the house.

"Hold on a minute," he said. "Is this what you want me
to be doin' right now?"

"Oh," she said, "I expect you might as well be earning
your keep."

The buggy clattered down the grade. The buggy wheels
rattled, the cross-reins and hame straps slapped, the bays'
hoofs drummed upon the ground. Tía Lupita said, "You are as
willful as your grandfather. As willful as I remember your
mother." *Oh, she is still thinking about that.* This morning
Lupita had laid out the blue serge dress upon the bed, but
Soledad had put on her black.

Soledad patted Lupita's hand. "It's all right, *corazón.*"

"The black crepe on the altar, yes. The candles for your
grandmother and your brother, of course. For the rest it is
sufficient to pray to God. You are too young to wear black."

They rode a long way in silence. Flat pads of cactus

skimmed by the wheel. The dead trunk of a scrub cedar twisted upward like stalled smoke.

Tía Lupita said, "¡Ay! I miss San Antonio! I miss your grandmother. Her on one side of the muscadine vines, myself on the other. And the evenings of chocolate and cards."

San Antonio. The white-columned gallery, the patio. The terror of the wasp! I still remember that.

Don Reyes and Abuelita María had sold their house in San Antonio. All the furniture had been put out on the lawn. The thing of the wasp had happened the day before. Had been helping Abuelita María take down the hanging flowerpots—a wasp had dropped down and stung Soledadita on her head. Soledad had not even seen the wasp. All she had known was the blinding light of pain that had coalesced on the side of her head, and the scream she let out. All the next day she had wandered from empty room to empty room in a drunkenness of pain, one eye closed, the side of her face puffed out like pudgy yeast dough. "Oh you poor child."

. . . The furniture had been carried out of the house. The bare tile floors looked naked and strange, as if they hadn't anything to do with her. The pieces of furniture, broken from their places, lay on the front lawn, waiting to be carted away. The hot sun of wasp-pain slapped against the side of Soledad's head, her swollen face made her feel lopsided. Sunlight flooded down around the pieces of furniture on the lawn, isolating each one like water around a rock. The furniture hadn't anything to do with her. The trees in the front yard, the cobbles in the drive hadn't anything to do with her. There was a new space between her and everything. In the driveway the great freight wagons waited to be loaded. Soledad thought of her mother's coffin. The huge white oxen waited. Later in the morning the wagons rolled away, their wooden axles creaking like thunder leaving heaven. . . .

The sun got hotter. Off in the distance, bushes shimmered and lifted from the ground. The courthouse and other buildings of Alto Springs appeared, floating in the air. Soledad and Tía Lupita rode into town.

In town Soledad picked up her mail. She read it in front of Van Zandt's racket store. It was a letter from Ian.

> *Dear Sister. Father sent Sam Foss up to Chero-*
> *kee. He came back today. He has smoked out that a*
> *man—a "greaser" according to his informant, some*
> *brush popper in a saloon there—was murdered in a can-*
> *yon near Cherokee last February and a prime black*
> *horse answering to a description of Águila sold up to*
> *Kansas on or about February the . . .*

"Oh!" Soledad cried. "Oh!"

When she came to, there was a crowd around her. Tía Lupita stood up over her, wide-eyed and anxious, a white handkerchief half stuffed into her mouth. The shock of the smelling salts still stung in front of Soledad's head.

Hands were everywhere. They tried to help her up. "No," she said. "No, I'm all right." She got to her feet. Someone tried to help her into the buggy. *Take your hands off me,* she thought or said. She managed to get into the buggy by herself. The letter was handed up to her. There was too much noise, too much confusion, too many hands. *Oh God, I think I'm going to go mad.* She slapped the reins at the horses' rumps as hard as she could. They started to trot up the street.

The letter burned in Soledad's hand. She stuffed it into her waistband. *No,* she thought, *I won't believe it. I won't. I won't.*

On the way out to the camp she managed to calm herself, though the grief seared like a hot stone in her breast. Tía Lupita tried to say something. "Please. I don't want to talk," Soledad said.

Soledad drove up to the cook wagon. Cook was scrubbing some pans in an agate bucket on the endgate of the wagon. "Mornin', Miss Lita," he said.

Soledad stared through him as if he weren't there. But she heard herself say, "I want you to break camp and fetch your gear back out to the ranch. Alfredo has more than he can handle cooking for the shearers, and we need you there. We can't have you spending all summer here."

"Why yes'm. If that's what you want. I arter be able to be back out there by Wednesday noon."

Headed back to the Tres Coronas. There was a moon to the east in the early evening sky, pale as a split pearl button in the thinned-out blue. Some thunderclouds were building in the northwest. Lupita was half asleep on the seat beside Soledad, her head back against the enameled drill, her eyelids drooping, her mouth open. She had wrapped the cords of her handbag around her wrist. Occasionally she came to with a start, if the horses changed pace or the buggy jolted on a rock. Her hand would lift abruptly to grab hold of a piece of air, hover a moment, drop back onto her lap. Then slowly her mouth would fall open again, her head tilt to one side.

Soledad brushed a patch of chalky dust from her skirt. *Wrist. Red hair on freckled backs of hands, white strips of cloth. The rust-splotched face looked up at her. "Claiborne Arnett."* Blood crowded Soledad's throat, constricted her breathing, pounded in her head. *The crave to hurt.* It felt as if it would lift her off the buggy seat. She had never felt such anger before. It frightened her. Her lungs were breathless, congested, the undersides of her arms ached. *To give hurt!* Spasms of sickness welled up in her. She sucked in a deep breath. It rushed in like a moan. Lupita stirred. "What?" she said, half awake. Suddenly Soledad was shaking all over.

Late in the night, in the dark of her room, pulled out of a dream that she could not remember though it still clung heavily to her upon the pillow about her head, Soledad was waked by a brief rain. It pattered against a window and dripped for a moment from the raised sash. Off in the southeast there was thunder, where they might be having a real rain. Then the night breeze blew across her bed again. The moon shone into the room.

The afternoon sun bore down. Soledad's skirt dragged in the dust and grass. The cuffs of her sleeves felt tight and binding, the high collar choked her. There was a weight of grief in her heart, heavy as her skirt. *Grandpapa.*

I want to know.

Grasshoppers scattered before the hem of her skirt. She walked into the orchard. Andrés and the man named Arnett—*Claiborne Arnett*—were cleaning the trash out of the irrigation ditches. On Soledad's left, under the plum trees, piles of pulled weeds and sticks and dead leaves lay alongside the *apáncle*, and water, brought down by a stone aqueduct from the springs, gurgled from whitewashed trunk to whitewashed trunk. A skin of dust and odd leaves floated on the surface. Claiborne Arnett stood in a dry ditch under a row of persimmon trees, scraping the ditch with a hoe. Farther on Andrés, on his knees, was pulling weeds from the ditch. Soledad walked between the rows of young fruit trees (they were in their first year of fruiting), a katydid scraped its bow in the top of one of them.

Claiborne straightened up to watch her. His shirt was soaked with sweat. For a moment Soledad felt frightened. "Good evening," she managed to say. She deliberately went on past. *Let him stand there until I've a mind to talk to him.*

Soledad walked over to Andrés. Andrés got up off his knees. "*Buenas tardes, Patroncita,*" he said. He took off his hat and wiped his face and the top of his head with a kerchief.

Soledad said in Spanish. "Andrés, what kind of man is this?"

"Who knows? He doesn't speak Spanish."

"He does the work though?"

"Yes, he knows the trees. He has learned that somewhere. He is a man who does not like to work on his feet."

Soledad smiled. "I expect not. But he *will* work. You are going to Mexico next week?"

"*Sí, Patroncita.*" Andrés' face grew round and sad. "Perhaps I will not go."

"You'll come back. If he knows the trees, I'll keep him until you do."

Andrés brightened again. "Yes, *Patroncita.* It's my poor mother. She's very old."

"Of course. God bless her and care for her. But there will always be a bed and a bowl for you here. Excuse me, Uncle."

"*Sí, Patrona.*"

Soledad turned and walked back to Claiborne. He was chopping furiously with the hoe. His sleeves were rolled up, his shirt pasted to his back. *White skin always seems to make more sweat.* He was not a small man yet his body seemed somehow slight, as if he'd just gotten out of a sickbed. His legs were bowed too. When Soledad looked at him a slight shiver went up her back. Claiborne grunted as he chopped.

"What are you doing, digging a hole to China?"

Clabe stopped suddenly and stood still for a moment.

"I never saw a body make such hard work out of nothing."

He straightened and turned to face her. He pushed his hat back from his forehead, wiped some sweat from his face.

"I reckon we got to," he said. He looked angry.

"What?"

"Work. It's all the style these days."

"That hoe does seem to fit to your hand."

"Only when I ain't thinkin'," Clabe said.

"How are you and Andrés getting along?"

"He works there and I work here."

"Oh?"

Where have I seen this man before? A face by a window. *A window by a face?*

"I need more elbow room," Clabe said. "I ain't used to this here kind of chores."

"Maybe I'll put you on the stock one of these days, when I'm short-handed."

"That'd suit me down to the ground. None of them blessed sheep, though."

"You don't like sheep?"

"About like I like hives or scarlet fever."

"Have you ever worked sheep?"

"I wouldn't admit to it."

"It might sweeten you up some. Where *is* San Sebastian County, anyway?"

"Up above San Antonio."

"Is that anywhere near Brady City? Or Santa Angela?"

"Brady City's in the next county. I been there."

"When was that?"

"Oh, three, four years back. Ran some stock through on the way up to Abilene. You ask a powerful lot of questions."

Soledad smiled. "Curiosity."

"That's what the cat died of." Claiborne swatted some more sweat from his face.

She could see the photograph as clearly as if it was printed in the air: the white summer dress, plaited collar, white, puffy shoulders.

Soledad closed her eyes to clear her head. *Train . . .* window!

Her eyes sprang open.

"San Antonio!"

"What?"

"Oh, nothing. I . . . have you ever been to San Antonio?"

He frowned. "Once."

"This spring. We had to cut back these trees so much this spring because of the blizzard. It killed so many branches.

It caught them just as they were beginning to show." Soledad stared at him. The train window slid past his face. *Who is this man? Why has he come here?* She was almost breathless. She knew that if she didn't get back to the house she would be shaking all over.

Claiborne blinked, lifted his hat and brushed back his red hair. Soledad said, "I've got to get back to the house." She forced herself to say, "When you're done with this Andrés will tell you what to do next."

"Am I supposed to be workin' for him?"

"*I think you'll do what you're told.*" Suddenly she laughed. "Oh, this heat!" She pulled the kerchief from her waistband and dabbed at her neck. "First the drouth. Then that blue norther. Then the twister. It looks like the weather is bent on tearing this country apart."

Clabe said bitterly, "I wouldn't care if it knocked it to smithereens."

Soledad sat at her worktable in the parlor. Behind her, on the *sofacita*, Lupita sat sewing and wheezing, her short, quick, indrawn breaths like the muffled chirring of a cricket. Soledad had a slight headache and when she looked up for a moment from her work, at the bright morning sunlight outside, it hurt more. There was a slight, knocking pain in the small of her back too, the dregs of a restless night. It seemed to exist by itself, a little fist of being there, right up against her backbone. She could almost hear its *tap tap tap tap tap.* Her pen made a splotch in one of the columns of figures. She put an "X" through it and wrote the numbers to the side. Suddenly the little knot of pain let loose of its clinging. *It's just as I thought.* She closed the stock ledger—the sheep, horse and cattle brands of the Tres Coronas

tooled on the cover—and set the pen aside. She pushed her chair back, stood up and said, "I am going down the hall."

Lupita said, "So it is that time again. Don't pour any milk today."

Soledad walked down the hall past the kitchen door— sunlight on the tile floor, Angelita in a bright red dress beating eggs with a wire whip—to the closet at the end of the passage. Blood flowed. It made her grief and powerlessness seem even heavier. *It is so bitter, being a woman. I wish I weren't a woman at all.* She pinned on a napkin. She washed her hands in a basin and dried them on a piece of flannel and walked back down the hall.

Too much silence! She stood alone on an endless prairie, in the hushed twilight that precedes a storm. Overhead an immense black cloud slanted upward. One breath could fill her lungs! One breath and the silence would shatter, the world change! Soledad woke. The moon was down. The wind had quit. She could barely make out the outline of the window. Stars sparkled. The darkness seemed to rustle in the ceiling corners.

Andrés was gone to Mexico. Soledad watched Claiborne as he propped up the lower branches of a fig tree with forked sticks. She said, "Where did you learn to tend fruit trees?"

"In Cherokee."

"That's in San Sebastian County?"

"I always had the notion it was." He propped up the last branch. A broken lateral bled milk.

"Were you in Cherokee when that blizzard hit?"

"Thereabouts."

Claiborne Arnett was pruning an apricot tree at the end of the garden. Soledad stood in the shade of a chinaberry tree nearby. She said, "I've brought you a pitcher of water."

Claiborne cut a water sprout out of the tree and dropped

it to the ground. "*Gracias*," he said. He stepped back from the tree and cocked his head at it.

"Thought you didn't speak Spanish."

"Not so's I know it. Is that what that is?" He pushed his hat back from his forehead and wiped his brow. He grinned. "I reckon I got a split tongue."

Soledad set the pitcher and a glass on the small, weathered bench nearby. Clabe came into the shade of the chinaberry tree and poured himself a glass of water. He said, "What's the name of them three hills?"

"*Las Tres Coronas*. The Three Crowns."

"Is that what they named this place for?"

"Who?"

"Whoever done it." He drank some water. Then he picked up the pitcher and took off his hat and poured water onto his head. It ran down his chest and soaked his shirt. "Mighty fine!" The tight, soaked, red curls, as wet as if he'd just come out of the womb. She half-expected to see a flat-tened face and soft, warped head when he looked up. She shook her head angrily. *No, I don't like that. What made me think that?* Claiborne put the empty pitcher on the table and dried his face with his kerchief. He said, "That makes a body feel some better."

"Maybe I should have brought soap."

"Aw. And a long-handled back brush." He kicked his boot heel at the dirt. "Who put in this chinaberry tree, any-ways? It don't usually grow in dry country like this."

"My grandfather planted it. It grows fast if you take care of it. This is my grandfather's ranch. Whatever's here is be-cause of my grandfather. Of course, these are all young trees."

"I don't know who that is."

"Don Reyes. Alvaro Reyes Ibarra."

"You're not Meskin."

"You act as if you have all the facts. I'm half Mexican. Let's take a look at that tree."

She touched a branch in the apricot tree. She said, "Maybe this one ought to come out." She said, "This tree was planted eight years ago. It grows so fast. If we don't keep cutting the top out it'll get out of hand. This other branch ought to come out too." She said, "My grandfather made this place. He had the house built. He had all these trees planted."

"Looks like he's got a hand in ever'thing."

"Nobody does anything important in Balcones County without asking *Granpapá*. He deeded one whole section for the county seat and had the courthouse built. He led in the organization of the county back in seventy-three."

"A body gets tired of them things."

"What things?"

"All them kind of things. What a man done and such. What Jesus done and Anson Jones done, I don't care which. They always make a law out of it. It gets writ up in the books. It makes a body want to lay down in the grass and quit."

Soledad stared at him a moment. A mustache of sweat started on her upper lip. She said, "Some people are just *born* white trash." Claiborne reddened violently. Soledad said, "Why'd you come here? What fetched you to this place?"

"Just . . . followin' my nose. Lookin' for work."

Soledad caught hold of an apricot switch as if she thought it was going to keep her from blowing away. "Looking for work? You say you've broken horses and run stock?"

Claiborne said sullenly, "I can do as good as the next man."

"You must need work awfully bad. That's quite a plug you rode out here."

Clabe spat on the ground. He said, "We can't all of us ride a prime black devil."

"Like what?"

"Like the one you got. The one with the stocking feet."

¡Ay! *Águila!* Grandpapa lit up into the saddle. The black horse with stockinged feet shifted under his weight.

So you have seen him!

The switch Soledad had hold of glistened like shivered light in her fist. She said, "Trim out this switch."

"I don't know as it needs it."

"Cut this switch!"

"That's a fruiting spur."

Her whole body was shaking. "I said cut it! Cut it!"

13

MORNING.

Spade, barrow, bucket, mattock, a pile of split tow sacks for balling the fruit saplings. Pale grayness of daybreak— the air was cool with the leavings of night. Some wetness on the steps and on the leaves of the sycamore, pressed Lord knows how from the dry atmosphere. It made her heart quicken. The cool morning air freshened her. Claiborne Arnett rode up on his brown tick mare. A dove called from the top of the sycamore, "¿Qué quieres, pastor?" From the drowned orchard another replied, "Comer comas, comer comas." Ramón had gone to open the water gates. Once more, from Tía Lupita's room in the east wing of the house, the pet rooster that Lupita kept tied by a leather thong to the foot of her bed at night crowed. Taste, still, of milky coffee in Soledad's mouth.

"Morning," she said.

"Mornin'," he said. He swung down from the mare. He was dressed in his rough jeans britches, brown ducking jacket and beat-up mule-ear boots. The boots listed at the ankles as he walked: too much time rounding the belly of a horse.

Soledad said, "The barrow and tools are here. Ramón's gone to open the water gates. He'll help you set the fruit trees. Do you want a cup of coffee before you start?"

"That'd suit me fine."

Soledad walked over to Lupita's willow chair and shook the small hand bell that was on the floor beside it. In a moment Angelina appeared at the door. Soledad said, "Trae una taza de café, Angelita, por favor."

"*Sí, niñita, ya viene.*"

Soledad pointed to the steps. "Why don't you come sit?" she said. Claiborne gave the reins a turn around the post and ring, his back to Soledad. *Come to think of it, in a way it's as if he's always got his back half turned to you. Like the time Raúl got kicked in the hip by that horse—all hunched up and turned away.*

"*Aquí está,*" Angelina said from the half-opened screen door.

"Thank you, Angelita," Soledad said in Spanish. "You may give it to me."

She crossed to the top of the steps and waited for Claiborne to take the cup of coffee. The dry porcelain heat stung through the folded kerchief with which she was holding the cup, the bitter coffee smell stained the air. Claiborne blushed when he took it. He did not look directly at her. He sat on a step. Soledad sat on one of the chairs at the edge of the gallery. *I don't think I can stand him.* The dove fluttered in the sycamore. Its mate, a patch of white on its wings, flew across from the orchard.

Soledad said, "Did you ever live in San Antonio?"

"No'm. I only been there once. Two, three days. Just passin' through."

"I grew up there."

"Is that so?"

"Papa owns a freight company there." She watched him lift the coffee cup. "You're left-handed."

"Well, they tried to keep me from it. My pa tied my arm to my side once for a whole week. He beat the bejesus out of me when I went to use my left hand. But I'll tell you what. If the state legislature was to make it a law you got to eat soup with the spoon in your right hand they'd have to jail me right off."

Soledad said, "I know what you mean."

Clabe shot a look at her from under his hat brim. Then he bent forward and began picking at a splinter on the edge of the step. He said, "Some things gets fat on contrariness."

Soledad watched his arm move in its sleeve. She could sense the workings of the muscles in his shoulder. Freckled skin where his collar touched his neck. She said, "How's that?"

"Folks put a name on ever'thing. They slap it in the books. But that don't mean it'll hold." He looked up. He said, "That's a pretty dress."

Soledad laughed abruptly. "I see you don't know much about the latest fashions. This is the blackest, plainest cloth a body can buy."

Clabe said sullenly, "You couldn't tell it by me."

"What do you know about my grandfather?"

"Nothin'. Exceptin' what I heard in town."

I will bring my grandpapa up to you until it sticks in your craw. "I guess you heard what happened. He rode out into a blue norther and hasn't been heard from since."

Clabe said, "It looks like a body'd have more sense."

Soledad got to her feet. She managed to catch hold of one of the gallery posts. Only a sudden brightening of morning light on the tips of the orchard trees fetched her back to her senses. She swallowed hard. She said, "There's the tools and the tow sacks." She didn't hear the words project into the air. They were locked-in clangings in her head. "You know the work that has to be done. I've a terrible headache. I'm going into the house."

Morning. Moro's ears were back, his neck stretched and head forward. His breaths came in hog-like snorts.

Fresh sweat, plastering the hairs, glinted off his shoulder. Knotting and unknotting of the tumultuous flesh. His hoofs pounded, the sun-drenched grass blurred by underneath, a ground dove flew from its nest. Strings of black mane stung Soledad's fists, the wind burnt past her face. A shriek of joy caught in her throat. She looked back. Angelita was on the fast strawberry roan. She was falling back fast. "¡Ven! ¡Ven!" Soledad cried. Angelita grinned, a slash of white. Her hair had come loose and was flying behind her. Her eyes were like a pursuing ferret's. She leaned forward and switched the roan even harder.

Noon. The two bays took their time. There was no breeze. Sunlight sliced in from the edge of the buggy top, pressed against her left side and felt as if it were working a finger into her ribs. *In heat like this you will your body to stay cool.* Beside Soledad, Lupita flicked her silk fan. Had spent the morning in Alto Springs. The mail and a sack of flour were in the boot of the buggy. Three miles more to the ranch. Up ahead, about a quarter of a mile off, a horse and rider came down a slope onto the trace. It was Claiborne Arnett. Soledad drove a little farther until he came up.

Soledad said, "Do you find anything interesting out here, Mr. Arnett?"

"I wasn't lookin' to. I've had enough of hoein' beans and sulphurin' bees. Had to get a chunk of horse under me."

"I'll say this for that mare. She's fattening up some. But you can't make a silk purse out of a sow's ear."

"Can't cut a preacher's coat out of bad manners, neither."

Soledad stared at him. For a minute she couldn't tell whether she felt hot or cold. Then her armpits broke into sweat and a streak of laughter skittered up her throat. She said, "*That* kind of cut my feathers!"

Claiborne grinned. He said, "I reckon we both got our noses caught in the crack." His horse, which looked to be suffering in the heat, shifted impatiently.

Soledad said, "I think we'd better call a truce."

"Suits me."

"I have to go. This heat's wearing Lupita to a frazzle." Soledad flicked the reins at the horse's rumps. "I'll leave you to your ramblings."

Claiborne swung his horse around. "Headed back my ownself. If y'all don't mind." He rode alongside.

"Where'd you get that mare, Mr. Arnett?"

He laughed. "Question is, how'm I gonna get rid of her?"

He tipped his hat forward and tilted his head back and rode along peering out from under the sweatband. His wiry red hair curled up off the top of his collar. He said, "I'd make a trade for one of them fat bays." They rode a while in silence. He rode his horse light and easy to the motions, the way ball moss rides a branch—weightless upon it, moving with it in a light or heavy wind. The way the Devil rides a thistle.

He was lightweight and delicate-boned.

Soledad said, "Have you ever broken horses, Mr. Arnett?"

"I've rid a few and been jilted by a few."

A bee shot across the shade of the buggy.

"Maybe I'll sell you my good horse Moro."

"That's the black."

"Do you admire his stocking feet?"

"He ain't got stocking feet."

Abruptly Soledad laughed. She said, "I'm about to swim in perspiration. This heat. We haven't had a wet spring in three years, except for that blue norther this spring. And that just killed everything back."

"It was a mean one."

"Where were you when it hit?"

"Up in Cherokee."

"I remember I was in San Antonio. It roared through the streets. It wasn't any weather to be out in."

"Not for two whole—not for *them* two days."

The buggy jolted on a rock.

Beside Soledad, Lupita closed her fan—"¡Ay! What a sad country!"

After a moment Soledad said, "Are you always contrary, Mr. Arnett?"

"What do you mean?"

"Oh—left-handed. But maybe it's just your disposition that's contrary."

"Maybe *I'm* straight and ever'body else's haw-handed."

"Hah."

"Maybe it's all contrary." Clabe flipped his hand in the general direction of the dirt and brush around them. "Maybe there ain't *nothin'* is what it looks to be. Folks figure they got it all cut and dried. Put a name on ever'thing and it's flat gonna *be* that. But that don't make it so. There ain't nothin' squares up at the corners."

"Sounds to me like you want to leave everything to chance. I'll tell you one thing. I never leave *anything* to chance. Couldn't run this ranch if I did."

"Look at that tree. Ain't that a wonder?" A mesquite tree blooming in the heat. "Oh, you don't have to leave nothin' to chance. Chance'll do what it aims to its ownself."

Evening.   Soledad opened the shutters and let light into the study. Motes of dust floated in the air. She watched a speck of it light onto the back of the horsehair settee. *It's so still in here. All the furniture is so—heavy. The chairs, the settee, it's as if they were bolted to the floor, as if they hadn't been moved in a thousand years. Oh, Grandpapa! But I shan't allow this room to be opened until you come back. Shan't permit a stick in it to be moved.*

He won't come back. *Oh, I won't believe that!* Not until I know. Not until I know!

The bass viol leaned in the corner. The locked desk stood up from the floor, four curved legs delicate as a gazelle's. It had been her Grandmother María's writing desk. When Abuelita María had died, Grandpapa had had it fetched upstairs to keep his papers in. "*She will not mind. I'll feel I've placed my papers in her care.*" There, evenings and Sundays, he had hunched over his account books and correspondence, which were still locked in the desk. *He'll come back. So long as that desk stays locked. ¡Ay, Granpapá! I've done everything! I've kept the books and run the stock. Your herds have grown, your sheep are on the hills. I've run this house and settled the quarrels between the men. Even your fruit trees—I've seen to them myself, they're pebbled with fruit. Everything is ready for you. Nothing is*

changed. Come home to me! Soledad's dark silhouette showed
in the polished surface of the closed, locked dropleaf. *Dark on
dark, like images of the dead.* Soledad squeezed her eyes shut.

Wax face on bolster. *Oh, come back! Come back to me!*

Soledad turned away from the desk. White squares of
Abuelita María's and Tía Lupita's laces and tattings on the
back of the settee. "*Sí, Cholita,*" her grandfather had said,
"*your grandmother was one of the most beautiful women I have
ever seen. Black hair to her waist. Small hands and feet. A small,
pretty woman.*"

Long string of perfect, luminous roundnesses—the pearls that
*Abuelita María had worn on her wedding day. They lay wrapped
in yellowed tissue in the lacquered sandalwood box on a chiffonier in
the next room.* In her mind Soledad walked into the room.
*Brass bedstead in the center of the room. Sheets of snowy linen,
hemstitched and embroidered, two inches deep. Lace counterpane,
pyramid of white pillows, eleven of them, each a little smaller than
the other and all decorated with the same lace, canopy of hazy lace.
On the table beside the bed a spray of paper roses*—ramilletes—
*discolored and dusty now, and the hand-hammered silver pitcher
that Angelita had always kept filled with fresh water when Gran-
mamá and Granpapá used to sleep there.* Often Soledad had
gone into the room to leaf through her grandmother's album
filled with tintypes of Abuelita María's kin, *la familia* Castrejon,
men and women, young and old, the girls wearing long curls
and hoop skirts, their hands on their waists, every finger outspread to show the gold rings. Often she had poked into
Abuelita María's things in the sandalwood box—the tissue-
wrapped pearls, the gold locket of raised flower design holding
a ringlet curl of Soledad's mother's hair, the crucifix of ivory,
the pair of earrings—*coquetas*—with gold dangles like a
fringe.

*Beside the sandalwood box, her grandmother's daguerreotype.
The bride is dressed in white, with lifted white veil, pearls tripled
about her throat, a wax wreath simulating orange blossoms crown-
ing her forehead, her dark, bold eyes.*

Everything the bride wears on her wedding day is the gift of the groom.

Noon. "Don't break the branches!"

Claiborne said, "Wait a minute. I got it now."

With a foot wedged in a fork of the chinaberry tree he leaned out on one of the lesser limbs. The bee swarm hung like a great, pulsing heart at the end of the branch. Claiborne held an open tow sack under the bees and managed to slip it up around the yellow cluster. He shook the branch. The bees dropped into the sack. He closed the sack and tied an end of rope to it. "Must weigh upwards of twenty pounds," he said.

Soledad said, "Hand it down to me." She dropped the pie plate she'd been banging down to the ground.

The sack, spinning slowly, swung down on the end of the rope. A few loose bees circled the sack or lit and crawled upon it and some lit onto Soledad's bee veil. "You've got nearly all of them," she said. "It's a wonder you didn't get stung."

"They don't bother me. What bothers me is I'm fiddlin' with 'em atall."

Soledad laughed. She said, "Where'd you learn to handle bees?"

"Old man and his woman that took me in. He kept bees. Had a few fruit trees. You could say I got it from the horse's mouth. That old man had been keepin' bees since the Year One. Always had that bee smell on him. He had me out there workin' 'em with him. I was just a young sprout and didn't know no better. Now you see where it's got me." He carried the sack over to the bee gums and stuck its rumpled mouth into the open top of one of them. "Oh well, he was good to me." He shook the sack of bees into the gum. They roared in the hollow and started to boil back up out of the opening. He put a lid on.

Soledad said, "I've got to get out of the sun."

In the shade of the chinaberry tree she lifted her veil and flung it back atop her straw hat. A few random bees circled her. *They're too confused to sting.* At the bee gum Clabe shook the rest of the bees from the tow sack onto the ground in front of the hive.

Soledad said, "What have you heard about my grandfather?"

"I don't know nothin' about him."

"Do you know where he is?"

"How'm I supposed to know that?"

"If you saw him you'd know him. I'm keeping this ranch for him until he comes back."

Claiborne came into the shade of the tree. He took off his hat and wiped his face with a dirty kerchief. "What if he don't come back?"

"He'll come back!"

"A man ridin' in that country—in particular one with a fancy horse and rig—you don't know whatall he'll meet up with. Them canyons are filled with men holed up from the law or hustlin' a few drifted cattle."

"What canyons?"

"Up around Cherokee."

"What makes you think that's where he was?"

"I don't know," Claiborne said sullenly, twisting and working a boot heel into the dirt. "But many's the man that's got shot off a Dick Heye or suchlike saddle."

"A fancy saddle with silver trappings."

"I reckon."

She looked away from him.

"Maybe he flat got froze in that norther. You got to wear somethin' more'n a yellow slicker."

Soledad looked up. Clabe's face was red clear to his ears. He said, "Like as not that's all a man'd carry with him on a warm spring day."

Soledad said bitterly, "Yes. Hand me that pie plate." Clabe looked at the ground as if he were about to step on a rattler. Soledad said, "It won't bite you."

He handed the plate to her. She brushed it off against her skirt. She fanned at a bee that was buzzing near her face. After a moment she said, "In a week or so I've got to go down to Ugalde to pick up a shipment of angora goats. They've got to be driven back up through the canyons. I'm going to need an extra hand. Have you ever handled goats?"

Clabe broke into a grin. "I'll tell you one thing—if it'd get me into a saddle, I'd drive *chickens* up through them canyons."

Oh, you'll come. I won't let you out of my sight until you tell me what you know.

To   Came down off the Plateau through the Breaks of
Ugalde. the Nueces River. At Blue Hole the water bil-
lowed out of the ground, swelled out of the deep earth lifting a ring of foaming water, a watery mouth boiling with small stones, and the widening circles sped over the skin of the deep pool and slapped at limestone walls. Bold-running stream. "¡Mira! ¡Mira!" Ramón and Faustino said. They lit down from their horses, ran to the rocks above the pool and jumped in, boots, hats and all. Ramón's sombrero floated down the stream. He barely caught it.

"¡Mójate por mí!" Soledad yelled. *Get wet for me.* She laughed.

Ramón and Faustino rode beside her, talking of water and of a great spring that runs through *ahuehuete* trees and red flowers that Faustino knew in Tamaulipas. Claiborne rode on his brown tick mare behind them. They rode under tall burr oaks and pecan trees.

At Truett's Crossing Soledad said to Claiborne. "Yes, for years my grandfather was a lawyer in San Antonio. He argued the famous Kolenberg case."

"I thought he was a Meskin."

"All the important families in San Antonio were Mexican, up to ten, fifteen years ago. Grandpapa's estate consisted of dozens of lots and properties. But the *gringos* were taking over. The old businesses in town, all the great land grants held by the old families—where are they all now? Grandpapa saw the handwriting on the wall. He sold all his holdings and came out here."

"He ought to of stayed in San Antonio."

"Yes, with his property gone and arguing Spanish land-grant cases to white juries."

They rode through the rough-bark settlement of Dixie Flats.

In the evening they trotted through a stand of cotton-wood trees. Five small brown owls were on the branches of one of them, turning their flat-fronted heads to watch them pass. "*¡Lechuzas!*" Faustino whispered. He and Ramón crossed themselves and murmured a prayer for departed souls.

Claiborne helped Soledad down from Moro. He said, "You got the blackest eyes."

"They're my mother's eyes. My mother was a Mexican."

They made camp under some trees beside the river. Soledad had her bedding laid out under a pecan tree a little way off from the men and a tent of blankets was put up around it. At the campfire Soledad said, "My grandfather studied law in New Orleans in the late eighteen-thirties. I think English law more or less applied after 1836. He could read Latin and Greek."

"He talk English?"

"As good as the next man."

Claiborne turned away from her. He said bitterly, "You'd think a man would stick to the tongue he was born with."

Late in the night, in the middle of the night, Soledad was waked by a noise. It was a panther screaming, way off on a ridge.

The next morning they rode into Ugalde. Soledad said, "My grandfather came down here from Alto Springs on business pretty often. He was an agent for the Cattlemen's Association and attended most of the meetings."

On the boardwalks, tobacco spit—ambeer. The streets were shoe-mouth-deep in dust. Inca doves called from the eaves of the *Ugalde Banner*. Soledad spoke to Faustino and Ramón in Spanish. She said to Clabe, "I've made arrangements for you and Ramón and Faustino to stay in the wagon yard behind Schultz's General Store."

Claiborne said, "You mean me and them two're gonna bed down in the same stall?"

"You can unspool your bedroll in the brush if you like."

Smells. Green horse manure on the square, bananas hanging rotten-ripe in front of Cloudt and Dolan's store, sacks of coffee, hard coal burning in the blacksmith shop, bread baking, beer and sawdust behind swinging doors, fresh-hung meat with its heavy flesh smell in a butcher shop. Wagons and buggies rattled down Main Street. They raised a haze of dust. Spurs jangled on the boardwalks. Women walked in and out of shops and grocery markets, wearing the new *havane* and pink and Napoleon-blue spring colors. The sun lay sprawled on all fours on the roofs and the boardwalks and the wooden awnings, on the dusty trees. Soledad took a room in Mrs. Henderson's hotel and ate her dinner there.

After dinner she took a nap. This was the same room her grandfather always stayed in when he came to Ugalde, the same bed. When Soledad came down to Ugalde with him she would have her own room, sometimes the one next to this. Today she had been given this one. She stared at the tea-brown stain on the ceiling. It looked like a doubled-up rabbit.

It was warm in the room, though there were pecan trees shading the building. Soledad's hair was sweaty on the bolster.

Down in the street some girls were having a "war," wrapping flower stems together and tugging them. Soledad fell asleep to their laughter and squeals.

First she was balancing on a stalk of grass, then she was hovering in the air like a moth or a bird. The air seemed to shake.

She heard the sound of hoofs, muffled as if in dust. Here came her grandpapa riding into the shade of a big pecan tree. He stopped under the tree. Águila shifted restlessly, lifting his white, quarter-stockinged feet. Spotted yellow leaves rattled underneath. A man climbed down the tree. It looked like Claiborne Arnett. The light shifted green and yellow on his back. Then it was a huge green snake climbing down the tree.

Soledad woke abruptly, in distress. Half her senses seemed still to be caught in sleep. The walls and ceiling of the room shimmered as from light reflected off water. Or maybe it was her own dazed mind.

In the evening Soledad saw Claiborne Arnett leaning against a hitching post down at the end of the street. She walked down a different street to avoid meeting him.

The next morning she stood on the station platform with a rancher from La Pryor and a Mr. Dollahite of the Cattlemen's Association. Both had been business associates of her grandfather.

"Want to see what them animules *looks* like."

"Steers going at four dollars a head, cows at three, and *that's* with the calf throwed in!"

"I've read the listings from Fort Worth," Soledad said. "It doesn't look any better there."

A crowd had come down to the station to watch the arrival of the town's one daily excitement. Spitting and popping, bell clanging and whistle hooting, the train came in. Brake shoes squealed. Cinders rained down onto the platform.

Soledad's goats were in an open car at the end of the train. They were dirty from dust and cinders and a little leaned-out, but otherwise in good condition despite the long trip from California. The buck was in good condition, cantankerous as if he'd never left his home territory. He had a good flat-lock fleece on his throat and belly. A boy fourteen or fifteen years old, his face streaked with cinders and sweat, his black felt hat tied down like a bonnet with a kerchief knotted under his chin, was in the middle of the bunch. His name was

Ned Davis, he said. He said, "Yes, I come all the way from Sacramento on account of my uncle sent me. Now I got to go all the way back."

The rancher from La Pryor looked at the goats. "You mean them things is supposed to make *money?*"

Ned and Clabe and Ramón and Faustino drove the goats out of the car and into a stock pen on the other side of the tracks. The men stayed to tend them and Soledad took Ned to wash up. She had him change his clothes and left the dirty ones with Mrs. Henderson to wash. Then she treated him to dinner at the Oyster House. He was filled with his visions of the Sierra Nevadas and the Great Salt Plains and the Rocky Mountains and Raton Pass and the Panhandle. "But I like Sacramento best."

The next morning, in Schultz's store, Soledad bought herself six yards of plain black lawn cloth and a bottle of calomel. When she came out of the store, Ramón had fetched Moro. "*Bueno*, Ramón," Soledad said. "Let's go home!"

Ramón grinned. His black mustache flared above his teeth. "*¡Vámonos por arriba!*"

Clabe rode out of the wagon yard on a new horse, a sorrel gelding with a white snip on its nose. It was already sweated. Clabe said, "He's a mite Roman-nosed, a mite pig-eyed and just a shade prick-eared, but he's got plenty of go."

Soledad said, "He does look mean."

Claiborne said, "I ain't paid for him yet. I've signed the papers. But when I get my wages I'm gonna pay on the barrelhead."

Soledad said, "I pay on the first of every month."

"I can wait."

They rode down Main Street to the station. The gelding acted jittery but it didn't shuck. Soledad said, "I notice you don't drink."

"I ain't got the money. I got the reasons but reasons won't buy whiskey."

□

And   Up into the canyons. The sun was as hot as a grid-
back.   dle. The goats picked their way up the rocky track,
          pausing now and then to browse on sumac and
guajillo. Soledad and Clabe and Faustino and Ramón took
their time. Moro lurched and swayed underneath, carrying
Soledad through the hot, thick air. Tick of the goats' deerlike
hoofs. Down below, to the left, the Nueces River tumbled
over the rocks of its riverbed, headed downstream.

Soledad said, "Grandpapa meant to go to the state legislature to get a road built up through here."

Noon.   In the front room the candles flickered in their
          small green jars. Soledad stood before the altar
          at the end of the front room. Angelita and Tía
Lupita had hung a sheet of white *manta* on the wall. On
the *manta* they had pinned ribbons—red, blue, orange and
yellow—in arches and arcades. Sprigs of cedar and oleander
and paper flowers were pinned to the arches. Pictures of saints
and angels formed a celestial host and at the back of the altar,
her hands outspread in the gesture of compassion, stood the
hand-carved, wooden statue of *Nuestra Señora de los Dolores*,
paint flaking from her blue robe.

The candles flickered in their jars. Two candles, one
for Abuelita María, the other for Edward. (The candle for
Soledad's mother was in front of the altar in the San Fernando
Church in San Antonio. Often as a child Soledad had been
led in to pray before it—mainly to stare at it. With the great,
hovering darkness overhead, the silence of arches and cold
tile all around—rustle of dresses and mantillas close beside—
the candle in its plain little tumbler-for-drinking-water tried
to talk to her. Soledad had it in her mind it was supposed to
be her mother: the light like a longing crying out, the con-
tinual motion as if it were alive, the little clear round pool
of melted wax—hot liquid of her mother's flesh? Warmth of
her mother's silk-gloved arm. It seemed cruel after that to
come out into the sunlight, always always always leaving her

mother behind.) The candle for Edward flickered. *Yes, it almost breathes. Oh,* she thought, *that means nothing at all. Nothing, nothing, nothing at all.*

Wagons creaked down East Commerce Street. Six rattled by. Soledad watched them with horror. The cholera—"Black Sunday." Oh, so hot and weary from the long train ride to San Antonio. Soledad had burst into the front hallway. Sunlight rose in dusty buttresses from the floor, but in the parlor the shades were halfway down. Soledad fell to the floor. She had to be helped to where Edward lay on the settee. They had to hold her to keep her from falling again.

Here is his face, the sunken features, the closed eyes, the blue lips, the gauze tied tight like a violent silencer under his chin, the pale, hurtable brow, sheen of dry sweat or death's wax upon it, the hair that is his hair and the creases motion has made at the corners of his lips. Edward! Dear! Open your eyes!

Her mother lay in her coffin.

And now Grandpapa?

Soledad was hardly able to breathe.

Night.   Tía Lupita lit the lamp in Soledad's room. She laid out Soledad's nightdress on the bed. Soledad felt nervous and distressed. She didn't think she would be able to get to sleep at all. Lupita undid Soledad's hair. She undid the buttons up the back of her dress. Then she went out of the room, her footsteps diminishing down the hallway and the stairs. Curtains moved at the open window. Outside, in the dark, the night breeze hissed through the leaves of the sycamore. Soledad started to undress. She had her hands at her neck to pull the dress up over her shoulders. She heard a *click.* Her grandfather had opened the door. He stepped into the room and closed the door behind him, but except for that *click* he did not make any other sound. She felt him staring at her. She closed her eyes, and now he was close behind her, on the other side of the bed. Her shoulder prickled where his hand was about to touch it.

For a long while she sat on the edge of the bed. He would not go away. Tears dripped from her chin. Longing and shame and confusion oppressed her. The lamplight flickered in its chimney. Finally she lay down in her dress and slept.

Noon.   Soledad poked the needle through the white, yielding weave of the disk of cloth stretched upon the embroidery hoop, caught it on the underside, the yellow thread writhing like a live thing, drew it tight and pricked the needle from below into its next position. Lupita sat in her chair at the end of the gallery, her handwork on her lap, her head back, eyes closed, a rose leaf pasted on her forehead to ease the headache that had come on her earlier that morning.

Soledad said in Spanish, "It will soon be time for dinner."

Lupita said, "It is so hot. I don't think I shall ever want to eat again."

Claiborne Arnett came around from the side of the house. He was carrying a crowbar and shovel, and his clothes and face were grimy with dust and sweat. He said, "I got them post holes dug."

Soledad stuck the needle into the cloth and set the embroidery on a book that lay on the floor beside her chair.

Claiborne said, "Where do you want these things put?"

"Leave them by the steps there. Ramón will take care of them."

Clabe leaned the tools against the gallery edge, pushed his hat back and wiped the sweat from his face.

Soledad said, "Why don't you come up out of the sun? Do you want a drink of water?"

"I'm doin' all right." Claiborne came up the steps and sat on the top step. He pointed to the book and said, "I reckon you like to read."

"Sometimes." It was a book that in two days of trying she had not been able to read past the first chapter. She did not seem to be able to concentrate on anything. Even the embroidery work irritated her.

"I reckoned you did. I reckon you take pleasure in it, too."

"I suppose everyone likes to read when they find something interesting, don't they?"

"No. It's darn tiresome to some folks."

"You don't like to read?"

"Folks keep pilin' words onto ever'thing. You can heap up your books until you get a mountain pile and it ain't gonna change howall things are."

"How are they?" *If you're so smart.*

Clabe leaned back against the gallery post. "Sometimes I feel like I don't belong in this world. Don't know where I come from, don't know where I'm goin'. Got the notion of a home somewheres, but it's a far cry from here." He closed his eyes and twisted his neck, rubbed the back of his neck as if it hurt. "Feel like I been kicked out and been hammerin' at doors and windows ever since."

"I don't expect there's anybody that's not a touch lonesome."

"Oh, I ain't lonesome, ma'am. I'm *alone.*"

Soledad flushed, she didn't know why. She felt annoyed. She said, "Then you ought to interest yourself in people."

"I'll tell you flat out, I don't trust nobody. Not in this world. Look at these hands. I had this one broke twice in the wrist. That's from doin' what I was told. Folks always want to put a bosal on your nose, lead you on a string right on down the line. This is this and that's that. Reminds me of a man on a pitch-black night cussin' and rowelin' at the edge of a bluff, tryin' to make his horse go."

"You figure you're so much better than most folks?"

Claiborne laughed. "I ain't no good atall and that's the God's truth."

Soledad stared at him. She said, "I think you're the

strangest man I've ever met." His face was a mask of freckles. She'd never seen such a freckly face, large coppery flakes drifting on the skin. His green eyes peered from between orange lashes—clear, liquid green, color of green of tincture of peppermint. There was a kind of animal distance in them. A queer, flat innocence.

Soledad said, "Why are you here? How come you to be here?"

He grinned. "Oh," he said, "I seen your picture in a pasteboard album somewheres and figured I'd come and see if you was real."

Soledad sat bolt upright in her chair. She unclasped her hands and began to rub the palms back and forth against each other. The tops of the orchard trees were suffused with an orange smoldering of evening light. She smiled. She said, "I really ought to wear white."

"What for?"

"Then I'd be 'pretty as a picture.'"

He shifted in the queer silence that seemed to be thickening around her. She said, "Oh, eligible men don't give me a second look when I wear black! I'm much too serious." She looked at him. Her throat hurt from the pulse thumping in it. She said, "I half think you came all this way just to court me." She never saw a face turn so red. The freckles fairly melted in the rush of blood.

Clabe stumbled to his feet. The noise waked Tía Lupita. "You'd think I'd offered to shoot you." She laughed and said, "I'm sure we've both got too much sense for tomfoolery like that." Abruptly she said. "Why *did* you come here?"

Clabe stared at his hat. He turned it around in his hands as if he didn't know what it was. He shoved the hair back from his forehead and looked at the palm of his hand. Three bent fingers rubbed at a pink scar. He said in a choked voice, *"I think a devil come out of the spring wet and had me to do it . . ."*

□

Evening, Soledad reined in Moro. "Mr. Arnett, I want to
the speak to you."
next Claiborne wedged the moldboard of the
day. hand cultivator into the ground and came over to
the caliche drive. The hard run through the heat
had left Moro salt-slicked and nervous. He kept shifting under
her. Clabe reached up and caught hold of the curb strap.

Soledad said, "No, I can handle him."

Clabe let go of the curb strap. He put a hand up to shield
his face from the sun, his eyes squinting. His face looked vulnerable, as if the sunlight were a switch, his hand trying to
ward off the blows. Soledad closed her eyes. In her mind she
came down onto his face with a stick. When she opened her
eyes Claiborne had taken off his hat and was holding it up to
shade his face. *Oh, I can't endure these thoughts. Fire him. Get
rid of him.* Moro's hip slumped under Soledad. Then the horse
shifted again and the other hip dropped. Soledad leaned forward in the saddle. She felt sweat prickling on her breast. She
felt light-headed. She said, "Where were you this spring when
that blizzard hit?"

"Up in Cherokee."

"I know that. But whereabouts?"

Clabe cleared his throat. "Well, I was out on a job to
round in some loose stock."

"Not in the middle of a blue norther."

"When it tailed off."

"Up in those canyons, I expect."

"That's where they'd got to. I was hired to round them in."

"All open and above board, of course."

"I can't say as there weren't a few mavericks amongst
'em. I wasn't gettin' paid to cut 'em out. Swing that horse
around to the other side, that sun's too bright."

"Did you see anyone else while you were up there? Any
strangers?"

Clabe laughed. "Well. We *might've* seen somebody for a
minute way up on the ridge."

"He didn't come down?"

"No, he didn't come down. Anyways, we were already startin' the cows down the draw."

"Did you see the same man in town?"

"What man?"

"The one up on the ridge."

"I don't know. *I* didn't see nobody up there. Somebody else seen him."

"But you *did* see him riding a big black horse with a fancy hull?"

"Did I say that?"

"No, you didn't say it. But you're going to tell me now."

"I don't recollect."

"Was he an old man? A Mexican with a white handlebar mustache?"

"I don't recollect."

Moro jerked at the reins. Soledad pulled his head up. She said, "Mr. Arnett, I want to send you back to Cherokee to track my grandfather down. I'll pay you for it." *I think you know where he is.*

"Oh, Christa'mighty, that's all I need." Clabe turned away and flung his hat onto the ground.

"That was my grandfather you saw up there on that ridge. *You know it was.*"

Claiborne bent down to pick up his hat. He said in a muffled voice, "I don't want nothin' to do with it. I don't know nothin' about it."

"Yes you do."

"I never seen that man. I don't know who he is. I don't know what he looks like."

"Oh? Would it refresh your memory if I were to draw you a picture?"

Claiborne laughed and shook his head and said, "I swear to God. This is like playin' snap-the-whip."

"Are you going to help me?"

"I ain't no federal marshal or Texas Ranger."

"You won't do it?"

"No I won't." He swatted the dust off his hat and chunked it onto his head. "It ain't in my line."

Noon.   Claiborne came up from the garden. He said, "Where was he goin'? What was he doin' up there?"

"Who?" Soledad said. She held some cuttings of pomegranate flowers she had taken from the bushes that lined the portico of the east wing, the leaves and orange-red blossoms bunched against her chest. Nearby, Ramón and Raúl had just killed a sheep and they were skinning it. The ewe hung by one leg from a limb of the big mesquite by the adobe wall. Blood dripped from its throat and hung in a coagulating beard from its chin. Flies buzzed around it.

Claiborne said, "That old man. Your granddaddy."

"He was carrying a petition from Santa Angela down to Austin. He and Mr. Peterson and Mr. Blackwell. Until he got to Brady City. In Brady City, he just walked out of the hotel and laced up his saddle and disappeared."

"What for?"

"How do I know what for?" Soledad said angrily. "He rode off into that blue norther. I've questioned everybody that was with him at the time. I've sent two men up to Brady City to nose around. I've been there myself. He just rode off into nowhere."

"What would've made him do that?"

"Nothing. Nothing at all. Look, he owned all this. House, land, stock, all of it was his and it couldn't be taken from him. He owned half the county. He was respected in town. All his help loved him. Some of them've been with him for years. He was a just and generous man. Everyone who knew him loved him. He didn't have any enemies."

"Maybe he just lit out for the hell of it."

You trash. The flowers at her breast shook. Soledad said, "He'd never do anything to hurt me like that."

Ramón cut off the head of the sheep. Raúl rolled the head and skin into a bundle.

Clabe said, "I reckon you . . . like that old man."

"I love him."

"On account of he's your granddaddy."

"That's not it at all. You don't know him. You don't know how gentle and strong-minded he was. If you ever saw him—if that man you saw near Cherokee was my grandfather—then you'd know what kind of man he was. Nobody stepped on his toes. But that isn't it. Everything he touched or had any dealings with seemed to open up and take on strength. I don't know why. Whatever he put his hand to turned out right. But he wasn't bossy or loud. It all came out of his quietness, his gentleness."

"How come you're always makin' such a fuss over him, makin' him out to be somethin' special?"

"I've never told you anything but what's true."

"They ought to put him in gold on top the state capitol!"

"*I won't have you talking to me like that!*"

"A man like that just can't *make* a mistake."

"Of course he can. Everyone does sometimes."

"*So good* he's got ever'body and his granddaddy cottoning up to him. So damn *smart* he's got the law in either hand."

"I never said that."

"Owns all this land, as like as not owns the air I breathe, has got hisself a law profession and an uppity granddaughter. Christ, you'd think he was a white man!"

The air hummed with flies. It sounded like a twister or a lifting blue norther. Soledad said, "*Whiter than you!*"

Clabe stared at her. Abruptly he said, "*Shit!* I wish I'd never *heard* of the sonofabitch!" He squeezed his eyes shut. They sprang open again. His head jerked to one side. "*Ha ha ha! He can sit there and you be talkin' your own tongue and not know he talks it atall! Can look at you like he was ignorant as a stick, not lettin' on who he is atall!"*

Ramón and Raúl stopped their work and looked at him. Clabe stuck his hands out as if he were pushing at something. "Christ! He don't leave me *be!"*

He spun away, bumping into the carcass. The two Mexicans stepped aside. Claiborne stood there a moment, swaying from side to side. His shoulders heaved. His breaths came in harsh gasps. "Christa'might! Christa'mighty! I wish he *was* dead."

He commenced to stumble down toward the garden.

14

THEY were airing the rooms and giving the ceilings and walls their once-a-year washing. It was cool in the dining room with its swiftly-drying walls and wet floor. Just outside the open windows, in the spring sunlight, Juana and Cruzita and Lucia were scrubbing the table and chairs. The room sounded so hollow with all the furniture taken out of it. The *trastero* had been washed and dried and rubbed with oil and fetched back in and Soledad was dusting china and putting it back into the cabinet. This was usually Angelita's chore but Soledad had been restless and irritable and craved some kind of busywork. The clear glass doors of the *trastero* reflected her movements.

Two translucent saucers floated upon a shelf like luminous ghosts. Soledad wiped a third saucer with a damp cloth and put it beside the others on the shelf. She picked up a teacup from among the set of them on the floor. This was Abuelita María's fine Meissen china. It was eggshell thin. Soledad could see her finger through the cup. To drink from it, which she had only done once on what must have been some very special occasion years ago in San Antonio, was to drink from paper, it was that *frágil* and light. She remembered that, emptied of its child's portion of tea and cognac, it had seemed as if the very weight of air could make it shatter. Its scalloped lip was gilded with gold, as was the handle. The inside of the cup was white, the outside cuckoo-egg green with a tiny landscape on the side—an ant-sized man and woman standing together under a tree, the man in knee-britches, three-cornered hat and scarlet coat, the woman in blue jacket and a lavender skirt that stuck out in back like a shelf, behind them a porcelain estate under a tinted porcelain sky. *When tea's poured into the cup the horizon lifts and darkens like a norther, and they'll still stand there. What are they talking about in the flat, glazed air?* Nothing serious. *No horseman will ride up that road out of a slant of snow into the calm under that tree. And men have died, screams torn the air, cries been sent up for one more, one more hour, Mama sunk down into the drownings of pneumonia, Edward's face on the bolster, Granpapá. And these two—these two ninnies still stand here.*

The cup went flat and out of focus. Freckles like flakes on Claiborne's face, the red hair. *What has he to do with my grandfather?* The cup shook in Soledad's hand.

The woman's tiny, flesh-tinted hand was on the man's scarlet sleeve. *Why must she touch? Why must men and women touch?*

If I were a man I could act, I could do something.

Oh, I wish I'd never been born a woman.

15

TODAY was the day to clean the up-
stairs. After breakfast Ramón and Vicente fetched the mattresses and carpets down from the bedrooms. They lurched
through the open doorway, hefting a double mattress, almost bumping into Soledad. "*Perdóneme, Patroncita,*" one of
them said.

Soledad came out onto the gallery. The early-morning
sunlight was from such a low angle it felt like it was pushing at
her. She put a hand to her eyes. *This stupid headache*—she had
waked up earlier with the front of her head pounding. *Maybe
work will help.*

"*Buenos días, Patroncita. Buenos días, hijita,*" Juana and
Lucía and Cruzita said. They were hanging rugs and blankets
over the gallery rails. A carpet, already soaked with water, lay
on the floor at the end of the gallery.

Angelita came out of the house with an armload of blankets. "*¡Estamos listos*—are we ready?" she said. "*¡Ay!* What a
lovely morning! Are you feeling any better, Cholita?" she said.

"I'm all right, *corazón.*" The pain pounded in Soledad's
forehead. *The thing to do is to get to work.* She supervised the
spreading out of a few blankets here and there. Then she
heisted the hem of her skirt and tucked it into her waistband,
fetched up a bucket of hot water that sat at the top of the steps
and carried it over to the carpet. Tía Lupita came out of the
house and sat in her willow chair.

The women scrubbed the carpet with suds of *amole* root
and rinsed it with fresh water. Soledad's black sleeves kept

sliding down her arms. Of a sudden she felt as if she were about to weep, her head hurt so and there was such a heaviness in her breast.

"You don't need to work so hard, *hijita*," Lucía said.

"I want to," Soledad said. She scrubbed at the carpet. It made her feel some better.

When the carpet was done Ramón and Vicente carried it around to the side of the house and spread it on the portico to dry.

The women commenced to scrub one of the mattresses. *Sacahuista* pads hissed. The iridescent brown suds had an earthy smell.

Juanita said, "You're so quiet this morning, *Patroncita*."

"She has a headache, poor dear," Angelita said.

"No. No. It's nothing," Soledad said.

Angelita said, "This afternoon I shall fix you a tonic— *un tónico*. It's this spring heat that thins the blood."

At noon, when the heat was lifting from the ground and the leaves of the sycamore were sodden with heat and all the insects were stilled and the mattresses had been laid out in the sunlight—the wetness shrinking almost instantly from the ticks—Cruzita and Juanita and Lucía, glasses of *agua fresca* in their hands, rested in the shade of the sycamore while Angelita went into the house to prepare dinner and Soledad and Tía Lupita retreated into the parlor.

Even in here it wasn't cool, but the darkness helped Soledad's headache. Lupita walked over to a window. She said, "I never thought the day would come when I'd have to speak to you like this."

She stared out the window for a moment, then turned back to Soledad. "You must get out of your black, Cholita. You must wear something bright, something with flowers in it."

"I've told you. I prefer black."

"You are so obstinate. It makes me angry. I know you're not wearing that black for your brother."

"What do you mean?"

"Please, dear heart, it isn't wise for you to keep on like this. Always sad. Always wearing black. A young pretty thing like you!"

Soledad crossed to the sideboard. She smoothed the scarf on the sideboard but the ironed creases kept springing up. She said, "*I wish I weren't young and I wish I weren't pretty.*" Her head hurt and she felt angry.

"You want to be old like me?"

"At least I wouldn't be pestered all the time with the notion that I've got to keep myself presentable for every stupid male that comes along."

"No, you certainly wouldn't be. I expect you think you're saving yourself for your grandfather. Is that what you're doing?" There was a momentary shift in the light in the room, as if a wing had passed.

"*No.*"

"*You're wearing that black for him.*"

"No I'm *not.*" *Oh, this is horrible.*

"It's what comes of not having a proper respect for religion, of not taking yourself to confess to Padre Cuevas when he comes here, as the rest of us simple folk do. It offends him when you don't come to him." Lupita's voice sounded exactly as Soledad had always imagined *las viejas brujas*—the old witches in the story—might sound when they spoke.

"*Leave me be,*" Soledad said.

Lupita took a step toward her. She said, "Well, your grandfather had no clean hands. He invited it. It's destroying you."

This is too too cruel.

"Mother of God!"

Soledad turned to see Tía Lupita sink to her knees. Lupita, hunched over like a crooked finger, rocked from side to side. "But I've sinned, too," she moaned. "I've stood by and watched this evil grow, this ugly toad squatting on my doorstep."

Tears rushed to Soledad's eyes. "Please. Get up. This is too much," she said. Lupita began to weep, sucking in her breaths with croaking noises. Soledad walked back and forth. Her head felt as if it would burst. She stopped before the hunched figure. "Please, please get up," she said.

Soledad knelt. She caught Lupita in her arms. She said, "It's all right. It's all *right, corazón*."

I wish the earth would crack open and take me into it. I wish my heart would stop right now.

Lupita made a muffled noise at Soledad's breast. "I'm so troubled for you," she said.

"No, I'm all right," Soledad said. Hot tears dripped from Soledad's chin. She helped Lupita to her feet and got her to the *sofacita*. "There. There. There," she said. She held Lupita and rocked her. The head against her breast was as small as a baby's. It felt like a baby's, the small, round hardness. Soledad blinked her eyes. The light in the room was old and motionless. Everything that stood up into it seemed turned to stone. The table. The rocking chair. Even her hand was stone. *This is stone blood forking from my heart.*

Lupita sat upright and looked at Soledad, her head wobbling, her eyes bleary, loose strands of hair sticking out from her filleted coil. She said, "My poor, dear child. You're so beautiful. Why should you ruin your life like this? I don't think even *he* would want that." *Please. Please don't talk to me of that.* Lupita said, "Will you forgive me, dear heart?"

"Yes, of course I do."

Flat. Flat. Flat. Flat. I wish they would lay me on the ground and put a board on me and pile on the stones—flatten out this ache, put a stop to my heart.

She persuaded Guadalupita to lie down on the *sofacita*— "Rest awhile, dear heart"—and planted a dry kiss on the top of her head. Soledad's forehead when she bent over pounded even worse.

Lupita said, "You do forgive me?"

"Yes, I do." Soledad patted the shriveled hand. Then she stood up and walked through the stone air to the rocker. She sat in it. The arms of the rocker were cold against her hands. The carved scrollwork at the back was as cold as ice against her head. She felt feverish. She got up in a moment and went over to the sideboard and opened the top drawer and took out a napkin and wet it with water from the carafe that sat on a saucer on the sideboard. In the rocker again she leaned back and spread the wet folded napkin on her forehead. She shut her eyes. They were gritty. Orange blood blared in her eyelids. She opened her eyes.

The mail lay on the worktable beside her. Copies of the *Galveston News* in yellow and the *San Antonio Herald* in brown wrappers, letters from Ian and Esperanza, various bills. Cook had fetched the mail from town late last night and Angelita had put it on the table. Soledad had been too tired to look at it. She reached across now and picked up the two letters. Tía Lupita seemed already to be asleep. Soledad let the letter from Esperanza drop into her lap and opened the letter from Ian.

> *Sister. Sam Foss came back from Cherokee again. Granpapá was killed last February, shot by a man named Claiborne Sanderlin who has lit out, according to all we can find out. Our informant is a man named Emmitt Tibbs. Father and Sam and I are going back up there.*

Soledad's blood stopped, her brain lay severed in halves. There was no feeling at all in her. She sat there for the longest time—hours, years—but they were years in which nothing changed, not even the horror of a rug or a table scarf. Then with a lurch her heart started to beat again. *Am I still here?* "Oh! Oh! Am I still here?"

Lupita moaned on the *sofacita*.

Claiborne Sanderlin? *Claiborne*—Arnett? Soledad's headache was gone.

She got up from the rocker. She'd forgotten the wet napkin on her forehead. It fell off and plopped onto the carpet. The letters fluttered from her lap. She started to cross to the doorway. Suddenly she felt light-headed. She stood still for a moment until her head cleared.

Lupita sat up on the *sofacita*. She said, "Where are you going, *corazón*?"

"Nowhere. I'm not going anywhere."

"Do you want me to come with you?"

"I'm just going down the hallway for a moment."

"Tell Angelita not to bring me anything for dinner. I don't feel well. Just a cup of tea will do."

Soledad's footsteps sounded distant in the hallway, disconnected and far away.

In the kitchen Angelita was folding a napkin over hot tortillas. Soledad said, "Tell Ramón to saddle Moro."

"But señorita, we're going to eat soon."

"Tell him to fetch my horse. Now. ¡*Ándale*!"

Soledad went up to her grandfather's bedroom. She pulled open a drawer in the chiffonier. She picked up a walnut box from beside her grandfather's starched, pressed shirts and set it on the chiffonier. She opened the box, took out a target pistol. It was her grandfather's pistol. Blue barrel and checkered walnut stock. It had a twelve-inch barrel and weighed three pounds. She'd used it before, had had to hold it with both hands in order to aim it. A box of cartridges was in the drawer—*J. Stevens Co., Chicopee Falls, Mass.*—and she took up a handful. She breeched the pistol and thumbed a cartridge into it. Then she went for a moment to her room.

The bush shook. Bark and dust and leaves flew in all directions. *Yes, it does work.* The silence after the explosion crowded Soledad's ears. She thumbed a fresh cartridge into the barrel.

The world stood still in the noon heat. Light fitted down onto everything, solid as an iron mold, and held it there. Only Soledad and Moro moved through the immense, white silence. The burning air had stifled the noise of insects, turned to gas in the lungs of birds. It hurt to breathe. Already Moro's flanks and withers were lathered.

Stones, hills, trees in their stiffness seemed to stare at Soledad as she rode through the heat. The pistol (twisted end of the pillowslip tucked into the double horn) swung at her knees. Moro crossed a bed of fossils, an open slope where shoals of stone oyster shells and ram's-horn coils of snails were locked in the chalky rock. He picked up the narrow track through the brush again. His hoofs made muffled noises in the powdery dust. Brush scraped his shoulders—hiss of whispery branches as they caught at Soledad's skirt. The sun was fierce, the brush a brittle sea of mirrors. Polished leaves fractured the light, which stabbed like splinters at her eyes. *Oh, it's too cruel.*

"Wearing that black." "Saving yourself for." Shot. By a man named.

¡Ay! ¡Ay! Soledad leaned forward in the saddle and vomited. When the spasms quit she pulled the kerchief from her waistband and wiped her chin and mouth and cleaned the clabbery splatterings from her skirt. Tossed the kerchief away. The horse hadn't changed pace. The pistol swung at her knee.

Grab hold of the saddle horn and it'll get you there. That much at least. That much at least.

Cow trails converged onto the main trail, widening the track. Moro topped a rise. Here was the water lot. They followed the stake-and-rider fence down toward the river. The lot, a large one of about seventeen hectares that included a quarter-mile section of the river, was dry and stony here, dotted with baked cowplops and an occasional mesquite. Some sheds and feed racks simmered in the heat. Clabe's sorrel stood in the thin shade of a mesquite tree, its head down, dozing, switching its tail. Soledad rode along the fence toward three live oaks. They were big trees, with long, horizontal branches, and cast a dense shade. The short, thick trunks rose out of pools of darkness. A small cedar-picket cabin was under the largest of them. Clabe's saddle was on the fence. Soledad rode past a dead campfire with dirty dishes alongside and a skillet and a blackened coffeepot. Flies lifted from the skillet. A locust chirred in one of the live oaks. Soledad rode into the shade under the trees. She reined in Moro. She said, "*Is there anyone here?*"

The flies hummed above the skillet. A lizard skittered up a tree trunk.

Soledad prodded Moro and rode up to the cabin. She dismounted and wrapped the reins around a post near the door. She grabbed hold of the post. She felt light-headed again. After a spell it was better. She went to the open doorway and stuck her head in. There weren't any windows—it was as black as pitch inside. It smelled of salt and musty tow sacks. She said, "*Is anyone here?*"

"You lookin' for me?"

Soledad stepped back out of the doorway.

Claiborne was outside, at the corner of the cabin. The sunlight was behind him and she almost couldn't make him out. She passed a hand in front of her face, trying to brush the glare from her eyes.

Clabe came toward her. She could see him better now. It looked as if he hadn't washed in weeks. His face was streaked with dust and sweat. Dirt rings creased his neck and a rash of orange stubble was cropping from his chin. His clothes looked as if he'd been sleeping in them. He stopped a few steps from her. There was a cut on his forehead, caked and black, that went from his eyebrow up under his hat brim.

Soledad said, "How'd you get that?"

"Fell down and knocked my head on a rock yesterday. Sonofabitch."

The thick, fat snake-like branches of the live oak slid through their leaves overhead. Clabe brushed a fly from his face. Of a sudden a rush of flies swarmed in Soledad's head. Her grandpapa lay on the ground. Flies lit on his face, ants and sow bugs crawled in the streaked, bloody grass. Streaked, bloody mustache. Claiborne's rust-flaked face hung like a petty sun above it. *The hand that brought Grandpapa down!* It was as if Clabe's hand were flinging flies onto that face. *He has killed Grandpapa. I will make him say it!* Soledad blinked her eyes. Flies buzzed above the skillet. The shade under the trees was a dark, heavy weight.

Soledad said, "It's stifling here, even in the shade."

"That ain't no news to me."

"This place is a mess. What do you do down here?"

"Get off your damn high horse."

The bush shook, bark and dust and leaves flew in all directions. Soledad took a deep breath. She said, "I didn't hire you to give me a lot of back talk."

"You hired me to twist my arm behind my back."

"You talk to me like that?"

"Get off your high horse."

"I'll get off my high horse," Soledad said in a rage. "I'll make you eat backwater. I'm not afraid of you or any man." She took a step toward him.

"No, you ain't, at that."

"I gave you work but I didn't hire your sass into the bargain."

"Christ, a shot of whiskey'd—"

"You're going to tell me where you saw my grandfather." Soledad was breathing hard.

"I don't know nothin' about him."

"Yellow slicker. Horse with stocking feet? You don't know 'nothin' about that?"

"How'm I suppose to know about that?"

"Out of your own mouth, Mr.—'Arnett.' I've got ears. A big black stud with quarter-stockinged feet."

"I never said that."

Soledad stared at him a moment. She felt better now. But her heart was still pounding as if it was going to jump out of her mouth. Her palms prickled. She wiped them on her skirt. They seemed to feel every wool thread in the weave. She said, "You were up in those canyons last spring. What happened up there?"

"Where?"

"Outside Cherokee. You know where."

Clabe kicked at a stone. It clicked and skittered across the ground. "I t-told you. We was roundin' in stock."

Soledad snorted. "Oh yes, in a blue norther. I've looked up Cherokee on the map. That's southeast of Tom Green and McClintock counties. There must have been plenty of cattle drifted down to there. It sounds like a profitable piece of thievery."

Claiborne said, "You keep puttin' words in my mouth."

I'm going to kill you, Soledad thought. "What happened when he came down?"

"Who come down?"

"The man you saw up on the ridge there."

"Goddamn you, get off my back."

"That horse was sold up to Kansas, Mr. 'Arnett.' My grandpapa's horse. It was sold out of Cherokee on the eighteenth of February. That's two or three days after my grandfather turned up missing. We'll find that horse—my father has sent up to Kansas to track him down. We'll find out who bought that horse and we'll find out who sold it."

Claiborne said, "You do that."

"Did my grandfather come down?"

Clabe shut his eyes. A big, humped-up vein pulsed his forehead. "I'm tired of talkin' about him"—spittle flew from his mouth—"tired of bein' told ever'thing he done. How he built this and run that, bossed this and bossed that, run for the state legislature for all I know, built hisself a fancy sawboard house, put up a courthouse, fetched water out of dry ground." His eyes sprang open again. "Fancy horse, fancy saddle, fancy duds. Goddammit, you'd think he rid out of the White House itself! I wish he'd of never . . . I wish . . ." He seemed not to be seeing anything.

Soledad took a step toward him. She said, "*Did he come down?*"

Clabe blinked. He stared at her. "*Who?*"

"*My grandfather.*"

Suddenly Claiborne began to laugh. "And him a *Meskin*! Who'd ever think I'd be—bound to a *Meskin*!"

"*I know you saw him.*"

Clabe quit laughing. He ran the tip of his tongue along his upper lip. He spat onto the ground and said, "No, I never."

Soledad trembled. She felt the sickness rising again in her gullet. She fumbled at her waistband and caught hold of the cabinet picture and plucked it out, thrust it at him. "*And what about this?*"

White dress, white face, white sleeves on spindle-stiff arms. It shook in her hand.

Clabe didn't say anything for a moment. He looked almost embarrassed. He shifted and cleared his throat and said, "What about it?"

Soledad flung the photograph onto the ground. She said, "*I'll* tell you about it! Your 'friend' Wash Delong fetched that out here. He found it among your belongings. Back in town there. You got that off my grandfather. He came down into that canyon. *You're going to tell me what happened to him there.*"

"S-s-s-s-send him to hell in a handbasket! He don't leave me be! Christ, I can't *breathe*. Come down and put his c-claim on me. He done it apurpose! He . . . He . . . He . . ." Clabe stood stock still, his mouth open, but nothing came out of it.

His eyes were dry and bright. Of a sudden he hit his fist against his thigh, gave a queer laugh. He said, "Soledad, Ma'm, please . . ." He took a step toward her. She stepped back.

"*What happened to him there?*"

Claiborne stared at her a moment. A nerve twitched on the side of his face. His left eye blinked. He said, "Christ, I'm done with it. To hell with it." He was shaking as if he had chills. "I ain't gonna break my balls tryin' to t-talk to you no more." He took off his hat and swatted it at his britches. He managed to get it back onto his head. The side of his face and the edge of his mouth were twitching violently. He turned and started to walk toward the end of the cabin, lurching like a drunkard.

Soledad swung around and stepped back to Moro. She jerked the pillowslip from between the double horn. The target pistol clunked as it slid across the saddle dish. She said, "Mr. Sanderlin! Mr. Sanderlin!" She got hold of the checkered stock and shook off the pillowslip. She pulled the hammer back with both thumbs.

Clabe turned to her. She said, "Oh yes, I know your name! You're going to tell me what happened to my grandfather. Or I'm going to kill you."

He started walking toward her. She held the gallery pistol in front of her with both hands, aimed it directly at him. She said, "I've knocked the necks off bottles with this." She said, "You got that picture off my grandfather. You're going to tell me what happened to him in Cherokee."

He kept coming toward her. He walked with a jerky, spastic motion, his hand out as if he meant to take the pistol from her. She said, "*You stop right there.*"

Clabe made a queer, croaking sound. He kept coming toward her. "*Do it,* if that's what you aim to. Goddammit, I won't take nothin' back. He *was comin' at me. He went to make me do it.*" He said, "*Give me that.*"

Soledad took a step back. Claiborne said, "*Do it, dam-*

mit, do it!" He was almost to her. He said, "Oh . . . my . . . god, woman . . ."

His face was drenched with sweat. He said, *"Yes. I. Done. It. I b-blasted the l-l-l-liver and lights out of him.* And you'n me . . ." His head jerked to one side. He half-turned in that direction, his hands groping. He let out a screech and fell to the ground.

I'll kill you! Kill you! Soledad went to him. His body was stiff and a slight, rhythmic trembling went through it. A wet splotch spread on his britches. His eyes were open. All that showed were the whites. His lips were pulled back from bared, clenched teeth. He seemed not to be breathing. He began to shake all over, arching his back and kicking his heels at the ground. His face of a sudden turned blue. He made a sharp, gurgling noise and lay still. Soledad aimed the pistol at him.

Killed Grandpapa! Oh, Lord God!

Clabe's chest began to heave. His arms and legs moved. The crusted cut bled on his forehead.

A fly lit onto his face.

Gaping mouth, the streaked, bloody mustache? What's— all—this—blood? Oh Grandpapa, it's you! Your face, your face, your face!

Oh, Mother! Oh, dear Edward!

All that dying.

Claiborne looked as flushed and pink as a new baby.

Soledad wept. She turned aside and aimed the pistol at the ground. Held back on the hammer so that it could not fire and pulled the trigger. She eased the hammer down.

She would have liked to put it to her own head.

THREE

16

CLAIBORNE reached down to stir the breakfast beans in the fry pan. A fly buzzed into the air. *Why didn't she shoot me?* The beans bubbled in the pan. *Shit, I ain't hungry. You ain't ate in two days. I don't give a damn.* The fly lit onto his knee. It rubbed its wispy forefeet together, then, propped up on its front legs, rubbed its hind feet along the outer edges of its wings. He brushed it from his knee. *I wish my brain was a slate. Wipe the slate clean! For certain sure I spilled everything yesterday. Why didn't she shoot me, wipe the slate clean?*

Soledad's face, the mouth and dark eyes. Clabe felt a grief beat in him. *Well, I feel some better since I told.*

Kissed her on the neck. Kissed her on the mouth. What I want to—.

The wound in don Reyes' chest crusted up. It closed like a mouth. Don Reyes sat up. He stood up and said, "Adiós." He turned and walked away. The wind blew. The yellow slicker lay across the withers of the big blood black.

It won't quit. I am plumb wore out.

The fly diddled its feet together on Clabe's sleeve. Clabe spooned a few beans into a dish and commenced to eat them. He stood up and his backbone popped. His joints felt stiff. *She aimed the gun at him. Wanted* her to shoot, wanted the kick of the bullet through him so he'd know he was real. *Got to connect someways. How was it Leona one time said?* "Sufferin' the wound for the sake of the blessin'."

Shimmer of midmorning heat off the stones and dried

cowplops in the water lot. Already late morning by the sun. The shade under the sheds and feeders was as black as the devil's ass-end. Not a lick of breeze. Clabe took a notion to walk on down to the river.

Here was the water trickling between rocks. *The body lay on the rocks. The rocks were stained red. It lay on the rocks as if it never had been alive, only that the blood around it said it had.* "Enough blood to paint a house." "You sure blowed the liver and lights out of him, Red." *Christ, what all have I gone and done?*

Clabe stumbled to the pond. Branches swatted his face and caught at his shoulders. He grabbed hold of a willow switch to get his balance back. Blue ducks lifted from the pond. Clabe sat on a rock. *Touch me, Soledad. Wipe the slate clean.* Tears rushed to Clabe's eyes. They came with a hot suddenness as if they'd been wrung directly from his blood. *A man don't cry.* Still his body shook.

After a spell he quieted. *Sunlight on Soledad's hands, sheen of the tight, black cuffs.*

Once Leona found me in the woodshed, wrung out from cryin' and all snucked up. On account of some mite little thing Mr. Sanderlin'd asked me to do and I'd gave him some sass. He hadn't said a word after that but looked like he thought a heap less of me, and I run into the woodshed where I figured nobody'd find me and opened up. Leona took me into the kitchen and washed my face and we had a talk.

Black apron and blue dress. Could find rest against that apron and dress.

The blue ducks lit back down onto the pond. They dove and skimmed away, scattering the water drops. Back behind Clabe some springs splashed down the bluff.

The sun beat down. Snake doctors hovered over the water. The surface of the pond was smooth. *Christa'mighty.* Clabe jerked off his boots. He fetched up from the rock, took two steps and bellyflopped into the water, shirt, britches and whatever all came along in his pockets. *That feels good.* He splashed around in the water for a spell. The pond was about three feet deep, warm on the surface and cold as a witch's tit underneath. Clabe waded out and shucked off his clothes, spread them on the rocks to dry and bellyflopped back in. He pushed off from the bottom of the pond, paddling like a coon. Water spiders skittered away on top of the water.

Water slicked past Clabe's skin, ticklings of weed. He stood up and waded ashore, drizzling water onto the rocks. Hot sun. He walked over to a buttonbrush and sat in the shade. The hot air dried his skin so fast it raised a chill. *Her body in her dress. Her body naked, slid through the water, white arms and legs, milk-white turn of her hip*

length of don Reyes washed in water or tears limbs smooth and wet sunken belly

skin looks younger there. Christ Christ Christ it don't look like an old man atall young man's self *like somebody'd washed ever' sign of time off him—what was in me to do it?*

"Whiter than you!" The skinned sheep swung in the air. *"How come you're always makin' him out to be somethin' special?" "I love him."* A terrible sadness came over Clabe. It was the sense of her tenderness, her self that waits by lamplight, that puts a plate down to the table for don Reyes. Yes, *for the señor don Reyes!* Claiborne had a sick feeling in the bottom of his stomach.

Back up at the cabin Clabe ate some more beans. Already his shirt was soaked again with sweat. *Get in the shade, you shikepoke. That's some better.* He sat against the trunk of one of the live oaks and shoved beans into his mouth with a jackknife.

Up in a corner of the lot Clabe's horse rubbed its nose against the fence, swished its tail. A ladybug lit onto Clabe's sleeve. Red back, two black dots. When he held his arm up it climbed up, when he held it down it turned around and climbed up.

Clabe blew on the beetle. Its back split open. Crinkly wings poked out and it flew away. *Soledad's hand on don Reyes' face, on the marble stare.* The hair lifted along the back of Clabe's neck, his skin tightened and pebbled. *I done that. What all did I do it for? It ain't only I shouldn't of. Somethin' brung me to do it. Somethin'—.* His guts knotted. *Don Reyes walked toward him, his black sombrero punching the sky. A dark fierceness was in his eyes—eyes that lit onto Clabe like a hawk. Yes I know you. From a long ways back. Ha ha ha. We're no strangers, no.*

Jesus Christ.

Clabe jumped up in a sweat. He went into the cabin. Inside, in the dark, he felt along the wall, pulled a corn shuck out of the sheaf tucked into a chink between two pickets. His hands were shaking. He fumbled in the pockets of his jacket on the wall and fetched out a plug of Little Rosebud. Back outside he shaved tobacco off the plug onto the shuck, scattering half the shavings onto the ground. Managed to roll the shuck and twist one end. *I'm gonna die before I get it lit.* Fished around in the ashes of the cookfire until he found a live coal. With a lot of sucking he lit his smoke. *This damn thing is half air.* Then the glow hit some tobacco and the hot, thick fumes filled his lungs. He could feel the easefulness of it going all through him. He let it out through his nose. The blue smoke held for a moment in front of his face then spread into a thinned-out veil as it began to drift away.

Toward dark Clabe parched some coffee beans in the fry pan, stirring them to keep them from burning. Ground them on a washed stone. Filled the coffeepot two-thirds full of cold water and dumped in a handful of the parched Arbuckle. While the coffee was boiling he chewed on some dried apples. *Sick to death of food.* He spat out the wad of rubbery, sulphur-tasting apple. *Nothin' sets right with me. This dark-brown taste in my disposition.*

Took the pot of coffee off the fire and added a dash of

cold water to settle the grounds. Poured himself a cup of coffee. Pinch of salt. *Think I could live on this and smokes.*

The round, white face. Soledad!

The moon came up out of the low, cedar-splotched hill
to the east like a clipped dollar through a slot. *She ain't done
with me yet. No, she ain't done with me yet!*

Moonlight flooded in through the cabin doorway.
Crickets were cricking outside like the makings of a Baptist
choir. Claiborne lay on his pallet. The night breeze hissed
through the cabin chinks. *Soledad's face, motion of her hand as
she brushed back a strand of loose hair.* A terrible grief came on
Clabe. *To have the knowing of her!* He shook as if he was
having a fit of chills. His grief and craving for Soledad took
the breath clean out of him. The sense of her being went
through him like a streak of light. Every parcel of Clabe's self
went toward her in a grief of tenderness.

The night breeze scraped the ground, hissed through the
live oak leaves.

She ain't done with me yet.

Birdpeep. Daylight. Coming up from under the water of
sleep. *What all have I gone and done? Killed a one that Soledad—.
Yes, that she—. Killed a one that walked the ground, that laid out
money to feed his get and kin, run a ranch a way I won't never
come in spittin' distance of, built a courthouse, made a town. Had
white folks cottoning up to him. Christ, I have laid that out. I have
put a hole through that.*

*What I've done is killed a man. Yes, goddammit, a man
better'n me.*

He went out to take a piss. The yellow stream darkened
the rock it spattered on. *Why'd I go to kill him? What brung me
to do it?*

      Coming at me

              no, it weren't only that. Shook it and

tucked it back in, tucked his shirt into his britches. *What brung me to do it? On account of I hate Meskins? I think I hate Meskins*

　　　round, white face: "I'm part Mexican"

　　　　　　　　　　　　　　　　those black eyes!

It's this restlessness.

　　The oil lamp chimney next the washbasin exploded like a firecracker. The world came apart like a busted bale. Nothin' fits anyplace for me.

　　The whole east was white. *Another damn day.*

　　It's myself I hate. Shit. Christ.

　　Regulated the sizzling contents of the fry pan with a sharpened stick.

　　Have parsed it out a million times before. How come I have them fits? Pitched onto the ground—that claybank horse out to Bradford's? No, it come before that. I know that. It's this meanness in me. Things fall apart. Never did like what I am. What all's that? Me. The me that don't fit nowheres. Like I done somethin' wrong somewheres a long ways back and've been regular kicked in the ass for it since.

　　Kicked out on my ass? Into this busted-apart world? Done what wrong? Bein' bornt? Ha. Ha ha ha!

　　Bornt! Crap. I didn't have no hand in the bid.

　　He put the fry pan aside. *Ain't got no taste for nothin'. Christ, that sun. Hot enough to sunburn a horned toad.*

　　Kicked out on my ass. Into this God-awful lonesomeness, where it don't nothin' fit, that's what is it. Alone: that's what bein' bornt is. Shit.

　　Don't want to think. I am fed up with thinkin'.

　　Clabe walked down to the river and rinsed his neck and face. The sunlight felt like it was coming out of the water or out of the weeds and bushes themselves. *And he don't get off my back.* "Goddamn you to hell," Claiborne said, shaking a fist at don Reyes. "I don't know whether you come to wreck me or just mop up the ground with me some. *Get the hell out of my life!*" Clabe picked up a good-sized rock and hove it at the water. It sent a few snake doctors scattering but didn't do a whole lot of good.

The sun moved on overhead. Clabe slapped a twine on his horse Lingo and snubbed him down. *Anything to keep from thinkin'.* Headstall and bit. Flung on the hull and drew up the cinch. When Clabe went to take the rope off the horse the bastard tried to bite his leg. Clabe swatted Lingo's nose with his hat and lit on up. Lingo started out on a straight buck then changed to a zigzag. He jumped all over the place. Clabe couldn't see for the dust. Finally the prick-eared sonofabitch got the kinks out of his tail and Clabe rode him out of the lot. Lingo didn't give him any trouble after that.

He has done his do. Clabe leaned forward and touched the gelding on the neck. *Good solid horse flesh. Horse brain and heart and lights. The all-to-hisself horseness.*

The thing is, Lingo don't know *he's alone. On account of he don't* remember. *Not like a man does. I seen a coyote caught in a trap once and it struck me—lookin' in his eyes—struck me he'd about made up his mind it hadn't never been no way but that. Figure this damn horse has clean forgot I ever lit up. I just been here forever. For now, anyways.*

It's this knowin' *that hurts.*

Way off on a flat, so far off and small it looked to Clabe like he could have held them in his fist— so far off he couldn't even *hear* it—somebody riding a horse. Racing through the huisache and cedar, trailing a cloud of dust. *It's that plump one from the kitchen, Angelina. Look at her go.* Her hair flew in a long black streamer behind her. *But no Soledad.* Had seen the two of them twice before, riding hell for leather, their shrieks floating through a mile of standing air, Angelina on the strawberry roan, Soledad on the big blood black.

The big blood black came down the side of the draw. White blaze. Three quarter-stockinged feet. And the yellow slicker, the tall black sombrero. Don Reyes' face was like dark, rained-on fieldstone. He came toward Clabe so terrible slow, like he'd come out of another country where nothing moves faster than a stone might grow and a bird hangs half a morning to a note.

Shit. Claiborne put the spurs to Lingo and galloped him up a slope. The heat cut the horse's wind. Clabe reined him in. Mesquite. Prickly pear. *Christ, this is poor country.*

A mile off, above the rolling limestone hills, an eagle was flying in a circle. It was acting mighty peculiar. It would drop to the ground and then rise and circle again. Is that a *bird*? Wingspread big enough to cover a horse. When Clabe got nearer, he saw it was after a young deer. It would drop down and catch the deer by its loins, just in front of its hips, and flip it head over heels. The third time the deer didn't try to get up.

The black came down the side of the draw. It was bad-gaunted. It rode the brush . . .

He ain't no stranger, no. Come out of that loneness, that no-wheres. I been there, too.

There ain't a man don't come out of that loneness, don't live in it. Christ, a body moves through this world, lays on his pallet and stands hisself up, and he don't touch no more than a bull-thistle blowin' through air. Come out of nowheres and goin' through no-wheres and gonna end up nowheres. A man might's well not live if he's gonna think on it. It'll kill him dead.

Is that what them long-necked preachers keep poundin' their bibles about? "Drove Adam out of Eden" with an all-fired sword up his ass. It don't tickle. It sure don't . . .

You sonofabitch, you have laid your claim on me.

Clabe woke. The explosion sounded in his head. He

fired again. *I know I shot twice.* The black sombrero flew off, the man's hair was scattered light.

Didn't go to do it. But it's like I had to do it.

That wind can blow. Buckshot sleet and powdery snow. Then it was quiet. And he come down, draggin' that white and quiet behind him—so white it's dark, like the new sun blinds your eyes. All that aloneness. It was like he was gonna rub my face in it! Flung myself back and pulled the trigger.

I want to quit this fuckin' thinkin'. Shit!

But I ain't never felt no wrongfulness for that. Not no wrongfulness. Not that I done it, but the horribleness. *On account of it's like I was made to do it. To be bornt into this hell of aloneness and him to rub my face in it!*

The head back, the white mustache streaked with blood, blood curling from the mouth. His shirt front was soaked red. San Antonio. Alto Springs. Tres Coronas. Soledad.

Goddammit! I want it to quit!

Come out of that high weather like he was aloneness itself. Like the dark had crossed him!

There ain't a man ain't crossed by the dark. It's all the same, Meskin or white. A man does his do and says his say, lives this way or thataway, has any color hair or eyes—his outward show. But in his guts it's the same damn thing. Alone. Wouldn't matter, if a body didn't know it. If a body didn't know a peck of things. That's the hell of it, that's the dark of it, the bruised black-and-blue of it: this damn knowin'.

Peeled off the yellow slicker and flung it over the saddle. He came toward Clabe. The black sombrero flapped.

It's myself comin' at me!

Shit, it's my own self.

Who all's gonna forgive me what I done? Who all's gonna forgive what all I am? Maybe when I was bornt I was pure as a new-dropped lamb. Now look at the piled-up shit of it. Shoved half-

assed into the come-apart world. One sonofabitchin', goddamned man. Christ, Claiborne, you ain't much. You are one damn poor show. So damn lonesome you'd take a polecat for company. Can't make nothin' fit. Keep havin' them fits. Got a hate in you big enough to black out the sun. And scared shitless. Yes you are, you sonofabitch—scared enough you went and killed a man. Christ, I could cry for the pity of you. Could cry for the pity of him.

There ain't a man ain't alone.

Jesus forgive me. There ain't nobody and nothin' gonna forgive me. She won't *forgive me.*

I forgive myself.
I forgive myself for bein' myself, for the damn heft and sonofabitchin' taste of me. For bein' all what I am. You poor show, somebody's got to have mercy on you. I do forgive you. I do. Forgive all what you are. Forgive what you went and done, the poor, scared meanness that was in you to do it. I do. I do.
I forgive these trees. And this dirt. And the hell-fired sun.
I do.
I forgive myself.
I forgive him.

The next morning Claiborne took a notion to shave. While he was lathering, the cook rode up on a small white mare. He was all dudded up, checkered shirt, kip boots, a flannel suit with the britches tucked into the boots, blue, leather-beaked fireman's cap. An alligator carpetbag was behind the cantle. Claiborne said, "Where all are you headed? Looks like a firemen's convention or a brush-arbor bible meetin', one."

"This here's my Fourth of July infare outfit," Cook said. "Don't you know day after tomorrow's Fourth of July?"

"I'd clean forgot about time."

"Fourth of July don't mean nothin' around here." The

cook took his teeth out of his mouth and then put them back in. "I'm headed into Krugerville to buy next year's fat and flour. While I'm there, I'll have myself one high old time. They have a big to-do Fourth of July in Krugerville. All them patriotic Germans there, you know. It's the one time a year I get to go on a good drunk."

"Wish I was goin' along with."

"I come out here to tell you you're wanted up to the house."

"What all for?"

"I don't know. Miss Lita said for me to send you on up."

17

SCRAPS of paper. Her grandfather's slight, Andalusian script on the backs of envelopes, on newspaper wrappings, on the edges of receipts, on whatever, apparently, had been to hand. She had found them in his desk three days ago. She had gone upstairs to Grandfather's study and unlocked the desk and let down the dropleaf. Pigeonholes stuffed with bills and receipts. Loose papers. Cork-tipped pens. A bottle of Sanford's ink with dried ink turned to rust around the rim. She had found the papers in a small, green, gilt-edged book at the back of the desk. *I don't want to remember that!* But she couldn't keep the words out of her mind.

pursuit of fate in the arms of chaos

as lovely as was once her grandmother

> *The mask of habit. Have clothed ourselves in all appearances. Eat with a spoon, the bed supports our weight, we have signed papers that force the leaves onto the trees. Have dressed ourselves in floors doors buttons clouds knives, in twelve o'clock and units of ten. This is the cause and that is the cause and the mockingbird sings all our reasons*

So weary. I do not sleep anymore.

□

El mundo solamente es—¡eventos! The world is only—
events!
¡Y vientos!—Winds!

Among the papers was a card

> A la sombra del árbol santo de la Cruz, ayer a
> las ocho de la noche, voló al seno de su Criador
> el alma del
> ## SR. AUGUSTIN GUERRERO SALGADO
> ## (ESPOSO Y PADRE)
> Sus atribulados esposa y hijo piden para él ora-
> ciones a la piedad de sus hermanos en Jesucristo.
> San Antonio, Septiembre 23 de 1876

on the back of which he had written *Three times I argued his
land-grant case in court. Still the Americans took everything.*

Soledad had taken the papers and the gilt-edged book
downstairs and burned them in the kitchen fire. She had been
ill for three days. She had spent the nights in her room and
the days down here in the parlor. "Leave me alone," she had
said. She had hardly eaten in three days. A hand bell and
some half-empty coffee cups and a silver water pitcher and
washbasin were on the low rosewood table in front of the sofa.
A fly buzzed in one of the cups. Soledad's hands felt hot and
dry. Her face and neck were as hot as if she had a fever. She
was wearing her nightdress and a black *stambre*, or jersey
shawl, as she had the past three days. She put back a blanket
from her lap, leaned forward from the *sofacita*, moistened a

napkin in the basin and dampened her face and neck. *Yes, I'll fire him.* The parlor windows were open. There was still a hint of early-morning coolness in the room, but she could hardly breathe. *I'll send him away.* The lace curtains at the windows, tied back by tasseled cords, hung motionless as nets. A dove called from a thicket down by the bluff.

Somebody coughed softly on the other side of the parlor door. "Who is it?" Soledad said.

"*Yo*," Angelina said. "The señor is here."

"Send him in." Soledad drew the blanket back across her lap. She pulled the shawl tighter around her.

The door opened and Angelina stood aside to let Claiborne in. He looked clean-shaven and washed but still in the same dirty clothes.

"Take out these cups," Soledad said.

"*Sí, Patroncita,*" Angelita said. She gathered up the three half-empty coffee cups and went out, closing the door behind her.

Claiborne Arnett—Claiborne *Sanderlin*—held his hat in his hands. His red hair was plastered down with water.

I hate you.

"Don't just stand there!" Soledad said.

Clabe came over to one of the straight-backed chairs on the other side of the table and stood awkwardly behind it.

Soledad said, "Why did you fall down like that?"

"Like what?"

"The other day. Out in the water lot."

Clabe stared at the seat of the chair. Suddenly Soledad had the sense again of his body—slight-boned and vulnerable and likely, under the shirt, white-skinned. She shook her head to get the image out of her mind.

Clabe said, "I was—havin' a fit."

She said, "I don't want to hear about it." She said, "What happened when he came down into that canyon?"

"Who?"

"You know who." It seemed airless in the room, hot and

close as if sound couldn't move through it, as if nothing could move through it, not here or anywhere in the world. The skin prickled on the back of her neck.

Clabe still held his hat in his hand. With his other hand he gripped the back of the chair. Red hairs at his wrist, the freckled backs. *This is the man who killed Grandpapa, had the shooting of him.* Soledad choked back her anger. Claiborne's face with its crowd of rusty freckles was almost like a mask. Abruptly Soledad was frightened, as if the knowledge of her grandfather were somewhere behind that mask.

She pinched the edge of the *sofacita* and took a deep breath. She said, "What happened to him there?"

"You don't want to hear that."

"I *will* hear it."

"He was comin' at me. I didn't know what I was doin'. I had a short rifle in my hand. When I come to he was layin' on the ground. I reckon I done it. They told me I done it. Christ, I wish I'd of never been out there with that bunch!"

Soledad closed her eyes. She pressed her head back against the wall. She had never felt such a grief and rage before in her life. *Blood for blood! I want to be judge and jury both!* She opened her eyes and said, *"Who are you? Why should you live when he doesn't?"*

Claiborne threw his hat onto the chair. He held his hands out to her. He said angrily, "Put a rope around them if you want."

Soledad stood. "Oh, I will, I will!"

Clabe took a step toward her, his hands out in front. "Wrap 'em with hemp. Drag me behind a horse." He held them out a moment longer, then dropped them to his sides. "Goddammit, woman, I been beat enough. You could string me from a cross-trestle, ain't nothin' to what I been through."

"And what about him? What about *him*?"

"One damn blessin'—he ain't got to think and hurt no more."

The room was suddenly so bright it hurt. "You sonofabitch!" Soledad stepped around the table. She hit her shin against the table and almost fell, but she flung herself at Claiborne with terrific force. The wildness of the rage in her was so blinding she couldn't see anything. She only beat against a wall of flesh with her fists.

Claiborne had hold of her wrists. She fought to get free. His face loomed in front of her. It was as bitten with anguish as anything she had ever seen. She threw herself against him and wept.

Claiborne held her. "Christ forgive me. I didn't go to do it. It grieves me what I went and done, what I brung you to." Her tears were bitter. They tasted bitter in her mouth. "Oh, my God," Claiborne said. "I wish I was dead."

Feet in the blue sky. Crisp, white, child's dress. For a minute she was on a swing, up and back, up and back, and Edward was pushing her.

I want to be quit of myself.

Claiborne was kissing her on top of the head. "*I love you, Soledad.*"

He was kissing her face and her hair. Their mouths caught. Her tongue went into his mouth as if it had its own life. She couldn't taste him deep enough—taste this fear, fear of the knowledge that she was all but certain in its clearest moment might kill her. *I want this death.*

He was kissing her on her neck and breast, where the buttons had come undone. Incoherent words were at the bones of her breast. His fingers moved upon her back and hips. Her skin pebbled. When he kissed her, she bit his lip.

He carried her to the *sofacita*. Now he was kissing her breasts and belly through her nightdress. *How can I be doing this?* She stood off watching herself in amazement as her nightdress came up, her knees went apart.

Oh! That hurts!

He pulled back and came into her again. It *hurts!*

He was kissing her on her mouth and neck. And she threw it all away—she threw away clothes and shoes and

words and cups of coffee and eating and needing hate and pin-
ning hats to one's hair and plucking off gloves and tears at
graves and tea at noon and clocks and sofas and cluttered
rooms. Her breasts strained against his chest. His tongue was
in her mouth.

She came up to him. Waves came over her, faster and
faster, deeper and deeper within. The waves were too high,
too often and too dark. They rolled over her and back, over
and back, each withdrawal dragging her back to her old life,
each shuddering-forward lifting her up into the terror, a cry,
collapse of power. Suddenly her body was fetching her out beyond any sanity of choice, the waves tossing her higher and
higher into more of chaos, silence and light, until for an in-
stant she was as clear as a window, transparent to everything.

The glass sh shattered. She

When she opened her eyes the room was stiflingly clear.
The light was of terrific silence and purity. She was stranded
in the calm and every object had the clearest, most definite
edges to it, each entirely a thing of emptiness and yet *here*.
Even the fringed runner of white damask cloth on the mantel
was substanceless and had always been here. Certainly the
ceiling was eternal, and she had a sudden, other glimpse of
herself. It was not what she had ever been before.

A fly buzzed. The clock ticked again on the mantel.

Claiborne's weight was upon her. He smothered her with
kisses. "Soledad! Soledad! Soledad! Soledad! Oh, the sweet-
ness of you! I ain't never loved nobody or nothin' like I do
you. I been dead till now. Oh, Christ, I ain't got a self to live
with no more. It's all gone over to you!"

To hold this flesh in this emptiness. Soledad was filled with
despair. *Her grandfather rode through the storm, the wind a hand
of sleet at his back, his slicker glazed with ice.*

Clabe's face close to hers, green eyes, the orange lashes,
freckles like rusty flakes. *What is it about him that is so—
innocent? The innocence of an animal? Like an animal—yes! It*

doesn't matter what he's done, he might have torn flesh and eaten it, he hasn't any sin.

What are you, an animal or a saint?

Smell of his hair, taste of the sweat on his neck. Sweat joined their naked bellies. "I hate you," she said.

He got right up off her. Soledad sat up on the *sofacita*. There was blood on her nightdress. She said, "I'll kill you for this."

Grandpapa! You rode out into that blue norther on purpose. You left everything to chance, and nothing to chance. Oh, goddamn you! I hope you're satisfied! I hope you sleep real well! Rage lifted in her. She said to Clabe. "Get out of here!"

The room darkened for a moment. When the light came back the room had a whole different aspect to it. It did not seem real at all.

Claiborne said, "Christ, Soledad, I do love . . ."

"I don't want to hear that. I don't want to love. I don't want anything ever to happen to me again!"

Claiborne stared at her. He brushed the hair back from his face and picked up his hat. He went to the door and looked at her a moment longer. Then he went out.

Soledad fell back against the *sofacita*. The sunlight flooded in through the windows. The silver water pitcher on the rosewood table shone. The silver crucifix above the door shone. Her grandfather stood near the door. I know why you wanted to die, she said to him. Nothing mattered to you any more.

Oh, I hate this room. I hate the world outside these windows. Oh, I hate everything.

18

LACED up his tree. The sun was well up, small and hot and bright. Dumped what grub he had— some Borden's Biscuit, a can of tomatoes, chunk of side meat, handful of coffee beans in a knotted blue kerchief—into a tow sack and tied it behind the cantle. Tied on his bedroll. Jabbed his knee hard into Lingo's gut and jerked the cinch tight. Tied on the fry pan and the coffeepot, the Sharps rifle. Lit on up. Lingo raised his usual Cain. Then Clabe rode him out of the water lot and down the track to the river. *Swick-swock* noise of the saddle, splash of water as they crossed the creek.

Clabe followed the river northward. The sunlight bore down. It burned on Claiborne's shoulders and britches. Birds fluttered in the bushes alongside the river. The river water talked across its rocks. Its changeable surface threw back the light in bits and pieces, flashings from an over-and-over broken mirror. Trees lifted up, showed their whole deck: spread of leaves to suck the light. Weed heads, prickly-tongued brush lifted up, cactus pads and stalks of grass poked up to suck the light. The light named the shape of everything.

Early in the afternoon Clabe hit a cattle trail. It crossed the river and looked to be headed north. He took the trail up into the hills. It was shoe-mouth deep in dust. Dust was on all the leaves, everything was powdery-white. Lingo's hoofs raised a wall of dust behind them. The sun held overhead and the world turned in the heat like a steer on a spit. In the brush and dead grass and scrubby-looking trees bugs were carrying on for all like they thought that was what kept the spit turn-

ing. It was all one noise, hum or buzz, squeal of the axle of
time. The hills rose and fell like stalled waves on all sides.
Lime-rock, brush-country hills. Only the motion of the horse
under him. Only the sweaty leather of the reins in his hand,
here and now and never ever anywhere other. Only the dusty
brush lifting up, dust of brush and bugs and birds and his
hands made live by the sun, song of sun-prodded dust over
everything.

Odor of cedar, sun's wax. *The man that invented God
ought to of took out a patent on it.*

Skittery rasp, black, half-moon shadow—with a crisp
snap a grasshopper lit on the horn of Clabe's saddle. He
brushed it off.

The trail went up over a ridge. At the top of the ridge
was a cedar thicket and a clump of mountain laurel. Somebody was sitting in the shade of a cedar. It was an Indian.
Clabe reined in Lingo. He couldn't tell if it was a man or a
woman, the Indian was so old, older than Clabe thought a
body could stand to be. The Indian was hunkered down with
his knees each side his chin, knees as polished and hairless as
a pair of bedstead knobs. The mouth in the dark-brown face
kept opening and closing, making smacking noises. There
wasn't a tooth in that mouth.

Clabe lit down. The Indian didn't look directly at him
but kept staring at a place above Clabe's head. When Clabe
got up close he saw it was a woman. Under a scrap of blanket
he could see her breasts, flat and dangling like a pair of
smoked shoe soles. Her hair, lice scooting in and out of it, was
a snarl of gray and white snagged with leaves and stickers, her
skin creased and wrinkled as a turtle's. A little wispy goat-
beard was on her chin. But it was her eyes that Claiborne
couldn't keep his own eyes off of. There was a kind of yellow
slough on them and he could just make out the ghosts of irises
underneath. Blind as a bat. That's why she ain't lookin' at me.

Her mouth opened and closed, opened and closed.
"Goda'mighty," Claiborne said.

She held out her hand. There were six or seven agarita berries in it.

"Jesus Christ."

Clabe walked back over to Lingo, fetched the can of tomatoes and the side meat and some biscuits from the tow sack. He put these on the ground in front of her, took out his jackknife and wrangled an opening in the top of the can. Her eyes followed the sound of the knife. The sun burnt onto Claiborne's back. You'd have thought the lice in the woman's hair would've popped in the heat of the sun. Clabe put her hand on each thing—the biscuits, the side meat and the tin of tomatoes. He put her fingers into the half-opened can. She felt around in the can a minute. Then she lifted her hand and stuck her fingers into her mouth. Of a sudden she began to rock and shake, let out a queer noise like a rooster being choked. She reached out her hand so quick, touched Clabe's jacket and then his face. She ran her hand wet with tomato juice up the side of his face, let out another queer squawk.

Claiborne stood up. He wiped the sweat from his face. His clothes were sticking to his skin. He looked around him and said, "You sure have picked one hell of a place. It looks like God made the rest of the world and dumped the leavings here." He walked back over to Lingo. "Adios," he said.

The old woman's mouth opened and closed again.

"I know it," Claiborne said.

He lit on up.

"Goddammit, I know it," he said.

Rode into Junction City late in the afternoon. Let Lingo drink from the town water trough and took a drink himself at the pump. Stopped at a little hole in the wall and bought himself a can of peaches, some Red X flour, a can of salmon and two cans of sardines. Ate some Borden's Biscuit and the can of peaches right there on the boardwalk. Bought some corn for his horse a little way farther down the street.

Rode out of town. There was not a lick of breeze. Off to

the left a patch of dust exploded, spun into a tight, swirling column and commenced to move slowly up a slope, spouting leaves and trash from its funneled top. Just as suddenly it dissolved. A shower of litter drifted to the ground.

Pretty soon Clabe hit the Lipan River again. The water was bubbling across the rocks.

He followed the river all afternoon in a northeasterly direction, sometimes right along the riverbed, sometimes up on the bluff. The crick and scrape and shrill and buzz of bugs made such a loud, steady racket Clabe stopped hearing it. Later, when the sun was down low in the west, the bugs quit for a spell and Clabe noticed. He heard the silence of the lack of it.

The dark rose in the east. Off to the east, from about a quarter of a mile off, came a low hum. A great black funnel rose out of the ground. It was millions and millions of bats in a funnel-shaped cloud that tilted and then flattened out as the flittering critters made off into the dark. When the sun went down they were gone.

Clabe rode down to the river and made his camp there.

Got up early the next morning and rode all day, more or less following the river. Early in the evening he hit a wagon track that commenced to run alongside the river. Fresh hoof marks and horse droppings were in the track—five or six horses, he couldn't make out which. About three miles farther up the track Clabe saw them up ahead, five riders, two men and three women. They had stopped and were watching him ride up to them. When Clabe got closer he saw they were young folks, the men in three-button cutaway coats and black cravats, the young women in riding skirts, trim waist-length jackets, high collars and pretty straw hats. One of them was wearing gloves.

"Howdy," Claiborne said as he came up to them.

"Howdy do," one of the young men said. He was a tall handsome fellow with clear gray eyes, a long face and full chin, dark eyebrows and light brown hair. His hair was brushed back into a ducktail above his collar. He sat ramrod straight in the saddle. He said, "Where are you headed?"

"General direction of Mason, Texas," Claiborne said.

"You haven't got too far to go," the other young man said. "We're headed for a ways in that direction our own-selves. Shall we keep each other company?"

"All right," Claiborne said.

"This is my brother Dud," the first young man said. Dud was the spitting image of his brother except that he had blond hair. He looked to be the younger of the two. "And this here is our sister Clara and this is Sybil Pope and Vernelle Pope. My name is Will Pope."

"Howdy," Clabe said. He lifted his hat to each of the women. "Howdy, ma'am. Howdy, ma'am. I have landed in a nest of Popes," he said.

"We're cousins," Will Pope said. "Vernelle and Sybil live on Big Bluff creek. We're headed to a dance up on Honey Creek."

"It's Mr. and Mrs. Frazier's wedding anniversary and they're givin' a party," Sybil Pope said.

"Twenty-five years," Clara Pope said.

"That's a good enough reason," Claiborne said.

"Mama and Papa left this mornin' and left us to do the chores. Clara and Dud and Will come over to pick us up after they done their'n," Sybil Pope said. She said it without taking a breath. She was about fourteen or fifteen years old and the pertest of the three girls, with gray Pope eyes, small cupid-bowed lips and honey-colored hair. Clara and Vernelle were older, darker-haired girls. All the Popes were on good mounts.

"What's your name?" Will Pope said.

"Clabe Sanderlin," Claiborne said.

The Popes wheeled their horses and started them on a trot up the track. It chanced Clabe was alongside Vernelle Pope. "Do you know anybody in Mason, Mr. Sanderlin?" she said.

"No'm. I'm goin' up past there."

"You're left-handed!" Sybil said. She came riding up from behind.

"Oh, it ain't that," Claiborne said. "It's if I don't keep somethin' in this hand my arm's gonna fall off at the shoulder."

Sybil laughed. She whipped her horse and ran it up past the others and whipped it into a gallop up the track. When she came back she looked flushed and happy and a mite showoff.

The girls rode their horses like they'd been born to them. There was a smell of florida-water in the air, from their hand-kerchiefs and gloves.

Clara Pope said, "I wonder if Charlie Pryor's gonna be at the dance."

"No, he won't be there," Dud Pope said. "You won't be there neither so I don't reckon he will."

"Quit it," Clara said.

Sybil said, "When Clara gets to lookin' at Charlie she can't tell a tortilla from a hot biscuit."

"Quit it, you all," Clara said. "Oh, I ain't gonna talk to you. I'm not gonna talk to a one."

"Gonna rust your jaw, Clurry," Sybil said. They all laughed.

"Charlie'll oil her jaw right quick," Dud said.

"Grease her ear, you mean," Vernelle said.

"Watch out, Clurry," Will said. "That boy'll talk a pump into believin' it's a windmill."

"He's got purty eyes, too," Dud said. They all laughed. Dud let out a whoop. He spurred his horse. Everybody choused up their horses and chased off after him. They ran their horses for a way. The girls let out a louder pack of war whoops than the boys did.

They reined their horses in to a walk again. Vernelle said, "We got to quit. This dust is gonna ruin our clothes."

"I wonder will it ever rain?" Sybil said.

"Rain's all wind and wind's all sand," Dud said.

Will said, "I hear tell the Greenback Party's puttin' up another man for governor next year."

Clabe said, "I been out of the world so long I don't know nothin' about it."

Sybil said, "Got so much dust in my teeth I can taste it."

They rode a long way, talking about rain, prices, weather, rain and weather.

It was getting well up on the shank end of evening. At a place where the track that went up Honey Creek came into the main track the Popes said, "Why don't you come up with us?"

"I ain't hardly dressed for a wingding like that."

"It don't matter. Ever'body'll be there. The Fraziers'll be mighty put out if they find you rode all this way with us and we didn't make you come up."

"More put out if you don't say yes."

"Around here a stranger don't go away without a light-you-down and some grub in his belly."

"It'll be all kinds of good things to eat."

"Venison, spareribs, chitlins, mince pie, green grape pie, jelly layer cake," Sybil said.

"It's bribery," Claiborne said.

"It's comin' night on you."

"Watermelon," Sybil said.

"You'd think I was about to die of starvation," Clabe said. "I got grub in my sack here."

"Pound cake," Sybil said.

"All right," Claiborne said.

They rode about two miles up the canyon. Dust way up high picked up the last of light. The sky turned plum-colored overhead. Stars were beginning to show as Clabe and the Popes rode up to a ranch house. It was a box-and-batten house with two big rooms and a breezeway in between. The fiddlers were in the breezeway. They were playing lively break-down music.

"Oh, they've already started!" Clara said. She spurred her horse forward.

Tall burr oaks and pecan trees grew about the hitching rack, where teams and saddle horses were tied. Safes, tables, bedsteads, chests, cupboards—all the furniture from the house had been carried out and left in the yard to make room for the dancers.

The Popes rode up to the hitching rack. "They're playing 'Fishers' Hornpipe'!" Sybil said. The girls slid down from their horses. The boys tied the horses and unsaddled them while the girls took off their riding skirts and straightened their hair and clothes and waited impatiently nearby. They started up toward the house and Sybil began to jump about in step to the music. When they came to the steps there was a crowd on the gallery. "Howdy, y'all!" "Howdy, Clara!" "Hey Will, you old poke!" "Food's already et!"

"Mr. Sanderlin, this here's Cap'n and Mrs. Sam Frazier," Will Pope said. A distinguished-looking gentleman and his wife were standing at the top of the steps. "It's their infare," Will said.

"Twenty-five years and he ain't been throwed out of the house but twice," somebody said. Everybody laughed.

"This is Mr. Clabe Sanderlin, ever'body," Will said.

"Take off your hat and coat and come on in," somebody said.

"You're most welcome, sir," Captain Frazier said. His trim salt-and-pepper mustache lifted in a smile. He held out his hand and Clabe shook it.

"Come up and join us, Mr. Sanderlin," Mrs. Frazier said. Her plump flesh shook.

Claiborne took off his hat. "Thankee, ma'am," he said. "Congratulations," he said.

"Congratulate us but thank the good Lord," Mrs. Frazier said.

Everybody went back into the house, and the fiddlers struck up again.

Salute your corners high and low
Then your partner and away we go.

Up the river and around the bend
Four hands up and goin' again.

Form a star with your right hand across
Dance back with your left and don't get lost.

Swing on the corner, swingin' on the gate
Then your partner and promenade eight.

Clabe stood in the doorway. There was a set in each
room. Old folks sat around the walls. Shy, lonesome cowboys stood in twos and threes, bunched in the corners. The
prompter's bugle voice held out the night dark. Lamps and
candles lit the rooms. Smell of Persian Lilac and Hoyt's Cologne, heat of the lamps and of bodies dancing. Feet tromped
the board floors. The curtains at the open windows moved in
a night breeze.

Swing on the corners as you heel and toe
Granny will your dog bite? No child no.

Bustles and bows. Girls in white dresses and pink and
cream and pale green. The long dresses swept the floor.
    Black hair. Done up like. Clabe's heart shook.
    The girl turned. *No, that ain't her face. There ain't no other*
face like hers.
    Oh Christ, Soledad.
    Claiborne went out onto the gallery.
    Later some of the boys built a fire out under one of the
pecan trees. Clabe went out there with them.
    "How's about a game of poker?"
    "I hear tell you're goin' to Mason," one of them, a raw-
faced fellow with slicked-back hair, said.
    "In that direction," Claiborne said.

"You can get up there by goin' straight up this canyon," another one of them said. "It's a rough ride. But there's a road up there. It'll take you straight into Mason. It's not but eight or ten miles."

One of the men dealt out the cards. "With the jick and not the left jack," another said.

"Draw poker."

The prompter's voice floated across the yard. The dancers danced. Their figures moved behind the open windows.

"How many cards do y'all want?" the dealer said.

"I'll take three."

"One to me."

"Same here."

The young fellow with the slicked-back hair put another cedar log on the fire. The sparks flew up.

"Won't be no moon tonight," one of them said. "Lord, it went by fast."

"Frank, you know Colonel Lowry that owns the mortuary down in Cherry Springs?" one of the men, an older man, said. "Well, I was down there to visit him the other day and that unreconstructed old Rebel is still mouthing things about 'before the war.' We was out walkin' along the road the night I was there and he carried on and on. 'Since the war the people of the South have got nothin' to live for,' he says. 'Ever'thing was better before the war,' he says. It was a bright moon up and I said something about it. 'Yes, John,' he says, 'but you ought to of seen it shine before the war.'"

The men laughed. "Deal me another hand," one of them said.

"I'm out."

"I'm out."

The cedar fire popped.

"Listen to Ot and Ollie go on them fiddles."

"Want some Little Rosebud?"

"No, I ain't chewin' tonight."

"What you got, Clabe?" the one named Frank said.

"A pair of kings," Clabe said.

"I got you beat," Frank said. "I got two pair."

"Well, it's your money," Clabe said as he shoved the pile of dimes across the saddle blanket.

At midnight everybody ate and then the dance went on.

Clabe took his bedroll up on the side of the hill and un-spooled it. The dance was still going on down below. The fiddlers shed their thin scrapings into the night air. The voice of the prompter held out, cricket in a lit box. Dancers danced past the open windows like a magic-lantern show. Clabe took off his boots and slid between the blankets. He picked out a few rocks from underneath.

Now it was a schottische down there in the lit box, a fast piece of stomping. Somewhere a coyote howled. Great dust specks of stars hung in the sky, drift of dust, drift of this piece of dust Clabe was on, motes glinting in the slant light of time.

A stone skipped down the hillside.

Sunlight through a window. Her face in sunlight. "I hate you," *she said.*

Clabe woke. There was not a sound anywhere. A dark-ness pressed onto him, solid as a stone. The terror was so fierce he couldn't breathe. A silence was on him, come on him like an animal with its nose in his ears, its tongue on all his senses.

A pinprick of light showed above his head. Of a sudden it widened, opening like a door, opening like the roof of a house took away, the top of the night plucked apart—light whiter than the sun, brighter than puff of photographers' phosphorus.

And Clabe saw all things: trees and bugs and birds, crit-ters and weeds—and his own kind, too, thicker than leaves, all who had ever lived, each alone, each in the one-time onlyness of its self, and he knew they were dead or going to die and a terrible grief came on him.

The roothairs of light reached out, lace lightning, like a net.
They touched all things.

Joy was a hot taste in Clabe's mouth. He went out of himself like water up the sun's ladders until he was joy itself touching its face to the top of the sky . . .

The flesh came back. Quick as whiskey, gracious as light, he was filled

        filled with a peace more pervasive than blood.

Clabe couldn't sleep. The world was too close, too solid and too real.

He crawled out of his bedroll and saddled Lingo, tied on his gear.

It was quiet down at the house. No lights there. But the great curve of stars glittered overhead, blinking like breaths. They gave enough light for Clabe to see by.

He rode up the canyon in the dark.

19

DARK red crusts of dawn.

The sun put the morning star out of sight.

Rode through Mason. Stone buildings. Shaded store-fronts and wooden awnings. The whole world had a different look to it.

Rode all morning under the track of the sun. About the middle of the afternoon Clabe checked Lingo at the edge of a brushy draw.

He spurred Lingo down the slope. He rode over to a live oak. Down in the grass, in the shock of the horse's hoofs and sudden, sun-killing shadow, bugs hushed, holding in their choiring, then, when he'd passed, opening up again.

Claiborne lit down and tied Lingo to the oak. He walked up the draw a way. A cedar bush spread its scaly branches and half-rusty, half-green needles. Clabe pulled apart the branches and kicked the trash out from underneath. His toe hit the cantle. He brushed off the cedar needles. The saddle lay on its side. It had been chewed by mice. The leather was cracked and turning black. The lacing had come loose from the rim of the cantle and the back housing was split. Good beechwood showed through. Borers had made a road map on the flat dinner-plate saddle horn. The silver conchos, still bright as rubbed dollars, shone in the sky of the rotted skirt like permanent stars. Clabe lifted a stirrup fender. A cottony ball of spider eggs was stuck to the underside. The ground seemed to shift under Clabe's feet.

He stood. Cedar needles ticked onto the rotted hull. Clabe climbed up the side of the draw, grabbing hold of cedar bushes and deer laurel to pull himself up. He walked over to a rise a little way off and climbed up it. He hunted around on the top. There was nothing there.

There was another rise a little farther off and Clabe walked over to that. Rocks skittered from under his feet as he climbed up.

He pushed his way through the thick brush on the top. *It's got to be here somewheres*—almost stepped into it. He stepped right on back.

Not a body in it. Not a pin in it. There was not a button or a bone in it. Just this hollow big enough to lay a man out in.

Had laid a man out in it

the bloody tucks

had laid him out shrouded in a yellow slicker, a black sombrero onto his face.

Rocks lay scattered all about. Cedar needles ticked.

The rocks heaved. Dark eyes, white handlebar mustache. Rocks scattered as the body lifted, wet and slick as a skinned rabbit or a pulled stalk of rain lily . . .

A string of ants with dirt crumbs in their jaws climbed up the side of the grave.

FOR RENT. HAVE GONE BACK TO SAN ANTONE.

Lord, when I die let me go to San Antone! Silk and good clean boards.

He ain't gone up on angels' wings, that's for certain sure. It's too much world.

Wherever all you are, you're here.

Forgive me, don Señor, what I done to you. Took the sun away. Took day and dark and sweat and hurt and ever' sweet thing away. Food in your mouth and noise in your ear and the name of Soledad. I was so damn scared. You was comin' at me. It was myself I seen. Oh Christ, to take a man's life and make him the any poor thing he finally is!

If I hadn't forgive myself, I couldn't live with it. She can't forgive.

Was you after me to do it?

Here's the stars ain't got no word for us. Here's your sky-blue heaven empty of comfort as ice up a man's ass. Here's brush and critters and trees and bugs have got their own ways and not a word of comfort and better off satisfied if we wasn't here atall. Here's the wall that says we got to die, where folks tack up the word "God" to hang their hats onto but a man walks across the dirt ground that's gonna soak him up quick as piss. There ain't nowheres a body can make a deal. It don't quit. A man is so damn alone he might could be on the moon.

Alone and not alone, that's what I know.

Christ, I am blessed!

There's somethin' about myself I ain't gonna tell even you.

I hope you got what you wanted, laid out in the long boards.

I ain't about to trade places.

EPILOG

Indian Territory
April 8, 1889

CLAIBORNE had just come in from
the horse trap and was washing his hands in the wash basin on
the stand outside the door when little Causey, sitting among
her pebble-and-twig houses and patted, red-dirt fences down
at the end of the house, pointed her fat baby finger and said,
"Look, Daddy!" Clabe turned and saw a horse and buggy coming down the prairie slope from the direction of Rush Springs.

Delia came to the door and said, "Come into the house,
Causey." But Causey just stood there with her thumb stuck in
her mouth, staring as tranced and curious as if it was the
moon rolling down the slope. The whole slope was carpeted
with wild indigo and sweet williams, at the top a mile-long
crest of flowering dogwoods and redbuds.

The buggy drifted through the axle-high flowers. It was
a Concord buggy, its top folded back, pulled by a scrubby
mouse-colored horse. The driver was in his shirt sleeves.
Sleeve garters, bow tie, derby hat. A drummer, likely. Halloo!
he yelled. Causey ran to her mama.

Crossed the creek and rattled up to the house. The man
checked his horse. He lifted his hat. "Howdy do," he said.
Scratched the side of his nose and put his hat back on his
head. "I seem to be away out from nowhere and I wonder if
you all might put me up for the night." He blinked. His ears
stuck out like jug handles and he had the mournfulest-looking
eyes. Kept tapping his long pale fingers on his knees. "All I
got in my feed bucket is one clean pair of socks and a Silver
King onion," he said.

"I think I know you," Claiborne said.

"You do?" The man looked a mite nervous. He cracked his knuckles and stared at Clabe.

"Aren't you Wash Delong?"

"Why, I do believe it's my old tentmate from Alto Springs!" Wash Delong said. "If that don't beat all!" His face cracked into a grin.

"Light on down," Claiborne said.

Wash missed the carriage step and almost broke a leg getting down. He lurched toward Clabe, his hand stuck out in front of him. "If it don't beat all!" he said.

They shook hands. Wash grabbed hold of Clabe's hand with both hands and pumped it up and down. "If it don't beat all!" he said again. He peered at Clabe. "I can't say as eight or nine years has made a lick of difference in you."

Claiborne said, "This here's my wife Delia. And this here's . . ." But Causey was hiding in the house.

"You've picked the cream of the crop, Red," Wash said, bowing to Delia. "How do you do, Miz—. I never did know your name, Red," he said.

"Sanderlin."

Wash knocked his hat off his head by tapping it under the brim. It flipped in the air and he caught it in his hand. "How d'ye do, Miz Sanderlin?" he said. He was half bald.

Delia laughed. "Now let's see you do that to your head," she said.

"I learnt *that* off the headhunters of Borneo," Wash said. "But I don't want to do all my good tricks first shot out of the bucket."

Delia said, "Come in to supper. I'm about to put it on the table." She had her hands folded under her apron. Now she held one out to Wash. "Shall we put up with him, Claiborne?" she said.

"So long as he washes up and don't tell no more jokes," Clabe said. "I hope he ain't as hungry as I am."

Wash hovered above Delia's hand and touched it briefly. "The pleasure's all mine, Ma'm, I'm sure."

Delia went into the house. Wash walked over to his horse and tied it to a blackjack tree.

"Where do you come from?" Clabe said.

"Up from Clay County, Texas, last. This is hog-wallow prairie if ever I saw it. I've seen more cows and less milk, more pasture and less grass. I never saw so much red dirt in my life." Wash pulled a sack coat off the buggy seat.

"No need to get dressed up."

"That's what the good citizens of Mineral Wells told me last year preparatory to riding me out of town on a rail, but I went dressed for the occasion, ha ha. It *is* a trifle hot." He tossed the coat back onto the buggy seat. He put his hat on the seat, slicked back a few strands of hair—turtle fuzz on the top of his head—and straightened his bow tie. "Got to keep up appearances," he said. A lark sang, up on the slope. It sounded like water gurgling from a thin-necked bottle. Wash cracked his knuckles. He washed his hands in the basin and he and Clabe went into the house.

The cookstove was in the center of the room and the dining room, the bedroom, the kitchen and the sitting room were in the four corners. The baby was lying on his back on a piece of domestic in the middle of the four-poster bed, teething on a thread spool.

Wash Delong said, "This your place, Red?"

"The T-4 ranch owns it. I work for the T-4 ranch."

"Doing what?"

"Breaking horses for Council Ames."

"Is he an Indian?"

"He's married to one."

"They call Oklahoma the Chickasaw Nation. But I ain't seen an Indian or any kind of human bein' since I left Wilson Town, sixty miles back. All I've seen is prairie, cows and mangy wild horses."

A jar of wild plum blossoms was on the table. The table had been set and an extra plate added. Delia said, "Come sit to the table." She put down a dish of fresh-opened watermelon preserves.

Chairs scraped under the table. Delia held Causey on her lap. Wash leaned toward Causey. "What's your name, Missy?" he said.

Causey stared at him as if he'd just dropped from a rafter. Delia kissed her on top of the head. "Tell him what your name is, honey," she said. She whispered to her: "Tell him what your *real* name is."

Causey plucked her thumb out of her mouth. "*Cow*-sey," she said.

"No."

"*Carisa*," she said.

"CaRISa?" Wash said. His eyebrows lifted way up toward the moon top of his head. Causey laughed.

"What's your little brother's name?" Wash said.

"Bub." Of a sudden she laughed again. "Bub's what on thop of the wox," she said.

"What?" Wash said.

"Yesterday," Causey chortled and churned on her mama's lap.

"I don't know what she's talking about," Delia said. She looked at Causey and laughed. Over on the bed Bub kicked his feet and gargled like he was laughing his ownself. Delia and Claiborne laughed.

Chicken—prairie chicken—and dumplings, biscuits six inches high, poke salad, leaf lettuce, radishes, watermelon preserves, wild plum jam. Later, coffee and vinegar pie.

Delia said, "Are you a drummer, Mr. Delong?"

"I been trying to."

"What do you sell?"

"Calicos, checks, plaids, muslins. Patent medicines. Soap. Snuff. Cookware. Hardware. Everything from soup to nuts. You name it and I ain't got it. Was headed out to West

Texas, trying to take orders for Wheeler Number Six reapers. Heard tell Congress finally come through and the new President's openin' up the Oklahoma Territory to settlement. Left my order books and balance of goods in Henrietta and wired the Company to come pick it up. I'm going to make the run into Oklahoma."

"April twenty-second," Delia said. "That's just two more weeks." She put Causey down onto the floor and commenced to clear the table.

"Plenty of folks are goin' into the Territory just to make cash. I'll take the train into Guthrie from the Cherokee line, peg down everything I can get my hands on, buy up lots and sell 'em for a profit. The real estate business. If that don't work I'll set up a chuck-a-luck table. A body's got to come out the big end of the horn once in his life."

Clabe said, "I'm going to make the run myself."

"Where to?"

"A quarter-section of timber and sod and sand-bottomed creek I ain't gonna tell you no more about."

"If somebody else don't get there first," Wash said.

"They won't," Clabe said. "The government has ordered the cowmen to get all their stock out of Oklahoma. They got 'til the day of the run. Council Ames' boys'll be fetchin' that stuff down from the Western Land District. Me and the boys've got a few appointments—I'll make the run across the river, pick up a fresh horse about five miles in, switch to another a little farther on. I'll be on my place before your train has blowed its whistle."

"It sounds real good," Wash Delong said.

"We're already mostly packed," Delia said. "Got all my jelly in that trunk there." She pointed to a pair of trunks in one of the corners. Some tools and two window sashes were leaning against the wall beside one of the trunks. "Have my pear saplings in washtubs and pretty soon I'll dig up my roses. All my curtains are packed and most of the dishes and bedding have been packed. Everything we don't need, we pack.

Next week we'll take the stove apart and load it on the wagon. Load on everything. Chickens on top and the cow along behind. Then Carisa and Stacey and me are going over to the ranchhouse to stay with Ella and Council until Clabe comes to fetch us."

They talked some more. The smell of the plum blossoms filled the room. Delia washed the few dishes. She put the beans to soak. She took off her apron and hung it on a nail. Claiborne watched her move about the room. Gesture of her face turning with—it struck him—a petal momentariness, motion of her hands, the silence of her breathing. Milk of her breasts, wideness of her hips. But it was the other thing that took him most of all, was on him so terrible powerful it hurt—the sense of *her*. It was as solid and real as a stone you could take in your hand and at the same time as untouchable as the smell of these plum blossoms in the air.

Delia bent to the baby, wrapping him in a fresh flannel. Her body in her blue calico dress. Hundred times more pretty naked than dressed! Clabe's guts kindled toward her. *Touched her face, cheek and nose and brow, kissed her eyelids and mouth, wet, warm, particular taste of her, ran his hand along her hip, kissed her naked breasts, penny-brown, goose-pimpled tips, kissed the white, naked belly, the warm, wiry hairs at her crotch. Cry in the dark, her body opening again and again to him . . .*

Delia looked up. She saw him watching her. She half smiled. She sat on the other side of the bed, with her back to them, humming *Daisies Won't Tell* and commenced to nurse the baby.

Claiborne lit the lamp. Delia made Causey blow her nose. She washed her face and hands and feet and put her in her flannel gown and sent her over to Claiborne. Clabe fetched Causey up onto his lap. He kissed her. He tweaked one of her big toes. "I didn't know you had two noses," he said. Causey laughed. Claiborne gave her another kiss. "Good night, Sissy," he said. Delia had pulled the trundle bed out from under the big bed and she put Causey into it. She gave

Causey her china-head doll and tucked the comfort up around her. "Good night, Sissy," she said. Clabe pushed his chair back from the table. "Let's go take care of your horse," he said to Wash.

Outside, Wash and Clabe unharnessed the horse. They hung the harness in the blackjack tree and backed the buggy under another, bigger tree. Wash put up the buggy top. "Want to buy a good buggy?" he said.

Clabe said, "Sell it to somebody on the Sac and Fox line."

They staked the horse out at the back of the house. The stars were already beginning to show. There was a late pink cast of light in the west—one long narrow streak—but it was fading fast. The prairie had a kind of phosphorous glow on it, and Clabe and Wash could still make out off to the north, about two miles off, the line of timber—sandbar willow and bunchy cottonwoods—marking the South Canadian River. All around them the chuck-wills and whippoorwills were making their complaints.

Clabe said, "Whatever happened to that one called Soledad, back in Alto Springs, that run that big ranch?"

"She sold the place and the last thing I heard she was gone to Mexico."

They fed the horse some dry corn. Wash gave her a short grooming. Then they went into the house.

The smell of plum blossoms filled the room. It was a room within the room. Delia was already in bed, with the baby beside her. She had laid down a pallet for Wash on the floor beside the stove. Clabe blew out the lamp and he and Wash undressed in the dark. Clabe climbed into bed. He listened to the general fuss of Wash getting settled on his pallet. "Good night," he said.

"Good night," Wash said.

Clabe's head sank into the bolster. His body sank into the tick. He was bone-weary. Tried to break that young sorrel this afternoon. It was a mean, long-legged, stiff-legged critter and could turn its pack. *Tomorrow I'll lock spurs on him.*

Peent of nighthawks diving, up over the house. Tree frogs trilled in the blackjack trees. The house shifted and creaked. The night air poured in through the open windows. Sounds of breathing—Causey asleep, and the regular in-and-out hiss and thumb-sucking noise of Bub pressed up against his mama. A low snoring commenced on the pallet. Clabe couldn't see a thing in the room, it was so dark. The dark went out through the windows. It held the trees and the nighthawks and the long prairie slope, it went up to the stars snapping and glinting like ice splinters.

Soledad said, "I don't want anything ever to happen to me again."

Smell of plum blossoms. Clabe turned to Delia. She made a low noise and moved up against him. Warm smell of her hair, loose now, next his face, thin shoulder blades at his chest, heat of her back, curve of her spine against his belly. His hand moved along the flannel cloth of her gown. Delia pressed up to him closer. The sense of her came on him again, her head beside his now half in the dimness of sleep, her motions as she bent over her sewing or her zinnias, carefulness of the way she sometimes touched things—a particular joy, a particular quiet. The longing ached in him again. To know the bones of her and the blood of her and the breath and the life and the self of her!

It can't be done.

The longing was in her too, he knew it. Her body opening again and again to him.

But you can't ever know.

Clabe lay an arm across Delia and Bub. The nighthawks made their faint noises up over the house.

A body has got to be satisfied. Clabe watched Delia come up from the creek with a jar of chilled milk in her hands. The sunlight was on her face and hands and the weeds catching at her dress. Even, as he made the shift closer into sleep, heard her voice, or someone's voice. *Christ, it's a grief, how a body goes his whole way on this earth, all his days, and his life is never known.*

AFTERWORD

"SOLITUDE, profound solitude," wrote novelist E. L. Doctorow, "as much as society, has been an overriding condition in American literary history." The reason is not difficult to isolate. Literature is inevitably a reflection of the culture from which it springs, and the central fact of American history is the profound solitude of the nation's frontier experience.

In the familiar myth first formulated by historian Frederick Jackson Turner, the American frontier is conceived of as a moving line on which the forces of savagery and civilization fought for supremacy. As long as neither held dominance along the line, there was danger but also boundless freedom. Into this mythic landscape came the archetypal pioneer American, an American who was free in a way that no American has been free since—free to choose patterns of conduct from an infinity of choices, free to move back and forth across the line that separated savagery and civilization, free to create his *self* from the materials of a totally unrestricted environment.

Though Americans have traditionally paid nostalgic homage to their frontier heritage, popular attitudes toward the frontier have always been characterized by ambivalence. In his well-known study, *Virgin Land: The American West as Symbol and Myth*, Henry Nash Smith demonstrates how Americans of the eighteenth and nineteenth centuries saw the frontier, at one and the same time, as a hospitable garden and a hostile desert. These seemingly conflicting images of the West were promulgated simultaneously in popular literature of the time. The frontier, to some, was an invigorating moral landscape, clean and uncorrupted because of its very wildness; to others, it was morally degenerating, promoting human degradation, even brutalization. If the frontier West was a place of freedom and unlimited opportunity, it could also, because of an absence of moral order and social discipline, generate terrifying loneliness—and aloneness.

In *Soledad*, R. G. Vliet superimposed on these rich mythic implications of the nineteenth-century American frontier experience a decidedly twentieth-century consciousness. Unlike many Texas writers, Vliet was thoroughly conversant with the philosophical and literary movements that have washed over modern European and American intellectual life. *Soledad* is a finely textured novel, and the existential angst of, say, Albert Camus is as much an influence on the book as is the myth of the frontier.

On one level *Soledad* is a kind of "Western" that conforms to a recognizable formula associated with the genre. The novel is about a wandering cowboy—a "lonesome cowboy," to use an appropriate cliché—traversing the landscape of Texas in the 1880s. It is, however, a Western with a difference. Any moderately informed reader of the genre knows something is up when a Western begins with an epigraph from Wallace Stevens: "We live in an old chaos of the sun."

The protagonist of the novel must find a way of existing meaningfully amid the chaos and savagery of nature—including human nature. He is a twenty-four-year-old cowboy known variously as Claiborne Sanderlin, Claiborne Arnett, Clabe, and Red—the uncertainty of his name presumably suggesting his uncertain sense of identity. Victimized by a brutal father, Claiborne has been on his own since he was a child, with no purpose in life and disoriented by what are apparently random epileptic seizures. He kills don Alvaro Reyes Ibarra, a stranger to him, in a violent and seemingly senseless action. Given Claiborne's personal history, however, the killing is hardly surprising. The surprise lies in his response to the photograph of a young woman in a white dress that he removes from don Reyes' body. His first glimpse of the photograph is the beginning of Claiborne's search for the woman—and for his own soul.

His quest carries him through central and southwest Texas in the spring and summer of 1881. The historical reality of frontier Texas of a century ago is recreated in the novel with wonderful precision and care; pains were obviously taken to make place names, even the smallest background details, right. As much a poet as a novelist, Vliet had a finely developed eye for the sensuous and the concrete; it served him well in this book, as it did in all his writing.

Claiborne's journey, though, as immediate and real as it is to the reader, is more spiritual than spatial. He is free in that the law will never punish him for his violent act; he is also alone, and in his freedom and aloneness he discovers fear, alienation, even a kind of terror. The landscape the novel explores, therefore, is not so much that of late nineteenth-century Texas as it is the landscape of Claiborne's mind. His search for the woman in the photograph is ultimately a search for absolution—and an attempt to create order and a sense of his existential self from the moral chaos of frontier Texas below and the merciless sun above.

The woman in the picture turns out to be don Reyes' granddaughter, Soledad, a complex and fascinating character. She is, as her name indicates, alone—as alone as Claiborne—though she does not accept the fact of her loneliness. Claiborne falls in love with Soledad, but she, needing her hatred more than love, sends him away. Thus Claiborne becomes another of those literary cowboys who ride off into the sunset. Except that he does not ride toward a beckoning horizon; he is consumed instead in a void of aloneness, made more intense by his ritualistic revisitation of the scene where he slew don Reyes. In his thoughts Claiborne rehearses what he has learned of the meaning of human existence: "There ain't nowheres a body can make a deal. It don't quit. A man is so damn alone he might could be on the moon."

Claiborne learns other things as well from his quest. He

never solves the mystery of his "fits," as he calls them—his seizures—but he does conclude that he killed don Reyes because he saw *himself* in don Reyes and was struck by an unnameable fear. "It was myself I seen," Claiborne decides, and it was himself he feared and tried to destroy. Claiborne further decides that Soledad cannot forgive him; God *will* not forgive him; so he must forgive himself. When Claiborne reaches a state of qualified self-forgiveness, his search for absolution, at least, is complete. In the end one of the most important things Claiborne learns is that it is better to be alive than to be dead; he is glad to be himself rather than don Reyes. "I ain't about to trade places," he asserts.

In her introduction to the novel, Ann Vliet poignantly describes her husband's lengthy and sometimes painful writing and rewriting of the story of Claiborne and Soledad, a story that was eventually published in 1977 under the title *Solitudes*. The final revision of the tale, finished not long before his death in May 1984, Vliet titled *Soledad*, and it is this revised version that the reader has just completed. Of the many changes, large and small, that were incorporated into the final version, two scenes that appear in *Soledad* but not in *Solitudes* are especially significant: Claiborne's encounter with the blind Indian woman at the beginning of chapter eighteen and the entire epilog.

The first of these scenes underscores Claiborne's newly acquired sympathy for other humans. He gives the old woman all his food and expresses, elliptically, his understanding of the common plight of all living things: we are all lost, and we are all going to die; our only salvation is to help each other along the way as best we can. The epilog, set eight years after the main events of the novel, shows Claiborne, once a wild, self-destructive cowboy, as a fairly ordinary, moderately ambitious family man. His past is behind him—and yet it isn't. The author's point is that what appears on the surface to be the most commonplace of lives is strange and complex in ways that no one—not even one's family and loved ones—can know.

"Christ, it's a grief," Claiborne thinks at the close of the epilog, "how a body goes his whole way on this earth, all his days, and his life is never known."

The critic Malcolm Cowley said of R. G. Vliet that his "writing is close to being a national treasure." Vliet was a gifted poet and playwright. His greatest talent, however, was in the writing of fiction. His three novels—*Soledad, Rockspring* (1974), and *Scorpio Rising* (1985)—are set largely in the nineteenth and early twentieth centuries on the Edwards Plateau, in and around the town of Alto Springs, which is the fictional counterpart of Rocksprings, the county seat of Edwards County, Texas. Had he lived, Vliet might well have become the Faulkner of Edwards County. Certainly the best of his fiction is worthy of being mentioned in the same breath as Faulkner's.

And, as is true of Faulkner's work, what the reader notices first and foremost in Vliet's novels is the style. Vliet wrote luminous prose that is at once poetic and colloquial, lyrical and concretely realistic. "To get a literature of the Southwest," the author once said, "to get an *image* of the Southwest, we are going to have to have poems and novels of such high linguistic and intuitive capabilities as to be able to probe and release, in their own idiom—reflecting the sky they are under and the land they are on, the past they come from and the present they are in—the individual communal psyches that, though they are at once all men, are also, and especially, of *this* time, *this* place." The "high linguistic and intuitive capabilities" to which Vliet referred are, I submit, displayed with consummate grace and skill in *Soledad*.

TOM PILKINGTON
Stephenville

ABOUT THE AUTHOR

Novelist, poet and playwright, R.G. Vliet grew up in Texas and attended Southwest Texas State College in San Marcos, receiving a B.S. and an M.A. in 1952. He attended Yale University School of Drama, studying under Robert Penn Warren and Lemist Esler, and received numerous awards for his dramatic works written between 1957 and 1962. *The Regions of Noon* was named Play-of-the-Year by the Southeastern Theatre Conference in 1961.

From 1957 until his death in 1984, Vliet also wrote and published three books of poems, one book-length poem, and three novels. Twice, in 1966 and 1970, his poetry was honored by the Texas Institute of Letters. His book-length poem sequence, *Clem Maverick*, recorded for public broadcasting, won a prize in the University of Wisconsin "Earplay Competition" in 1973. His novel, *Solitudes*, earned the Texas Institute of Letters Fiction Award in 1977.

Vliet also received several important fellowships. In 1960 he was named a Ford Foundation Fellow in playwriting and in 1969 a Rockefeller Foundation Fellow in Fiction and Poetry. In 1983 he was the Dobie-Paisano Resident in Fiction at the University of Texas. During his career, he lectured and read from his works at many colleges and universities throughout the United States, and in 1983 he was honored with the Southwest Texas State University Distinguished Alumni Award.

Vliet's last work, *Scorpio Rising*, was published posthumously in 1985.

SOLEDAD
was set in Goudy Old Style type by
G & S TYPESETTERS
printed and bound by
EDWARDS BROTHERS
designed and produced by
WHITEHEAD & WHITEHEAD